A BAD PLACE TO BE

Huntington City Township
Public Library
255 West Park Drive
Huntington, IN 46750
www.huntingtonpub.lib.in.us

JOHN HANSEN

outskirtspress
DENVER, COLORADO

Outskirts Press, Inc.
http://www.outskirtspress.com

ISBN: 978-1-4787-6429-8

Outskirts Press and the "OP" logo are trademarks belonging to Outskirts Press, Inc.

PRINTED IN THE UNITED STATES OF AMERICA

Chapter One

August 5, 1870

The image of the rider off in the distance shimmered in the midday heat. But, this was of no consequence to the shooter as he had picked a comfortable spot and could wait until the rider got closer. Unknowingly, the man on the horse moved steadily towards his fate. Other than the incessant horseflies that he swatted at, he didn't appear to have a care in the world. In fact, life was good; he had been one of the lucky ones to locate a producing gold claim in the Idaho Territory. Unfortunately, he was not alone in this knowledge. And on he went, marking time with the rhythmic creaking of his saddle and each step that his horse took. He was getting much closer now to the spot that the shooter had selected for him to die. It was time; the shooter had long ago secured a dead rest for his rifle and even chambered a round. He settled his cheek onto the rifle's stock. It was smooth and comfortable and his eyes aligned perfectly with the buckhorn sights. At this range, with this rifle, it would be a difficult but not impossible shot. He thumbed back the hammer. And then, for reasons known only to the rider, he stopped. "What luck," whispered the shooter as he placed the front bead on the rider's head. His heart was pounding so fast that he couldn't distinguish the individual beats. He took a deep breath and released it slowly, but it did not achieve the calm that he had hoped for. The rider had presented him with a golden opportunity; he had to act now. The bead was fully in the notch of the rear sight as he began to squeeze the trigger. He was in that neutral state of neither exhaling nor inhaling, but that was just seconds away from changing when the rifle roared and bucked upward. The shooter lost sight of his victim. Black smoke hung in the air. Frantic, he rose from behind the big rock and looked for the rider; his horse was there, prancing nervously in a half circle, its saddle empty. The shooter's legs and hands were shaking and he felt as if he might be sick to his stomach. He'd killed a man before but not like this. He was reluctant to leave his hiding spot for fear that he'd only wounded the rider and he would get shot walking up on him; so he waited for the man to hopefully bleed out.

The big slug had hit the rider in the stomach, just below his heart. He tried to get up, but couldn't. Death was imminent and he knew it, but so would it be for the coward who had shot him, if only he would show himself. He struggled to pull his pistol from its holster and cock it; finally he succeeded. And then he waited, with his left hand clutching his wound and his right the grip of his pistol, but it was a losing proposition. Blood steadily seeped from beneath the palm of his hand and down his side onto the dirt where it was beginning to puddle. The pain, which had been intense, seemed to be easing off now. Just above his head, at the edge of the road, he could see the grass gently sway in the breeze and above that, white, puffy clouds. He was feeling really tired and wanted to close his eyes but he fought it until suddenly, like the last of the grains of sand in an hourglass, he was through.

Chapter Two

Josh Morrow gently nudged his horse onward. The clouds overhead were a charcoal color, almost black and piled high. It didn't take a genius to know that a real frog strangler was in the making. Josh had been caught in these types of storms before and it wasn't a pleasant experience. But the task at hand precluded him from even considering looking for shelter. On either side of the wagon road, the wind swayed the yellow grass amongst the short gray sagebrush that covered the rolling hills. It was monotonous terrain. Not much cover here for bushwhackin' a guy, thought Josh. Sheriff Hollis in Bear Creek told him that his friend had been found dead about ten miles south of town on the road to the Salmon River country. "Looked like he got shot right outta his saddle. Probably never knew what hit him."

If this was the sheriff's attempt at consoling Josh over the loss of his friend he had failed miserably, not just in his choice of words but the look of indifference in his eyes. There wasn't a hint of compassion. Not the slightest bit of "I'm sorry about your friend." Instead, Hollis was quick to point out that money was owed to the undertaker. "You need to go see Willie Magee over at the barbershop. He does the undertakin' around here and he done your friend up. Wasn't nothing fancy 'cause he didn't even know who it was he was burying or if he was gonna get paid or not."

"Yes, sir. I'll do that straight away." No sooner had these words left Josh's mouth than he regretted having addressed the sheriff as "sir." He had just met Hollis but his first impression of him wasn't good. He was well dressed, handsome by some accounts with a neatly cared-for mustache and goatee. To Josh, Hollis looked like a dandy, but his parents had schooled him to respect his elders and people in positions of authority—and Hollis fit both of these categories. Even more, it had become second nature for Josh to address people of authority as "sir" during his five years in the army, which had ended only six months ago. He, and his now dead friend Seth Jacobs, had served in the 2nd Calvary down south in Texas and Oklahoma fighting Comanches and Mexican bandits. Josh had joined the army, in spite of his parents' objections, at the age of twenty-one. He'd had a comfortable life prior to that, having grown up in Galveston the son of a storekeeper. But for Josh, that was part of the of the problem. There was an Indian war going on and people were dying while for him life was good, maybe too good, too soft. The papers were full of stories about Comanche raids on ranches to the north and the atrocities committed. From time to time, some of those surviving settlers would end up in Galveston looking for a safer way to make a living. All of this caused Josh to take stock of himself as a man and where he was going in life. Being a storekeeper was an honorable line of work, and it probably would have made his father proud had he chosen to stay on and take over the family business. But deep down, right or wrong, Josh simply felt like being a storekeeper wasn't the manly thing to do, not when folks weren't safe on the frontier. Of course, he could never tell his father this, which only made it all the more difficult to explain why he wanted to join the army and leave home. His mother cried and his dad, exasperated, told him, "Just be sure this is what you want to do. Five years is a long time. Plenty long enough to get yourself killed by the Indians." Nothing was certain in Josh's mind, only that he wasn't content with what he was doing with his life at the present time and what would be coming his way in the foreseeable future if he didn't make a change. It was only a few months after joining the army that the prophecy of his father's words became more apparent.

There was a small coulee up ahead, maybe a half mile, that had a few ponderosa pine trees with snowberry bushes growing beneath them. Josh spurred his horse into a gallop, figuring that it made more sense to go to where the terrain lent itself to an ambush than waste what little time he had before the storm set in looking for the spot where his friend had been killed. Sheriff Hollis could've obviously been more helpful, but his attitude was Seth was just another dumb miner looking to get rich but got himself killed for probably what few personal items he had with him. There were a lot of out-of-luck miners, reasoned Hollis, that would kill to get another grubstake—anything that would enable them to stay on in the Bear Creek gold-fields. The rain had just started to fall when Josh spotted the bloodstain in the road. It had been a little over two weeks ago that Seth's body had been discovered lying at the edge of the road in a pool of blood. His horse, weapons, and anything of value had been taken. His murder and robbery came as no surprise to anybody in the area, as Bear Creek and the new gold strike near there had fostered a lawless environment. Josh stepped down from his big paint horse and dropped the reins, knowing that it would stay in that place until he either whistled or came for it. He knelt beside the bloodstained earth. He could see Seth's face and hear him laugh and go on about the cattle ranch they were going to start. Seth had been a true friend, even having saved Josh's life. A Comanche warrior had knocked Josh from his saddle. The blow from the Comanche's war club had left Josh semi-conscious on the ground, with his assailant standing over him with his knife drawn. The image of the Indian poised above him was like one of those bad dreams where you sense overwhelming danger, but you're paralyzed and your body just won't respond. Then, at the last second, you wake up and realize that it was just a dream—except in this case, as Josh's senses started to return, the Comanche warrior had put a knee on his chest and was grasping for his hair. Josh could do no more than flail at the Comanche's hands, when suddenly, a blow from Seth's rifle barrel pitched the Indian violently to the side. He was stunned, desperately trying to regain his senses but it was too late; Seth's .52-caliber Spencer roared. The

385-grain bullet slammed the warrior back to the ground. It was at this point, finally, that Josh had his wits about him.

There stood Seth, rifle in hand with a nervous, adrenaline grin on his face. "Damn. Thought you was a gonner." Josh looked up at Seth's outstretched hand and took hold of it. "Yeah, me too." At the time, that was all he could think of to say. Maybe it was the gash in his head, or the realization that he had been only seconds away from a hideous death, but words just wouldn't come to him. Days later, over a beer, he had tried to offer a sincere "thank you" but Seth jokingly laughed it off with: "Buy me a beer. Maybe you can return the favor someday. Enough said." And now three short years later when his friend needed him most, Josh had not been there. He'd received a letter from Seth saying that he had succumbed to the temptations of the goldfield and that he had what he thought was a promising claim. He was confident that if Josh would help him for just one year that they could make enough to buy a ranch on the Salmon River. Although he already had a job on a ranch in the Salmon River valley, Josh couldn't bring himself to turn his friend down. He owed the man his life, but even more, Seth had been a true friend, which as Josh had discovered in life, was hard to come by.

The rain was steady now. It mixed with the dark bloody soil, at first just making it damp, but then it created little puddles and finally the puddles gave way to tiny rivulets flowing down the gentle incline. It wouldn't be long and any evidence of exactly where Seth had been killed would be obliterated. From the bloodstains at the mouth of the shallow coulee it was, Josh reckoned, about 300 yards to a small stand of ponderosa pine trees that had taken root, probably due to the moisture that accumulated in the coulee. Most of the rest of the nearby country was sagebrush and grass. The stand of trees wasn't real big, but big enough to conceal a horse and its rider. There had been too much horse-and-wagon traffic on the road since Seth had been killed for there to be any clues that might be of value. Josh looked at the stand of trees and whispered aloud. "It'd be a pretty fair shot at that distance, but if I was going to ambush someone on this stretch of road that's where I'd be."

Josh gathered the reins of his horse, Thunder, which on this day was more than appropriately named, and began slowly walking up the coulee looking for anything that might give him a clue as to who the shooter was. The sagebrush in the coulee was taller than on the flat ground to either side of it. This caused Josh to meander through the brush. He went slowly, in spite of the rain, peering down at the ground searching for something that he wasn't even sure what it would be. Thunder provided Josh with a good vantage point. He was sixteen hands and moved slowly as if he knew the task before them required it. Josh was nearing the trees and hadn't seen much of any consequence other than some old horse tracks which could've been the bush-whacker's horse, but there was nothing about these tracks that would distinguish them from any other.

Josh stepped down from Thunder. There were about a dozen big ponderosa pines and maybe twice that many small ones in the thicket at the head of the coulee. It was a different feel in the trees. It made the hair on the back of Josh's neck stand up. The sky had darkened such that with the falling rain and being within the trees it was difficult to see. For a moment Josh rested his right hand on the butt of his pistol. It gave him comfort, not that he was any *pistolero* but his knowledge of the world, men, and death and dying had come a long ways since he'd left home five years ago. Josh surveyed his surroundings. The rain had abated slightly, but his view was punctuated by rhythmic drops of water from the brim of his hat. He was soaked and beginning to shiver. Josh moved further into the trees. Good, clear tracks of any kind were hard to come by due to the heavy needle cast and fall of pine cones from the trees. Droppings from mule deer and elk, although not numerous, were evident but little else. And then he saw it: a pile of horse droppings on the back side of the thicket. The ground near the droppings had been churned up by numerous horse hoofprints like the horse had been tied off there and made to wait for a good while. From the droppings Josh looked back into the trees. The road was not visible from here. He began to walk back through the trees looking for the place that he would set up if he were going to ambush somebody on the road below. He hadn't taken more than a few steps when he spotted it. It was on the east edge of the trees, about halfway up the north side of the coulee: there were a couple of good-sized rocks. Josh worked his way over to the rocks; either of them would make a good rest to shoot from. He dropped to one knee. The view from the rocks to the road was unobstructed, yet someone crouched behind them would be very difficult to see. For one thing, it was a long ways to be able to see no more than the top of a man's head and a rifle barrel. Suddenly, something on the ground slightly off to his right caught Josh's attention. It had been pushed into the forest duff, possibly by the killer's boot heel, but there was no mistaking a fairly new copper shell casing. Josh brushed the decomposing pine needles aside and picked up the empty cartridge. He recognized it as a .44 Henry even before he looked at the stamp on the end of the case. Josh smirked and shook his head as he eyed the empty shell casing. If this was what Seth's killer had used, it said a couple of things about him. One, he wasn't very smart when it came to the capabilities of guns. Josh hadn't been either prior to serving in the army, but he soon found that knowing the limitations of various rifles and pistols could mean the difference between life and death. The .44 Henry Rimfire was not a good rifle for shooting long range; it was at best a 200-yard weapon. This fact led Josh to surmise that maybe the killer wasn't stupid as much as he was a coward. Josh had killed men, both from a distance and on one occasion in hand-to-hand fighting. Killing someone at a hundred yards was far less emotional than looking into someone's eyes and pulling the trigger—or worse, having them in your grasp, as Josh had done once, and plunging a knife into their heart. Seeing the stunned look on their face and the light, the gleam in their eyes, retreat gradually until suddenly you realize it is gone and you are responsible. It wasn't the long-range killing that haunted Josh's dreams so much; it was the other, mono on mono. This required a brave man or a desperate man with no other options. Josh reckoned that the killer was desperate but not willing to confront a man like Seth face to face. Based on what he'd heard about Bear Creek before coming there, that description could fit quite a few people. The area had a reputation for being lawless despite having a sheriff.

Josh and Thunder hunkered down as best they could in the trees at the head of the coulee and waited for the storm to die down. Being near the tall trees with the lightning popping all around might not have been the smartest thing to do, but the wind had picked up considerably and the rain was now coming almost horizontally. Riding back to Bear Creek under those conditions just didn't appeal to Josh.

The storm raged for close to an hour before finally subsiding. Water dripped from all of the vegetation, and mud puddles dotted the ground wherever there was a depression. The wind, the thunder, the lightning; they were all gone. The land had been rejuvenated, so to speak, and the commotion of the storm had been replaced by silence save for the melodic call of a western meadowlark.

"All right, Thunder. High time we was gettin' outa here," said Josh as he rose from his spot beneath a big ponderosa pine. Thunder snickered softly as if in agreement. To say the road was muddy would be an understatement. The soil was clayey and the surface of the ground had turned into a slippery, treacherous mess. In many places Thunder's hooves sunk in several inches. Josh had not gone far on the road back to Bear Creek when he decided that it would be easier going if he rode in the short brush and grass next to the road.

Josh was about an hour into the ride back when he thought he heard a voice from up around the bend in the road. "C'mon, mules. Git your lazy asses movin'." This was followed by a whistle and more words of encouragement. Soon the source of this racket came into view. It was a small freight wagon drawn by two mules. A dog was running along behind. Josh had no sooner reined Thunder in to watch the procession headed his way when the driver saw him up ahead and to the side of the road. Instantly, he dropped the mules' reins in his lap and reached for his rifle. "State your business," he commanded over the barking of the dog, which had now come up alongside of the wagon.

Josh eyed the driver for a moment. He was a slender, scruffy-looking guy who hadn't shaved in about a week to ten days. His whiskers were salt-and-pepper and he had on a slouchy felt hat that had lost most of its original shape. His demeanor was somewhere between nervous and sorely agitated. "Pleased to meet you too," said Josh with a smile.

The wagon driver kept his right-hand thumb on the hammer of his Sharps repeater—a fact which hadn't gone unnoticed by Josh. He must already have a round chambered, he thought.

"A fellar can't be too careful these days, especially around these parts," replied the wagon driver with just a hint of civility in his voice. "Lots of folks takin' stuff that don't belong to'em and killin' good folks in the process."

"Yes sir, I know what ya'll mean," said Josh, still mindful of the driver's thumb on the hammer of his rifle. "Ya'll reckon it'd be okay if I rode on up so's we could stop hollerin' back and forth."

The driver paused for a moment. He seemed to be taking stock of Josh's youthfulness and relatively clean-cut appearance as well as the fact that Josh was on the edge of effective pistol range where he was currently at. Finally, satisfied that Josh posed little risk, the mule skinner summoned him. "Come ahead on, mister. Just keep your hands near your saddle horn."

"Much obliged." And with that Josh closed the distance to the freight wagon under the watchful eyes of the driver. When he was within about twenty feet of the wagon, he reined Thunder to a halt. "Name's Josh Morrow. I'm headed to Bear Creek."

"Lester Scoville's mine," replied the driver. "And this here is Rufus," he said, nodding to the dog who was now sitting on the seat next to him. Rufus appeared to be a mutt mix of some sort, but he most closely resembled an Australian shepherd.

"Pleased to meet you both." It was obvious to Josh that there was a warm bond between Lester and his dog.

"So you're headed for Bear Creek, are ya?" said Lester rhetorically. "I try to spend as little time as possible in that hellhole. It's a good place to lose your money, your life, or both."

"Ya'll travel this road very often?" asked Josh.

"Oh, ever' now and again when I need supplies in town," replied Lester. "Hate to leave my claim for very long. Course if somebody was to want to take it my being there probably wouldn't matter. Some young fellar had a claim up on Moonshine Creek. I seen him workin' it a time or two and then next thing I know is somebody murdered him, just up the road here," said Lester, nodding his head in that direction for emphasis.

Josh had his arms crossed near the wrists and was resting both his hands on his saddle horn well away from his Army Colt .44. "I think the guy you're talking about was my friend. A big guy, blond hair, always had a smile."

"Yeah, that sounds like this guy."

"I was supposed to meet him here and help work his claim," replied Josh.

There was a look of genuine concern on Lester's face. He had moved his thumb away from the Sharps' hammer— an obvious gesture of trust that Josh noted. "Sorry to hear that," said Lester. "Far as I know, they ain't caught the guy who done it. But to be right truthful, with the sheriff we got here, they never will."

Josh had only been in Bear Creek a couple of days, and what he had heard from folks there pretty much coincided with what Lester was saying. If there was to be any justice for Seth it would be up to him, but that was beginning to look like a tall order. "This claim you said you saw my friend working, how far is it from here?"

Lester's eyes widened a bit like he had something important to say. "You thinkin' agoin' there?" he asked.

"I am," said Josh. "In his letter to me, my friend Seth said he had a good claim and that it was no pipedream. He said that he'd filed on it in both our names, but when I went to the claim office in town they said some other guy named Leroy Bates had took over the claim due to it being abandoned. I told'em Seth was dead and I was on my way here but that didn't matter to them."

Lester turned his head to the side and spit a stream of tobacco juice. "Don't mean to rile you but I already seen a couple of other guys workin' your friend's claim. They been there upwards of a week. The way the law reads in this here mining district is a fellar can be gone from his claim for three days without losing it; after that, unless you're sick, it's fair game for anybody else."

"Yes sir, that's what they told me in Bear Creek at the claim office, but it still seems like a lot of horse crap to me," said Josh somewhat angrily. "What's to prevent this very thing from happening over and over? If a guy wants a claim all he has to do is knock off a guy who owns one, wait three days, and then move in. Don't seem right to me."

"It ain't," said Lester, "but the miners here was the ones that made up the laws of the mining district. So I'm a-guessin' that unless your friend left a will you ain't got a snowball's chance in hell of gettin' any part of that claim."

Josh sighed heavily and adjusted his hat slightly to block the sun which had now come out and was shining brightly. "Lester," he began in a somewhat serious tone, "this ain't about me getting rich. I was happy workin' cattle and fixin' fence over on the Salmon River. It might have taken a little while, but in time I reckon me and Seth could've got us a place of our own. But now I feel obliged to at least try to get back what was taken from my friend. It was his dream.

At best his family back east should get something from his work and losing his life."

"Can't say that I blame you," said Lester, "but I think you're swimmin' upstream agin' a pretty fast current."

"Maybe so," replied Josh, "but I gotta try." Josh paused for a moment to consider what he was about to ask. "I don't want to drag you into this fray but I'd be obliged if maybe tomorrow you could show me where Seth's claim was. I'm not lookin' for you to side with me or anything, just point out where his claim was."

Lester didn't seem to be surprised by the request. In fact, his facial expression seemed to suggest that he was kind of honored that his new acquaintance would ask. "I got me a little shanty and corral about a mile up Porcupine Creek from where this here road crosses it. Be about another six-seven miles on up the road. I'll be there tomorrow. Got me a claim on the creek, so I'll most likely be down there when you come."

"Much obliged, Lester," said Josh. And with that the seeds of a friendship appeared to have been planted.

Lester set his Sharps in the wagon box behind his seat, and then taking up the reins to the mules he said: "I best be gittin' home, Josh. Watch yourself tonight."

"I'll try," said Josh.

Lester snapped the reins. "Git up, mules," he shouted. Rufus barked twice for added encouragement and the freight wagon lurched forward.

Chapter Three

It took Josh about an hour to reach the small town of Bear Creek, which was situated on, as the name implies, Bear Creek. It was a bustling concern with a number of businesses located along its main street, the majority of which were intended to satisfy the miner's social needs. The town had just recently been established a couple of years earlier when gold had been discovered on Bear Creek and in a number of the surrounding streams. It had a look and feel of newness, but at the same time somewhat unorganized due to the numerous tents and shanties associated with the mining claims along the creek.

It was nearly dark as Josh rode up Bear Creek's main street. Pale yellow light from lanterns spilled out onto the street from the various businesses that were still open—mainly saloons. The light from the lanterns shimmered on the surface of the mud puddles that dotted the street. The summer evening was warm. Mosquitoes from the creek nearby had taken up their quest for dinner. Josh slapped the back of his left hand, ending prematurely the dinner plans of at least one mosquito. There weren't many people on the street, certainly no women. Boisterous voices punctuated by occasional laughter and honky-tonk music from several of the saloons drifted out onto the street. There was a smell of smoke in the air from the cooking fires up and down the creek. Here and there, in the distance, Josh could see people squatting around fires that periodically illuminated the outline of a wall tent. There was an obvious contrast between the tent people and the town people—not necessarily one of the haves and have-nots but rather, Josh reasoned, one of potential. There was potential for both groups to advance to either a more elevated "have position" of wealth or complete failure; the only question was the path that they would choose to get there; some would not survive.

Josh rode directly to the livery stable. He unsaddled Thunder and fed and watered him and brushed him down. He'd not been a horse person before joining the cavalry, but there he had come to appreciate, if not love, his horse, as he realized that his life could depend upon it.

Knowing that Bear Creek's only restaurant was just about to close for the day caused Josh to quicken his pace. It had been early that morning since he last had anything to eat. To say that he was hungry would be an understatement. Josh took a seat at a table near the window. There were only two other customers in the place and they appeared to be about done.

"Dinner bell rang a long time ago," said the portly, middle-aged woman who had now approached Josh's table. "We got a little beef stew left and some apple pie, or I could maybe cook you up a venison steak with a few taters. What'll it be?"

"I'll have the stew, some coffee, and biscuits if you got-tem, ma'am," replied Josh.

"Young man, it's your lucky day," said the waitress. "Usually by this time of day we don't have any biscuits left. I make'em fresh every morning and they tend to go pretty fast, especially with some fresh-churned butter and honey." The waitress's eager-to-please attitude reminded Josh of his mother.

As Josh waited for his coffee he took in his surround-ings. The restaurant wasn't real big; there were six tables with three to four chairs at each table. Red and white oil-cloth with a nondescript pattern covered each tabletop. Several, but not all, of the tables had chimney lanterns that burned coal oil. Lighting in the room was uneven and shadowy, but not so much so that Josh hadn't observed the badges on the two men across the room. They had been talking in low tones to one another, but in Josh's opinion, they seemed to have taken a special interest in his presence as they frequently glanced over at him.

"Here you go, young man," said the waitress as she re-turned with his coffee. "Your food'll be ready real shortly."

"Thank you, ma'am," replied Josh.

"So what brings a well-mannered young fella like you to a place like this?" inquired the waitress in a friendly tone.

Josh paused a moment to consider his response. After talking with Lester he wasn't certain who he should trust. He reasoned that since he had already talked to Sheriff Hollis about his purpose for being in Bear Creek that the deputies across the room were probably privy to this information as well. Josh looked the waitress in the eye. "I came here to meet a friend of mine. I was going to help him work a claim that he had filed on for the both of us, but I've found that he was murdered a couple of weeks ago. So now, I have no friend and no claim."

"I'm sorry to hear that," said the waitress sincerely. "But you're not alone. This kind of thing happens all the time. Decent folks around here really have to watch out for road agents."

"Pretty sad state of affairs," said Josh.

The waitress's eyes darted left towards the deputies and then refocused on Josh. They had stopped talking and were definitely concentrating on what was being said between her and Josh. There was some concern in the waitress's eyes but she continued, "So, what are you going to do now?"

"Several years back, my friend saved my life. I think I owe it to him to try and find out who killed him, and not to mention, who stole his claim."

"You better watch yourself, young man," said the motherly waitress. "You could be barkin' up a pretty tall tree and no tellin' what's in it."

Josh laughed. "Ma'am, you're the second person, in so many words, that has told me the same thing."

From across the room, the sound of chairs being slid back from the table could be heard. Josh and the waitress turned their attention in that direction. The deputies were on their feet and headed towards Josh. Their demeanor was stern but not threatening.

"Evenin'," said the first deputy as he neared Josh's table. "Didn't mean to eavesdrop but I couldn't help but overhear what you was sayin' about your friend."

Josh eyed the two men briefly. His immediate impression of them was that they were far from being any kind of dedicated public servants. They were somewhat unkempt and their eyes and facial expressions lacked sincerity or respect for Josh. "Yeah," said Josh, "I talked to the sheriff yesterday. He was the one who told me that my friend had been murdered on the road south of town."

"These parts is pretty rough, mister," said the second deputy. "Especially with all the gold that's being mined, and then you got folks that figure they can just up and go wherever they want with a big shit pot of the stuff and nobody's gonna bother 'em. It just ain't gonna happen. People like that is just askin' for it."

Josh couldn't help but wonder if what he had just heard from the deputy was his personal philosophy, which seemed to border on justification. It was like, how dare one of the "haves" tempt the "have-nots" with a bunch of gold, especially when this transfer of wealth could be affected with a single bullet. Looking the second deputy squarely in the eyes, Josh said: "You may be right, Deputy. The longer I'm here the more I realize just how much bushwhackin' scum there is in this country. They seem to get away with just about anything they want to do."

Josh's words had the desired effect. There was anger in the second deputy's eyes. Josh had struck a nerve; whether it was because the deputy was one of the bushwhackin' scum or he had taken offense to Josh's implication that the law wasn't doing their job was not quite certain to Josh.

The first deputy sensed the anger in his partner. "Mister, we just wanted to let you know that it'd probably be best if you let the law sort out your friend's murder. You never know what you're dealing with. A guy could get his self killed pokin' around something like this."

"Thanks for the advice, Deputy," said Josh. "But I reckon two heads might be better than one."

"Suit yourself," said the first deputy. "But you can't say that you wasn't warned." And with that the two lawmen walked out.

"You don't want to rile those two hooligans," said the waitress. "They're bad news."

Josh took a sip of his coffee. "I suppose they are," he replied. "But I intend to find out which side of the street those guys walk on."

After he had finished his meal Josh stepped out into the street. It was totally dark now. It had been a long day and his muscles were tired and kind of achy. Just going to bed over at the hotel and getting a good night's rest sounded good, but so did having a drink to relax before he turned in. Having a drink won out.

Josh entered the first saloon that he came to. It was summer and warm so the door to the place had been left open. The room was longer than wide. It was illuminated, although poorly, by multiple coal oil lanterns atop two crude wooden chandeliers suspended from the log beams overhead. As he entered, his senses were bombarded by a variety of sights, sounds, and smells. Cigar and cigarette smoke hung heavy in the air. At times it was almost overwhelming to Josh, who was a nonsmoker. Yet counter to this he detected a hint of fresh pinewood, owing to the fact the building hadn't been in existence all that long. But as he moved toward the bar and in closer proximity to its patrons, the brief respite of pinewood was replaced by body odor mixed with the tobacco smoke. Taking an actual bath was a luxury not readily available to a lot of the miners.

The saloon was lively. A piano was being played by a man with slender features at the back of the room. His audience appeared unappreciative as they never clapped, but not long ago the piano player had been sick for a few days and there was no music. Some of the miners complained, but when the piano player returned nobody seemed to acknowledge it. Numerous men lined the bar on the left side of the room, while even more sat at tables to the right; some who were playing poker were pensive and quiet except when a particular hand necessitated an outburst from either the winner or the loser. The poker table was like a simmering cauldron that periodically boiled over. A dark stain on the rough plank flooring near it was evidence that this had happened in the not-too-distant past.

Amidst all of this gruffness and potential depravity were three barroom girls. They all wore heavy makeup and dresses that displayed cleavage sufficient for the prospective client to complete the image. On the surface the saloon girls were like white lilies in a field of ragweed, but it was clear to Josh that for at least two of the girls a guy might not want to look too far beneath the surface. One of the girls, however, didn't appear to fit this category. She looked younger, awkward, and kind of out of place.

The bartender—a big no-nonsense-looking guy with dark mutton-chop sideburns and a thick moustache that covered his top lip—had seen Josh enter the saloon. He could see that Josh was making his way to an open spot at the other end of the bar and started in that direction. The bartender arrived first. "What'll it be?" he asked as Josh stepped up to the bar.

"Whiskey," replied Josh.

The bartender took a small glass from the shelf behind the bar and poured a generous amount of whiskey into it and then set it in front of Josh. "That'll be two bits," he said as he sized Josh up.

Josh shoved a quarter across the bar towards the bartender without speaking. He felt that since entering the saloon there were several people, including the bartender, that had taken more than a casual interest in his being there. This was only his second night in Bear Creek, so other than the sheriff and the undertaker there really wasn't anyone else who had any "long-term" knowledge of who he was or why he was there. Josh took a sip of his whiskey. It almost made him grimace. It was rotgut, not smooth tasting at all, but he reckoned he was in the wrong place if he wanted some quality whiskey. It'll do for a nightcap, he thought, so long as I only have one. Josh smiled to himself as he recalled some of the cheap whiskey hangovers that he and Seth had experienced at different army posts. He could smile about those times now. They were fun in the making, but the morning after was usually totally lacking in humor.

The men to either side of Josh were sitting on high stools, as were most of the other bar patrons. Providing a stool so the customer was comfortable encouraged more drinking. The man to Josh's right had obviously taken advantage of this. Both of his forearms rested heavily on the bar, and his head was either hanging down or from time to time it would jerk upright in synchrony with one or the other of his arms and point with curled fingers towards the mirror behind the bar and mumble: "Those sons a bitches'll get theirs. Jus' you wait." He appeared to be a working miner; his pant legs were muddy below the knees and torn in places. His cotton shirt was sweat-stained under the arms and down the center of his back, and there was dried, white, salty-looking sweat around the base of his hat. He had bags under his brown eyes and his face was thin and drawn—the latter condition possibly due to the man having lost a number of his front teeth, while those that remained were heavily stained by chewing tobacco. His beard was extremely sparse, confined mostly to some sporadic chin whiskers. The man looked like he could be part Indian. "Hollis, he's a worthless bastard," announced the drunken miner in a voice clear enough and loud enough for the bartender to hear.

The bartender stepped closer to the bar and leaned over to where he was face-to-face with the drunk. "Henry, you keep on talkin' that kinda shit and you're gonna wind up dead or in jail. What's done is done so let it go."

"You ain't the one that got robbed," replied the drunk defiantly. "I busted my ass for that gold dust and then some lazy no-account crook sticks a gun in my face and takes it. And then Hollis tells me, let the law handle it. They can't handle shit. Been a month and nothin'. I tell you what, though," said the miner, patting the .36-caliber Navy Colt that was tucked under his belt. "If I find the worthless bastard that got my gold he's gonna be a sorry sonvabitch."

The bartender looked at the drunk with disgust. "You're drunk, Henry. Take my advice: shut your mouth and get outa here." And with that he turned and walked to the other end of the bar.

In the mirror behind the bar, Josh could see that a stool several places to his left had become vacant. Figuring that even being in close proximity to Henry might not win him any points with Hollis or his deputies, he picked up his drink and moved to the unoccupied space. Josh began to reflect on his experiences of the past couple of days. It seemed to be a common consensus among decent-working folks that the law in Bear Creek was worthless, if not corrupt. However, actually proving that might not be an easy task and it might be downright unhealthy.

Josh noted the time. A clock situated on the back bar above a painting of a nude woman lying on her side indicated that it was 10:15. A pendulum encased in glass that swung back and forth beneath the clock face metered the time. It made a fairly loud ticking sound, and when the bar was quiet it served as a reminder that time was wasting, like there should be more useful, productive things that a person could be doing than just sitting there drinking and telling lies or daydreaming about getting rich. But it wasn't a quiet time. There was a steady din of noise such that the ticking couldn't be heard above it, and so that mournful guilt trip wasn't played upon anybody's conscience save for the bartender occasionally when there might be a momentary lapse in the noise.

It had been a long day and Josh decided that it was time to turn in. As he brought his glass up to finish his drink, his eyes made contact with the younger saloon girl in the mirror behind the bar. She was walking towards him. Josh swallowed the remains of his drink and turned to leave. The saloon girl was squarely in his path. "Hi mister, buy a girl a drink?"

At slightly over six feet, Josh towered over the girl. "Ah, no thanks," said Josh. "Got a lot to do tomorrow." And with that Josh started to step around the girl, but she grabbed his left arm lightly, causing him to pause. The girl looked up at him and said: "Please, just one." There was desperation in her voice and in her eyes. Earlier, from across the room she didn't appear to fit the image of a saloon girl but now, up close, Josh was even more convinced of that. He was torn. He had no desire other than to go back to his room at the hotel and get some rest, but now he was suddenly feeling some strange moral obligation to buy this girl a drink. He had a sense that to leave would be akin to turning his back on a person in need. And then it was as if the moment had become so pregnant with awkwardness, Josh couldn't help himself when he said: "Alright, just one." There was an immediate look of relief in the girl's face. Conversely, Josh inwardly berated himself for having committed to the drink. The two of them stepped back to the bar. Josh summoned the bartender with an upward nod of his head. "Whiskey for the lady and me," he said. The bartender turned to the back bar and poured the drinks from separate bottles. Josh smiled derisively. It was a common scam: he would be drinking whiskey (getting hopefully more drunk and looser with his money) while the lady drank tea; the price, however, was the same.

Noting that the bartender seemed to be lingering in front of them, Josh asked the saloon girl: "Ya'll want to sit at that table by the door?"

"Sure, lead the way," she replied.

Josh's upbringing dictated that he pull the lady's chair out for her. Clearly this surprised her, but she was appreciative. "Thank you," she said. "I haven't worked here long but you're the first gentleman that I've encountered."

Josh laughed. "Does that surprise you?" Instantly, he regretted the tone of his words. He sounded judgmental but he didn't apologize. The girl seemed to take it in stride.

"The only thing that surprises me," said the girl, "is that I'm working in a place like this. My circumstances left me with no other choice."

"I suspected as much," replied Josh. "Ya'll have a look of innocence about you that your coworkers don't."

The girl took a sip of her tea, obviously nursing it so it would last, which was contrary to what she had been instructed to do. "They don't like being here either but they got no choice. In this part of the world unless a woman has a man to look out for her she doesn't have many options," she said defiantly.

Josh had not ever given this much thought before now, but he could see that from a single woman's perspective, making a living, especially in a rough place like Bear Creek, would be difficult. But on the other hand, for a man to make a living was no cakewalk either. This fact might account for why there was so much thievery and murder. It took grit, determination, and hard work along with a little good luck for a man to make a living. A man lacking in any of those areas could succumb to the temptation of taking from someone else that had been more fortunate. Undoubtedly, there were instances of desperation that might seem to justify breaking the law, but generally society saw this as a fine line that shouldn't be crossed. Desperate actions such as stealing and killing would not be tolerated. On the other hand, folks seemed to be more tolerant, almost indifferent, to desperate measures causing a person, such as a saloon girl, to destroy their reputation and health.

"So how long have you been workin' here?" asked Josh.

"Four days," replied the girl, "but it seems like eternity. I don't know that I'll be able to take it much longer, men pawing at you every night."

"You mind me askin', but what caused you to take up this line of work?"

The girl's eyes began to tear up. "I came here from San Francisco with my husband a couple of months ago. He was intent on searching for gold and he finally found a fairly promising claim west of here in the mountains, but before he could file on it, he was murdered. Then some other people filed on it and I ended up with nothing. We were penniless at the time and I lived off of handouts—pity mostly—for a time, but then people's generosity dried up. I had no place to turn to."

"You don't have any family that could help you?" suggested Josh.

The girl shook her head. "None with any means. Besides they're back east, in Boston mostly. It'd take considerable money to travel that far and they don't have it and neither do I, obviously."

Josh took a sip of the whiskey which he hadn't wanted and pondered the girl's situation. She could be playing him for a handout. He'd known guys in the army that had fallen for a saloon girl's sob story and it had cost them a lot. But there was something about this girl that told him she was on the up-and-up. But even if she was it wasn't his problem. He had his own problems. He'd quit his ranch job to come here to work Seth's claim, but now that wasn't going to happen. He was living off of his savings, money that he'd set aside to buy a ranch; that couldn't continue. At some point, he was going to have to find a job, preferably not in the goldfield. Josh was aggravated and frustrated. Why didn't I just go to bed after supper? he said to himself. Little did he know, but his aggravation was about to get ratcheted up a notch.

"Oh no," said the girl in a low tone to Josh. "This guy's trouble."

Josh looked to his left. A big guy—bigger than Josh, who was about six foot one and 210 pounds—was headed towards his table. He had long stringy hair and a dark, full beard. He had a gun belt with a .44-caliber Colt on his right side and a Bowie knife on his left side. There was a menacing look in his eyes, as if he knew he was about to cause trouble but didn't care. The big stranger stopped close to Josh's table such that he towered over both Josh and the saloon girl. "Evenin'," he said in a coy tone. "Mind if I dance with the lady here?"

Josh could see the fear in the girl's eyes. There was something different about this guy that seemed to terrify her. "Sorry, pardner, the lady's having a drink with me," said Josh in a deliberately cordial voice.

The big man instinctively wiped some tobacco juice from the corner of his mouth. His eyes glared at Josh in a threatening manner. "Don't mean she's your property, mister. Hell, she ain't nothin' but a whore and whores git passed around."

Given the circumstances, Josh felt awkward in arguing the saloon girl's virtue. "Maybe so," replied Josh. "But right now she's drinkin' on my dollar." From the corner of his eye Josh could see the girl was slightly insulted.

The big guy scoffed. "I don't rightly give a shit 'bout your dollar," he said in a mocking tone. "This little hussy has been ah-dodgin' me ever since she started here but not tonight." And with that he grabbed the girl's arm and started to pull her from her chair.

Josh jumped to his feet. "Let her go," he commanded.

And with that the big guy, who had grabbed the girl with his left hand, suddenly released her and then swung across his body with a big left hook intended for Josh's chin. Unfortunately for the big guy he'd telegraphed his intentions and Josh stepped back slightly, allowing the punch to miss. At the same time Josh snapped a left jab out that caused the big man's nose to explode. Blood immediately began to stream down over the big man's lips. The taste of his own blood seemed to enrage him even more. "You sonovabitch, I'm gonna kill you," he seethed. And with that he lunged at Josh, only to be met by a left-right combination that dropped him to the floor. The big man lay prostrate, face down. Blood began to pool around his face. The room had become quiet save for the ticking clock on the wall and the gurgling breathing of the unconscious big man. But the quietness was only temporary; it was broken by the bartender: "Mister, you best git the hell outa here. 'Cause when the Swede there wakes up he's really gonna want to kill you and I don't need any gunplay in here."

Josh looked up from the Swede to the saloon girl, who was now crying quietly. Tears had begun to cascade from her eyes. Those from her right eye had made it all the way to her jawbone. Her heavy makeup was streaking. Her face had a forlorn look about it that seemed to belie the realization that her escape from this insanity was about to walk out of her life and that tomorrow night the big Swede would probably be back.

To his left, Josh heard the sound of steel on wood. It was the bartender laying a sawed-off, double-barreled,

12-gauge shotgun on the bar. "Mister, I meant what I said. The Swede's gonna be comin' around any second now so take the gunplay outside."

Josh looked the bartender in the eye. "I'm not lookin' for any gunfight."

"Good," replied the bartender. "Now get the hell out and take the sniveling bitch with you. She ain't nothin' but trouble."

For a brief second the irony flashed through Josh's mind of how wanting a nightcap to relax before bed had become anything but. There would be time to sort things out later but for now, the bartender with the sawed-off shotgun was calling the shots. Josh looked over at the girl. "Let's go."

The girl's demeanor brightened slightly. She nodded her head and turned toward the door, as did Josh. But time had run out. "Look out!" yelled someone in the crowd. Instinctively, Josh's right hand went for his pistol as he turned towards where the Swede was lying. His gun had barely cleared his holster when he heard the roar of the Swede's pistol and instantly felt the burning in his left side. But it did not stop Josh from turning completely around to face the Swede, nor did it rattle him as he quickly aimed and fired a well-placed shot into the Swede's forehead. Once again the room was enveloped by a temporary silence save for the ticking clock above the back bar and Josh's pounding heart. Josh stared at the Swede through the gun smoke that hung in the air, making sure he was done.

"Someone go fetch the sheriff," said the bartender in an irritated voice.

The saloon girl's focus was on Josh's left side. "Oh my God, you've been shot."

The adrenaline still raged within Josh, and his breathing was somewhat rapid and heavy. He'd killed men before and it had never been a good feeling; this time was no different. It was like a mild form of shock. Looking at the saloon girl he said matter-of-factly: "Yes ma'am, it appears that way." Josh was not trying to be smug or cavalier about the situation, but his experiences in the army had taught him to control his emotions at critical moments.

"We need to get you to a doctor," said the girl.

"Not before the sheriff sorts this mess out," said the bartender, who had come out from behind the bar and was standing near the dead Swede.

Josh eyed the bartender for a moment. His demeanor and the tone of his words caused Josh to wonder if the bartender was looking at the shooting as something other than self-defense. "The guy tried to back-shoot me," said Josh sternly to the bartender. "Not much to sort out."

The bartender was indifferent. "We'll let the sheriff decide that."

At this point one of the other saloon girls stepped around the bartender and handed a bar rag to the girl. "Maybe this'll help stop the bleedin'." The bartender scowled at her but she ignored him. Normally, she wouldn't do anything to antagonize the bartender, as he could play heavily in her future well-being, but it seemed the court of public opinion in the room at that time was on her side. Besides, she hated the Swede. He was a mean drunk. He'd taken her upstairs one night for a poke and had gotten rough, slapping her around and blackening her eyes. She had no recourse; she was a whore. The bartender had warned the Swede that he'd be cut off if he continued to abuse the girls, but there was no punishment, just the threat of the loss of pleasure. For the girls, it was adding insult to injury.

"Thanks," said Josh as he took the rag from the girl. With his left hand he lifted his shirt to reveal a deep furrow across his side. There was considerable blood, which made the wound look worse than it actually was. Josh folded the rag and pressed it to the wound.

"Does it hurt much?" asked the girl.

"I've had worse," said Josh stoically. He was apprehensive about the sheriff's take on the shooting. He'd killed people before, but only in an army uniform on the field of battle; there he had been ordered to kill.

A voice could be heard behind the people who had gathered in the doorway to stare at the dead Swede. "Make way here," said the sheriff, who was being followed by his two deputies.

The crowd parted to reveal the Swede and Josh with the girl at his side. "Well, Mr. Morrow, we meet again," said the sheriff somewhat sarcastically. "And just to be straight up with you, it don't surprise me none that we're meetin' over a dead body. So, since he can't," nodding towards the Swede, "why don't you tell me what went on here."

"It was self-defense, Sheriff," said Josh. "As you can see, I been shot and there's plenty of witnesses here that'll tell you that I had my back turned when it happened."

"That so," said the sheriff as he eyed Josh's wound. A man dressed more like a cowboy than a miner stepped forward. "That's a fact, Sheriff. I seen the whole thing. It was more plain than a fresh brand that the Swede was lookin' fer trouble when he went over to this here fellar's table and tried to horn in."

From the crowd there were several shouts of "that's right" and one dissenting "all he wanted was a dance." It was an informal referendum that the sheriff was quick to acknowledge. It wasn't what the sheriff had wanted to hear as he felt that Josh could potentially upset the balance of things in Bear Creek. He'd just as soon give Josh a necktie party, but clearly the public sentiment for that wasn't there.

Conspicuously absent in the discussion was the bartender—a fact that hadn't gone unnoticed by Josh. He'd seen what had happened and he knew of the Swede's past behavior. Why wasn't he speaking up unless he'd just as soon see Josh go to jail?

Turning to Josh, the sheriff said: "Well, Morrow, appears you're in the clear this time but let's not make this a habit. Next time things might not go your way. In fact, just a friendly suggestion, you might want to consider movin' on."

Josh could tell by the look on the sheriff's face that he was irritated having to let him go. This baffled Josh somewhat, as the facts concerning the shooting were pretty clear-cut. The sheriff had no reason to be suspicious of him unless he thought Josh would interfere with some other agenda of the sheriff's. "I'm free to go?" said Josh.

The sheriff sighed with disgust. "You are for now."

Josh turned to the girl. The look on her face was beyond sadness; it was more like hurt, embarrassment, and shame all vying to win out. It was because of her, she reasoned, that the Swede was dead; not that she was very sorry about that, but it had brought pain and trouble to someone else, who for a brief time was treating her with respect, like a lady, and not a would-be whore. She wouldn't blame him if he just walked out—she was trouble. Josh could see the wheels of anticipation and uncertainty turning furiously in the girl's eyes. "You comin'?" he asked.

For a brief second there was a look of hesitancy in the girl's eyes as she re-processed in her mind the echo of Josh's words. Had he really asked her to go with him? Ironically, for something that she wanted so bad to happen, it was difficult for her to speak. There were lots of eyes upon her, waiting to see what "the little hussy" was going to do. The room had become quiet to hear the sheriff's decision, and now it had been awarded a bonus event. The girl could not look at the crowd; she felt naked before them and their judgment of her. But, once again in her life, desperation overcame pride. She nodded her head and whispered, "Yes."

Outside the night air was free of the tobacco smoke, and Josh and the girl were enveloped by the darkness save for the occasional shaft of light from a building. "We need to get you to a doctor?" said the girl as she looked up at Josh.

Josh shook his head. "It looks worse than it really is. The bullet just grazed me. I think it'll clean up okay and heal on its own."

"Are you sure?" asked the girl in a concerned tone.

Josh laughed. "I fought Comanches for five years. I saw my share of bullet wounds, some of 'em on me, so I think I got a pretty fair idea which ones need doctor'n and which ones don't."

The girl sighed in exasperation. "Well if you say so but sounds just like a stubborn man to me."

Josh smiled, although in the darkness it was doubtful if the girl could see it. She seemed to have a wholesomeness about her. There was something about her speech and mannerisms that said she was from good people. From Josh's perspective, her saloon-girl attire was definitely out of character. "You know, ma'am, it seems like we been through a lot in the last thirty minutes and I don't even know your name."

"It's Sarah, Sarah MaGinty," she said.

"Josh Morrow, pleased to meet you."

There was an awkward pause between them, precipitated by the obvious question at hand: what was to become of Sarah? Josh had very mixed feelings about getting involved with her any more than he already had. But what was he to do with her—just leave her standing on the street? She wasn't welcome back in the Gold Strike saloon and whorehouse. On the other hand, it wasn't his job to look out for her.

Sarah broke the silence. She knew that it had been too good to be true that a knight in shining armor would rescue her from the Gold Strike, but it had felt good, if only for little while, to believe that it had actually happened. "Well,

I guess this is where we go our separate ways," she said in a halting voice.

Josh was caught off-guard. He'd expected Sarah to be more presumptuous, even though he thought she was basically a good person. "You got any place to go?" he asked rhetorically.

Sarah reasoned that she could lie and say yes, but what would that get her—pride? Pride didn't ease the hunger in your belly or keep the rain off your head. But there would be expectations; was she prepared to meet them? Looking up at Josh, she said: "You know I don't."

"Well, I got a room at the hotel. You're welcome to spend the night there," said Josh. And then he added: "There'll be no foolin' around."

Sarah would not have believed most men about not fooling around, but Josh seemed different. "I accept your hospitality, Mr. Morrow." There was a sense of relief in her voice. Her dilemma of being penniless and homeless was solved for at least tonight.

There were no fancy accommodations in Bear Creek, and Josh's room was no exception. It had one bed with a straw mattress that was barely big enough for two people, but not comfortably. A small dresser with a pitcher of water and washbasin was situated along the wall to the left of the door. A mirror hung above it. Beyond the bed on the opposite side of the room was a window that looked down on the street. A wooden chair was situated next to it such that a person could have a relaxing drink while watching the comings and goings on Bear Creek's main street. At the head of the bed on the side closest to the door was a small night table. It had a coal oil lantern sitting on it. As Josh and Sarah entered the room, Josh left the door open long enough to allow light from the hallway to illuminate a shadowy path to the lantern in the room. He struck a match and lit the lamp. Its pale yellow light projected distorted caricatures of him and Sarah on the wall opposite them. In the far corner of the room, on the floor, were Josh's saddle, bedroll, rifle, and saddlebags. He'd brought them to the hotel for safekeeping rather than leave them at the livery stable with Thunder.

Josh swung the door shut and locked it on his way to his saddlebags. "Have a chair," he said to Sarah without looking at her. "I'm just going to clean this wound up a bit and call it a night."

"Let me help you," said Sarah. "It's the least I can do."

Josh was about to decline her offer of help but then thought better of it, as it would allow Sarah to reciprocate for the kindness that he was extending to her. "OK, just a second," he said as he rummaged through his saddlebags. "Here," said Josh, holding up a white cotton undershirt and handing it to her. "We can use this."

Sarah took the shirt and then watched with some embarrassment as Josh took off his blood-stained shirt. She couldn't help but stare at his muscular chest and arms. Beneath the fine black hair on his chest and stomach, she could see scars suggesting that he had experienced wounds of this nature at least twice before. The bloody rag concealing his current wound had fallen to the floor, revealing a shallow furrow about four inches long in the flesh on his left side. The wound oozed a little fresh blood but it had mostly stopped bleeding. Sarah poured some water in the washbasin and soaked a piece of the clean shirt in it. "Hold still," she said firmly as she dabbed at the dried blood. She felt goose bumps and her heart pounded being so close to this man who had just walked into her life barely an hour ago and who had killed for her.

"Am I gonna live?" teased Josh.

Josh's words made Sarah feel more at ease. Continuing the playful repartee she replied: "That depends on if you keep squirming around like a schoolgirl."

Josh laughed. "Here," said Sarah, handing a fold of cloth to Josh. "Hold this on your wound while I tie it in place."

"Yes, ma'am," said Josh in an exaggerated tone of respect.

Sarah tore a long strip of shirt and extended it around Josh's midsection and over the bandage that he was hold-ing to his side. In the process, her face brushed against his chest as she struggled to reach around him with the cloth. This closeness not only heightened her excitement but it allowed, ironically, her to feel good about herself; she was helping another person. Her mind and body were awash in emotion and physical sensations, for in the short time that she had known Josh they had likely violated societal norms by her coming to his room, and now on a personal level she had transcended that personal space reserved for select individuals.

Sarah tied the bandage in place. "Well, that's about the extent of my doctor abilities," she said.

"Looks good," said Josh. "I appreciate it." And, true to his word, he turned and knelt down to take the bedroll from his saddle. "I'll just spread my blankets on the floor over here. You can take the bed," he said over his shoulder.

Sarah wasn't really surprised as much as she was a bit taken aback by Josh's actions. Deep within her there was a part of her that had hoped he wouldn't be the total gentleman. "Are you sure?" she asked. "You're injured. You'll rest better on the bed."

Josh had taken off his boots, and except for a shirt, crawled between his two blankets clothed. He'd bunched up his slicker for a pillow. "If ya'll don't mind, blow out the lantern when you're settled," he said in deference to her admonition of hospitality. And then he added as he closed his eyes: "Good night." His behavior had been almost mechanical; it had to be. Sarah was a pretty girl and he was after all a man, but the evening had been a calamity thus far and, Josh reasoned, there was no point possibly adding to that.

It may have been because she was exhausted from her relatively sleepless, stressful nights at the Gold Strike, but Sarah slept soundly. If not for some ravens perched in a ponderosa pine outside her window, she might have slept longer, but their incessant babble had finally lured her from the depths of a good dream. It had been of Boston where she and her husband had known happiness. As she lay there feeling the warmth of the sunshine coming in through the open window and smelling the freshness of the morning air as a gentle breeze teased the curtains, she was struck with a sudden awareness that she was alone. Instantly, she sat up-right to confirm her feeling. It was true—Josh's stuff was gone. A sick, empty feeling came over her. She had thought he was different. Her eyes were welling up with tears when the door opened.

"Thought you was gonna sleep all day," said Josh.

A wave of feel-good emotion swept over Sarah. Relief did not adequately describe her feelings in seeing Josh return. "I thought you were gone," she said and then added: "for good."

Josh paused. A serious look came to his face. "Thought about it," he said. "Got up with the chickens this morning so I had plenty ah time to think. Drank enough coffee to make a dead man jittery, but the long and the short of it is I just couldn't bring myself to leave you high and dry."

They weren't exactly the words that Sarah had hoped to hear, but they were better than the deafening silence, save for the ravens, of the room just a moment before. A single tear had emerged from her left eye and was beginning the journey down her cheek, leaving little doubt that she was crying. "I appreciate what you've done for me, Josh. I really do, it's just that I'm so tired of being at the mercy of other people's pity."

"This ain't pity," said Josh as he set some boots, a hat, and a bundle wrapped in brown paper on the bed. "You're gonna pay me back some day."

Sarah's attention was diverted to the items on the bed. "What's this?" she asked, somewhat mystified.

"Well, ya'll can't wear that saloon-girl gitup out on

the trail," replied Josh. "As soon as you get changed and maybe some breakfast, we're gonna part company with Bear Creek."

"Where are we going?" asked Sarah.

"I got some business to attend to south of here, and when that's done we'll head for the Salmon River country. There's a ranch there that's been lookin' for a reliable cook. It'd be respectable work and you'd get room, board, and wages. Give you a stake in life."

Sarah was not ungrateful. It may have been more that she was not a spontaneous person and that she had an innate fear of the unknown that had been made worse ever since she had left San Francisco to participate in her husband's adventure in the Bear Creek goldfields. In any event, she replied: "What will you do?"

This was not the response that Josh had expected. Gratitude was more along the lines of what he was thinking, but he indulged her. "I don't know. I quit a job in that country to come here and help my friend work his gold claim. Like your husband, he's been murdered and now there's no claim to work. All this get-rich-quick in the goldfield doesn't seem to come to any good end for a lot of folks. I reckon I'd be better off workin' a ranch back over in that Salmon River country, if I can get on."

Sarah looked relieved. She picked up the package and felt its heft as if she were a little kid at Christmas. She looked at Josh. "Thank you," she said warmly. "I'll get changed."

"I'll be downstairs," replied Josh.

Josh hoped that he wasn't making a mistake taking

on this relative stranger. Initially her hard-luck story had struck a chord with him, but then with the Swede entering the picture it seemed there was no turning back, that his commitment to the girl only deepened. His out-of-pocket costs for trail clothes and a horse with the necessary tack had been considerable. These were purchases he really couldn't afford, for at the time, he was living off of his savings from his time in the army, and that was supposed to go towards buying a ranch. Josh's second-guessing himself had reached a near frenetic pace when suddenly there stood Sarah in the doorway of the hotel, dressed in the clothes that he had given her. At first glance she looked like a teenage boy. She'd pulled her dark hair up under the slouch hat and washed all the makeup from her face. It gave her a look of innocence and natural beauty that, up to this point, Josh hadn't seen.

The cotton shirt and pants that she wore were a little oversized, further disguising her shapely body such that from a distance, she would likely be mistaken for a boy.

Sarah paused a short distance from Josh. Her attire was definitely foreign to her, and she appeared embarrassed and in need of approval.

Josh smiled broadly. "Best-lookin' trail hand I ever saw," he said lightheartedly.

Sarah frowned. "I'll bet."

Chapter Four

By the time that Josh and Sarah had breakfast, purchased some supplies at the mercantile, and retrieved Thunder and the horse that Josh had bought for Sarah, it was close to noon. This was more than ample time for the residents of Bear Creek to recount the events of the previous night at the Gold Strike and form opinions as to the correctness of what had taken place. As if this hadn't been enough to prime the gossip mill, you now had the Swede's killer and his recently acquired harlot girlfriend, dressed like a man, parading around town like they were respectable folks. Except for the matronly lady who ran the restaurant, what few other ladies that resided in Bear Creek wouldn't even walk on the same side of the street as Josh and Sarah. And so it was that when they departed Bear Creek, the sun was high overhead and the little town was abuzz with the un-folding scandal. All eyes seemed to be upon them as they slowly rode out of town, especially Sarah. She wasn't riding side-saddle as was the expectation for ladies on horseback, but instead sat astride as a man would.

From the sheriff's office, Hollis and his two deputies could be seen lounging on the front porch. Their attention

was focused on Josh and Sarah. "Lookie here," said the sheriff to his deputies in a sarcastic tone. "Here comes the Texan
and his whore girlfriend." Being the paid lackeys that they
were, the deputies laughed. But then the bigger deputy
said, almost as a compliment, albeit a lascivious one, "She
don't dress down all that bad," suggesting that even without the skimpy saloon-girl dress her feminine features were
obvious. This prompted a snicker from the other deputy
but not the sheriff. He had a dislike of Josh that seemed to
be rooted in a thinly disguised fear. Conversely, the deputies exhibited a bravado that was spawned from ignorance
that the badges they wore made them immune from any
retribution by the people that they were sworn to serve
and protect.

As Josh and Sarah's horses passed directly in front of
the sheriff's office, Hollis called out to Josh: "Glad to see
you're takin' my advice and gittin' outta town."

Josh had little respect for the sheriff. There was simply
too much robbing and killing going on in the area that the
sheriff and his deputies just couldn't seem to ever solve.
Josh looked over at the sheriff somewhat smugly: "Yup,
Sheriff. I had enough ah Bear Creek."

"You know," began the sheriff coyly. "You coulda dis-
armed the Swede after you knocked him out, thataway he
wouldn't-ah been able to shoot' ya and you wouldn't have
needed to kill him."

"I suppose," replied Josh, and then added: "At least not
then, anyway."

The sheriff scowled. "You know, Tex," slurred the

sheriff in a mocking tone, "you got a smart mouth and I don't like people with a smart mouth."

Josh wanted so badly to respond with, "So what?" but he could see that the situation was about to go to hell in a hand basket and so he said, "Sorry, Sheriff, didn't mean to rile ya." It galled Josh to apologize to Hollis, but he was holding the trump cards.

The sheriff gave Josh a dirty look and then glanced disapprovingly at Sarah. He had a big chaw of chewing tobacco in his left cheek. With deliberation he mustered up a large quantity of tobacco juice and spat it in the direction of Sarah's horse, clearly intending it as an insult to her. "Get the hell outa my town, the both of ya. Don't come back or you might find yourself in the hoosegow or worse."

By this time there were a number of townspeople that had paused on the street to see what was going to happen. Peripherally, Josh sensed these people. He knew that spectators could sometimes make men do irrational things. It was time to leave, discretion being the better part of valor on this particular day. Looking at Sarah, he said: "I guess we best be movin' on." And with that they nudged the sides of their horses to a trot and rode out of town. For a good distance, probably close to a mile, neither of them spoke. The incident with the sheriff had impacted each of them in a different but yet connected sort of way. The sheriff's insult directed at Sarah was the third such transgression upon her reputation since last night at the Gold Strike. The Swede had called her a whore, the bartender a sniveling bitch, and now the sheriff had spat at her; was she deserving of this kind of treatment? It had only been a few weeks ago that she had been treated like a lady. And for Josh, he wondered if there would be others—a miner or cowhand that had known Sarah during her brief stint at the Gold Strike that would feel free to take liberties with her reputation in his presence. He had already killed one man because of her and he didn't want there to be a second.

It was a hot day. The crackling noise of grasshoppers springing from one spot to another in the sagebrush on each side of the wagon road seemed to accentuate the growing heat. Josh and Sarah had slowed their horses to a walk only to discover that they had become a less mobile target for the hordes of deer flies. It was shaping up to be a semi-miserable ride, when off in the distance behind them, Josh and Sarah became aware of a rider approaching. He was coming fast. Both Josh and Sarah turned their horses to face the oncoming rider. Josh pulled his Spencer repeater from its scabbard and chambered a round. There was a look of fear in Sarah's face, while Josh's was more reflective of bewilderment and concern. Who could be approaching them this fast?

As the stranger neared Josh and Sarah, he slowed his horse to a trot and finally to a walk when he was about 50 yards away. Josh eyed the man. He looked familiar. He was of medium build, but shorter than Josh and had a large black handlebar moustache. He wore a Stetson hat that had multiple indentations, causing the crown to be sharply peaked. A small round paper tag affixed to the drawstrings of a bag of Bull Durham tobacco dangled outside the man's right shirt pocket. He wore his pistol in a cross-draw position on his left side and was careful to keep his right hand filled with reins.

"Afternoon," said the stranger in a loud voice while keeping both hands on his saddle horn. "Mind if I ride on up?"

And then it came to Josh. The stranger was the one who had spoken up last night in the Gold Strike. "Come ahead on," replied Josh.

The stranger reined his horse in just short of Josh and Sarah. "Didn't mean to cause you no alarm," he said, eyeing Josh's rifle. "Name's Marshal Caleb Johnson. I'm outa Boise." The stranger paused, waiting for the effect of his identity to register.

There was obvious surprise in Josh's eyes. "Well, I reckon ya'll know who we are." Sarah remained silent but her face conveyed an uneasiness with the stranger.

"Yessir, I do. You made quite a name for yourself for no longer than you was in Bear Creek," replied the marshal.

"It wasn't by choice," said Josh. "Sometimes a crap-storm comes your way and you just can't get outa the way quick enough."

Sarah looked hurt. *So that's what I am, a crap-storm*, she said to herself.

"Yeah," said the marshal, "the Swede didn't give you much wiggle room. But truth of the matter is if it hadn't been you it woulda been someone else. The Swede was a bully just lookin' to get his ticket punched."

"So what brings you out here, Marshal?" asked Josh.

"Well sir, the Bear Creek gold strike is in Idaho Territory, and that means it comes under the jurisdiction of the federal court in Boise." The marshal paused momentarily while he fished his tobacco and cigarette papers out of his pocket. "The reason I'm here," continued the marshal as he plucked a single paper from its small packet, "is I'm at the beck and call of a federal judge named Charles Higgins. Ever hear of 'im?"

"Can't say as I have," replied Josh as he watched the marshal shake a small amount of tobacco from the pouch onto the cigarette paper, which he had formed into a shallow trough with the fingers of his left hand. Josh couldn't help but notice that the marshal's hands were as steady as a rock. Here he was casually rolling a cigarette in front of a man with a loaded rifle that he had watched kill a man less than twenty-four hours ago. The marshal was either a fool, a great judge of character, or, Josh reasoned, maybe he was just that fast with a gun.

"Well, sir," continued the marshal as he dabbed at the edge of the cigarette paper with his tongue to complete the seal. "Higgins is a no-nonsense kinda guy. He don't abide stealin' and killin'. And so when he kept hearin' all these stories about the goings-on in Bear Creek, he sent me to check it out. Only thing is I was instructed not to let on to anyone who I was or why I was here." As the marshal concluded, he glanced at Sarah. Their eyes met for just an instant, with Sarah diverting her attention downward and the marshal quickly back to the task of lighting his cigarette. This recognition, this unspoken communication, had not gone unnoticed by Josh. It was as if it was an awkward moment for the marshal and a desperate plea for secrecy from Sarah. It was one of those totally unforeseen feelings that comes over a person, but Josh felt as if he was an intruder. It made for a pause in the conversation that was rapidly becoming an uneasy silence. Josh decided to remain quiet and let the marshal rescue himself.

The law man puffed gingerly several times in rapid succession to bring life to his cigarette. It was a dead calm day and for a brief moment the blue smoke obscured his face; perhaps it was fortuitous given the situation. "Mr. Morrow," he continued , "I'm looking for an ally, someone who's honest and that I can trust, especially if things go to hell."

Josh smiled. "And you think I'm that man, a guy who was just told to get outa town by the sheriff."

"I do," replied the marshal in a deliberate tone. "In fact that's all the better. Nobody would suspect you was helpin' me, not with that kinda reputation."

Josh felt anything but proud of last night's events, but the marshal's words served as an unnecessary reality check. In these parts he would forever be known as the guy who killed the big Swede in a fight over a saloon girl and was ordered by the sheriff to get out of town. These weren't exactly desirable attributes for a lawman. Josh adjusted his hat in a casual manner and sighed. "So what would you want me to do?" he asked with some hesitation.

"Be my eyes and ears mostly," replied the marshal as he took another drag from his cigarette and exhaled the smoke such that it briefly looked like he was talking smoke.

"The sheriff and his deputies is up to no good." The marshal paused and then added: "I will tell you something and I guess as far as that goes, the lady here as well, if I have your word that you're sidin' with me and whatever I tell you is just between us."

Josh pondered his options for a moment. He was determined to find Seth's killer and bring him to justice, however that might happen. He reckoned it would be better to have the marshal on his side in case things went south. "Alright, Marshal," said Josh, "count me in."

"Good," said the marshal; he paused and looked directly at Sarah: "What about you? Can I count on you to keep to yourself whatever you hear today or on down the road?"

Sarah didn't really want to get involved with anything that might involve another confrontation with the sheriff or violence, but she'd stepped off into this quicksand when she came to Bear Creek with her husband and now the only helping hand appeared to be in one or both of these men. She replied meekly with as little eye contact as possible to the marshal: "Yeah, I guess so."

"Can't be no guessin' about this," said the marshal, looking at Sarah. "This is deadly serious business, gotta be yes or no."

"OK, yes," said Sarah firmly.

Apparently satisfied, the marshal turned his attention to Josh. "The thing that prompted the judge to send me up here in the first place was the sheriff comin' down to Boise with bags-a gold dust."

Josh's eyes widened. "Anybody ask him where a sheriff

gets bags of gold dust?" he said sarcastically.

The marshal scoffed. "Wasn't necessary. Hollis freely volunteered to the people at the bank the fact that he had an interest in a mining claim that his partner was workin'. Said he worked the claim on his time off and that the gold he was depositin' came from that claim."

"I suppose you already checked to see if he really does have a claim," said Josh.

"Yessir, I did," replied the marshal, "and he does have a claim up on Bullwhacker Creek. I been by there; didn't see a whole lot of activity. Definitely not $40,000 worth."

"$40,000," exclaimed Josh.

"Yup," stated the marshal flatly. "The judge is friends with the president of the bank so that number is the gospel truth."

Josh shook his head. He wondered if some of that gold had been Seth's. It was probably a good bet that some of it had been, but proving it might be difficult. "So what's next?" asked Josh.

"Well, sir," began the marshal as he took another drag off his cigarette. "I got me a plan that hopefully will play upon the sheriff's greed and stupidity. Several months ago a merchant from Boise come up to Bear Creek with about a half dozen wagons full of dry goods, mining supplies and such, and sold it. He had upwards of $30,000 in gold when he headed back to Boise. And since he'd been in Bear Creek a couple of weeks a-tradin' it was pretty common knowledge that he was bound to have a lot of gold on him when he left town, and with six wagons you don't exactly sneak out. Well anyways, the trader gets robbed about halfways between Bear Creek and Boise. One of the mule skinners tries to stop the affair and he gets killed for his trouble. Course there's a big uproar about the deal and the sheriff and his deputies supposedly went out and tried tracking the robbers but somehow lost the trail and that was that." The marshal paused while he took another drag off of his cigarette, which was pretty short now—so short that he had to pinch the butt of it between the index finger and thumb of his right hand, being careful not to touch the burning end, and purse his lips such that they could grasp that tiny portion available for that last inhalation of smoke. He had contorted his face and squinted his right eye, as if these machinations were reflective of the satisfaction he was deriving from that last bit of tobacco smoke. Exhaling, the marshal began again: "I don't think the sheriff nor any of his cronies are very smart, and I'm hopin' not very observant either for I intend to trick them. The merchant from Boise is in Bear Creek now with another load of goods to sell. He'll conduct his business as usual and then leave for Boise, probably a couple days from now. I'm hoping that somewhere along the way he gets robbed again, except this time no one will resist and the robbers will only be getting iron pyrite for their efforts. Iron pyrite, or fool's gold, looks very similar to the real thing. Hopefully, the thieves won't look too closely at their take and I'll be able to tie the robbery to whoever shows up with some fool's gold."

"What about the real gold? How does this merchant get that back to Boise?" asked Josh.

"I'll be takin' that on a pack horse," replied the marshal. "Gonna leave Bear Creek the night before the merchant. I'll be stayin' off the main route to Boise. Hopefully, any desperado types will just take me for another prospector lookin' for that big strike. Besides, they'll be payin' more attention to the merchant and when he leaves than a single person."

Josh shook his head slightly. "I don't know, Marshal. I ain't no expert on rocks or gold or any such stuff, but I got my doubts."

The marshal scowled. "Well if we don't use some kind of trickery like this, then a fellar's pretty much got to catch 'em red-handed, actually committin' the crime, and that'll probably involve considerable gunplay. And when it's all said and done I still might not be able to tie this back to the sheriff, if he's involved."

"Maybe so," said Josh doubtfully. "But what's my part in this?"

"Well, sir," began the marshal, "I saw the way that you handled yourself at the Gold Strike last night. I need someone like you to back my play, somebody that'd be good in a tight spot. So, I was wonderin' if you'd be interested in being my deputy?"

The marshal's offer caught Josh by surprise. He sighed thoughtfully. "Never have gave much thought to being a lawman. Always pictured myself workin' a ranch."

"Pays seventy-five a month," added the marshal. "You can always punch cows on down the line."

Josh thought of his commitment to find Seth's killer.

Being a deputy marshal might actually be useful in that endeavor, but he also had Sarah to consider now. He'd made a commitment of sorts to her even though he was beginning to have second thoughts. Regardless, he was living on his savings now, money that was supposed to go towards buying a ranch. That was not a situation he liked being in. "Alright, Marshal, you got yourself a deputy." The words seemed to tumble from Josh's mouth as if he had no control over them. They were propelled by gut instinct.

"Glad to hear it," said the marshal as he dug into his shirt pocket for a badge. "Raise your right hand."

Josh raised his right hand. He couldn't help but remember the last time he'd raised his hand to take an oath; it had been to join the army. That had resulted in five years of fighting and killing, mostly hard times, but he had become a man during that time and he had made a good friend—a friend who was now dead. Taking another oath might just help him avenge his friend's death.

"Usual way ah doin' this would be for you to put your left hand on the Bible," began the marshal, "but since I ain't got one with me, I guess just bein' out here in God's creation will have to do. Repeat after me: I Josh Morrow do solemnly swear to uphold the laws of the Idaho Territory to the best of my ability, so help me God."

Josh parroted the words back to the marshal while Sarah looked on, almost as if she was a privileged guest. "Congratulations, Mr. Morrow," said the marshal as he handed him a deputy's badge. "I'd be obliged if you'd keep this in your pocket for the time being. We don't want to be tippin' our hand just yet."

Josh looked at the badge briefly and then stuck it in his shirt pocket. "You know, Marshal," said Josh, "the only thing keepin' me from ridin' on over the mountain is my friend's murder. I mean don't get me wrong. I'll lend you a hand however I best can, but that can't take away from me settlin' the score for my friend."

The marshal frowned and sighed heavily. It was obvious by his facial expression that he was crafting his response carefully. "Josh," he began, "I know we ain't exactly dealin' with the cream in the milk bucket here, but we can't step outside the law. We gotta try to have due process."

Josh scoffed. "Due process," he said coldly. "Ya'll suppose that's what my friend got down the road here when he was bushwhacked and left to bleed out."

The marshal shook his head. "I'm sorry 'bout your friend but he ain't the first good man that's been killed by some riffraff. The problem I see is when the good people drop down to the level of the riffraff tryin' to get even. A fellar's walkin' a fine line there."

"Maybe so," replied Josh. "I guess we'll just have to see how it shakes out."

Chapter Five

It was early evening when Josh and Sarah started their descent down the gentle ridge overlooking Lester Scoville's claim. They were following the tracks that Lester's freight wagon had made through the sagebrush and grass. Scattered ponderosa pines partially obscured from view Lester's cabin near the edge of the creek. Smoke coming from the stovepipe that protruded through the roof suggested that he was home, probably cooking his supper. A Steller's jay perched in the tree near the cabin screeched noisily at Josh and Sarah's approach. Not to be outdone by the jay, Rufus came bounding out of the cabin to sound the alarm, albeit a little late, of the approaching company. Shortly, Lester appeared in the doorway with rifle in hand, and then recognizing Josh, he leaned the rifle against the wall of the cabin.

"Evenin'," hollered out Lester.

Josh could see that Lester had a bit of a puzzled look on his face. "Hey Lester, how ya'll doin?" he said as he and Sarah reined their horses in near the cabin and dismounted. Josh knelt down to greet Rufus. He seemed to remember Josh and was mostly tail wags and a few excited licks. Josh scratched Rufus' ears and gave him a couple of pats on the side. "You're a good dog, Rufus. Good dog," he said as he rose to shake Lester's hand.

"Well, boy, you timed it 'bout right," said Lester in a friendly tone of voice. "Supper's just about ready."

Josh could see that Lester was almost beside himself with curiosity over who this woman dressed like a man was and why she was standing in front of his cabin. Josh assumed that since Sarah was with him that she would be welcome. Josh turned so that he could divide his attention between Lester and Sarah. "Lester, this here's Sarah MaGinty," he said. And since Josh had told Sarah all about his meeting Lester, he did not reiterate Lester's name to her.

In the brief time that it had taken to walk from the doorway of his cabin to where Sarah and Josh stood, Lester had surveyed the person standing next to Josh closely. He thought that he recognized her as one of the girls from the Gold Strike but not by the name of Sarah MaGinty; she had been Pearl then. He was conflicted as to whether he should go along with the girl's ruse or call her on it now, but then he said: "You know, ma'am, you look an awful lot like a woman I met about a month ago in Bear Creek but she went by the name of Pearl."

A look of embarrassment quickly came over Sarah's face. She could feel Josh's stare upon her. Her heart began to pound as she frantically processed her options. She wanted to just melt away into the evening shadows and rid herself of her legacy at the Gold Strike, but she knew that would never happen; what was done was done. She took a deep breath to steady herself. "You are right, Mr. Scoville,

I did go by the name of Pearl while I worked at the Gold Strike. I only told Josh my real name after I was forced to leave there." Sarah paused. "What I wasn't truthful with him about was how long I'd been at the Gold Strike and how it was I came to be there."

There was disappointment in Josh's eyes but not surprise. Earlier in the day, he had sensed there was some history between the marshal and Sarah. He'd felt similar then to what he was experiencing now, but he rationalized what did it matter to him as he was just helping her out and not necessarily because he wanted to but more due to the circumstances being what they were. Besides, as soon as they got over to the Salmon River country, he would hopefully be shed of her. But deep down where it really mattered—where a guy, regardless of what he told himself, just couldn't shake free—he knew he was developing feelings for her. The real question was whether Sarah's past would destroy these feelings. It was a question that Josh couldn't truthfully answer, at least not at this point.

Sarah looked at Josh with a sadness in her eyes that was genuine. It was a look that was rooted in something beyond mercy or sympathy; it spoke more of regret. "I'm sorry, Josh," she began in a voice that was lacking any energy. "I kind of deceived you. I've been working at the Gold Strike for a little over a month." She paused and tried to speak but couldn't.

Josh sensed where she was going with this, and although he was a little angry that she hadn't been totally truthful, he saw no need for her to grovel. "Maybe some things are best left unspoken," he said in a sympathetic tone.

"No," she said more assertively. "What I don't tell you now, other folks will at some point." Sarah paused. "The truth is my husband didn't have a promising gold claim and he wasn't killed near Bear Creek. We spent most of our savings taking a sailing ship to get to San Francisco. We were broke and down to living on the street. My husband couldn't find any work and so out of desperation he tried to rob a wealthy man and was killed in the process." Sarah paused, and then in her defense, she said: "I had nothing, no one to turn to," and then in a forlorn tone she added: "I signed on with Madame Ruth and her girls and came to Bear Creek."

The silence, save for the babbling of the small creek a short distance away, was, for Sarah, overwhelming. She searched the faces of Josh and Lester for an acknowledgement of some kind but Lester shifted his eyes downward, leaving it for Josh to respond. But Josh seemed frozen in place. Here was the first assault on the fledgling feelings that he had for Sarah, and it had come from her. For an instant, when the particulars of what Josh suspected all along became known to him, he felt revulsion. But then, it flashed in his conscience something that his mother, who was a religious woman, used to remind him of: "Judge ye not for ye shall be judged also." Sarah had begun to tear up when Josh broke the silence: "Sarah, sometimes desperate times call for desperate measures. Your husband turned to robbery and paid the ultimate price. And no doubt you've paid a heavy price for your decision but life goes on." It was difficult for Josh to sound convincing but it was the best that he could do, considering the fact that he was still trying to convince himself of Sarah's future.

Sarah stood before Josh and Lester, naked in her shame. She had bared her soul and there was nothing more to give. At what price would acceptance come? It was an awkward moment, a painful moment with no easy way for anyone involved to extract themselves. But then Josh said: "That invite for supper still stand?" And just like that the healing process seemed to have begun.

"You betcha," replied Lester in an exaggerated tone of cordiality. "Got beans and venison and some baking-powder biscuits too. Even got some honey for them biscuits. Me and Rufus found a bee's nest up the creek the other day. Got stung a few times but we made out okay." Lester laughed.

The tension that had existed only moments before was lifting rapidly like a morning fog under the onslaught of the sun. "Are you hungry, Sarah?" asked Lester in a purposeful gesture of kindness.

Sarah could see that both Josh and Lester were making an effort to console her, but what wasn't apparent was what their true feelings were; most importantly, would they ever respect her? She'd experienced pity before. It was a hollow fix that temporarily satisfied your physical needs but left you painfully devoid of self-respect. She was hungry; she hadn't eaten since breakfast but her thoughts took flight, as a person's mind sometimes does at inappropriate times, to the past when she and her husband had been dinner guests of family or friends. Dinner then had been preceded by polite conversation and laughter, but tonight her surrender of what little self-respect that she possessed had been the topic of that conversation. What a difference two years can make, she thought. The irony of the situation would have been laughable to Sarah had it not been so deadly serious. And then the kaleidoscope of events in her mind was ended when a gray jay flew down from a nearby tree and began calling noisily as it hopped about on the ground. Rufus gave chase to the intruder, barking wildly.

Sarah glanced at Rufus and the jay and then made eye contact with Lester. "I am hungry, Lester, thank you for the invitation."

"Good," said Lester jovially. "Let's eat."

"I'll be along shortly," said Josh. "I'm gonna tend to the horses first."

"I'll help," offered Sarah tentatively, not knowing if Josh would want to be around her at this very moment.

Josh looked at Sarah. For a brief moment he considered declining her offer, as he felt the need to be away from her for a short while so he could ponder this revelation of hers. He had no need for any more emotional discussion where there just didn't seem to be any good answers. But then he saw that same innocence in her eyes that he'd seen at the Gold Strike. Her body language seemed to evoke a fragileness of her being. Josh knew the recovery of Sarah's self-respect would be a long process, if it ever occurred at all, and so he said: "Sure, bring your horse. We'll unsaddle by the cabin and then take the horses to the creek for water."

Sarah nodded but she did not smile. "Okay," she said simply. Earlier that day there had been a playful, almost teasing tone in Josh's voice; it was not there now.

"Don't be long or me and Rufus'll eat your share," said Lester with a chuckle.

Josh laughed. "Ya'll don't need to worry 'bout that. I'm never late for supper," he said, continuing the good-natured bantering.

Sarah gathered the reins of her horse and followed along behind Josh and Thunder to a place on the south side of the cabin. Without speaking, Josh began to remove Thunder's saddle. From the corner of his eye he could see that Sarah was struggling to remove her saddle, but he didn't offer to help. At five foot three and 110 pounds, lifting the saddle from the back of her horse was a bit of a challenge for her, but she finally got it done. At that moment Josh felt less than a gentleman, but his ambivalence towards Sarah had left him incapable of doing things for her that prior to their conversation a short time ago, might have been spontaneous. He didn't like this feeling but he couldn't help himself.

After watering and picketing the horses in a grassy area, the conversation between Josh and Sarah was still minimal, at least from Sarah's perspective, and lacking not so much in sympathy because she didn't really expect that, but just simply any kind of warmth. She felt certain that the spark between them that had been present in Bear Creek was gone.

Lester's cabin was small; it had only one room. He'd built it himself from Douglas fir trees that he'd cut down up the canyon a ways. After trimming the branches off and cutting them to length, he used his mules to snake the logs down to his cabin site. It had been a tremendous amount of work, but he reasoned that he was going to be on his claim for a good while and he might as well be comfortable. Towards the front of the room along the wall opposite the door was a stove and wood box. Near the stove was a table made from rough-cut pine and two chairs. A coal oil lantern sat in the middle of the table. There were no cupboards on the walls, but instead numerous shelves that revealed everything that Lester owned. A fair-sized bed took up most of the room along the back wall. A half-full metal water bucket sat near the door. A metal ladle hung on the edge of the bucket, and if a person looked close he could see a few small shreds of chewing tobacco clinging to it. There were windows in the north, east, and west walls, but given the time of day they did little to alleviate the increasing darkness within the cabin. As Josh and Sarah entered the cabin, Lester removed the chimney from the lantern and struck a match. The lantern was slow to come to life but eventually it did, pushing the darkness into the corners of the room.

"Sit yourselves down," said Lester, knowing that there were only two chairs in the room.

Josh was quick to note the shortcomings of the accommodations. "Have a seat, Lester," he said as he went out the door.

Sarah looked at Josh's sudden departure somewhat perplexedly, but said nothing, assuming there was some logical explanation. Lester began dishing the steaming hot beans and venison onto plates that he had taken from the shelf near the table. "Sarah," said Lester, nodding his head towards the oven compartment of the stove, "you wanna grab that towel and pull them biscuits out of the oven?"

Sarah had just risen to get the biscuits when Josh reappeared in the doorway carrying a stump length of firewood under one arm and his rifle in the other. "Got a couple of visitors up on the ridge," he said with some indifference. "Not sure what they're up to."

Lester set the pan of beans back on the stove. "Where 'bouts are they?" he said as he stepped to the door.

Josh edged in near Lester. "Just below the skyline near that crooked ponderosa. One of 'em's ridin' a sorrel and the other a palomino."

Lester could barely make them out in the fading light. They were a good 500 yards away—too far for either party to make an effective shot if that's what it came to. Lester sighed. "You know I ain't fer certain, but them horses kinda look like the ones that I seen over to your dead friend's claim."

Josh's pulse quickened. His first impulse was to ride up there and confront the two strangers, but then he exclaimed, somewhat in disbelief, "The hell you say."

"Well, like I say," said Lester in a tone that was markedly calmer than Josh's, "I ain't dead certain but the buckskin especially looks familiar. I only seen 'em once before, though."

Josh watched the riders who, perhaps sensing the alarm that they had created at the cabin, spur their horses and ride up and over the ridge out of sight. "I reckon there'll be time enough tomorrow to locate them two hombres," he said.

"Yeah, if I'm right about them two being the ones that's on your friend's claim," said Lester in a gravelly voice, "you won't have to look too hard for 'em. They're too full of themselves to have any common sense." And then he added: "Let's eat 'fore them whistleberries get cold."

Inside the cabin, Sarah began dishing up the rest of the food and handing each of them their plates. She had voluntarily assumed this role, and it made her feel good that Lester did not object. It gave her a sense of belonging if not wholesomeness.

Josh leaned his rifle against the wall near the door and set the piece of un-split firewood on its end near the table; this would be his stool. "Y'otta let me set there," said Lester, who was distributing coffee cups.

"No, sir," replied Josh. "I'm good. Besides, it wouldn't do to have the host sittin' on a stump in his own house."

"Oh, horse feathers," said Lester. "Ya want some coffee to wash that stuff down with?"

"That sounds good," said Josh.

Lester started to get up from the table to get the coffeepot from the stove behind Sarah. Seeing this, Sarah said quickly: "I'll get it, Lester," and then she added, "I'm sorry, I should have already done that. Don't know what I was thinking, empty coffee cups aren't much good."

Josh extended his cup to Sarah; as she poured his coffee, he could see that her hand had a slight tremble to it. She wanted badly to be accepted. "Thanks, Sarah," said

Josh, looking deliberately into her eyes. There was an unspoken communication between them, and Sarah could see that Josh's demeanor had softened from when they were caring for the horses. Nonetheless, it had been a long time since a smile came naturally to her, and now was no exception; she said simply, "You're welcome," and turned to pour Lester's coffee before sitting down.

Everyone had just begun to eat when Lester noticed Rufus sitting patiently near his side. "Ah dammit, Rufus. I'm sorry. I plumb forgot to dish your plate." And with that Lester got up and went to the stove, where there was a cast-iron skillet with two good-sized venison steaks that were cooked. He quickly went to work with his fork and knife, cutting the meat into bite-sized pieces, and then dumped it into a metal pan for Rufus. "Here you go," he said as he put the pan on the floor and patted Rufus on the head.

It was obvious that Lester cared a lot for Rufus. "So how long ya'll had Rufus?" asked Josh.

Lester paused from eating and sat back in his chair with a pensive look on his face. His hands, filled with a knife in his right and a fork in his left, rested on either side of his plate. He continued to chew his steak, and when he'd created sufficient space to speak, he said: "Purty darn close to ten years. Got Rufus when he was just a little guy. His mother was a stray runnin' the streets in Boise. Somebody there decided he didn't like dogs and shot her. Left Rufus to fend for himself and that's when I found him. We been pardners ever since."

Josh had already taken a liking to Lester, but learning of

his devotion to Rufus made him all the more confident that Lester was a good man who could be trusted.

Supper continued with small talk, mostly between Josh and Lester about the finer points of sluicing gold in the stream near the cabin. It sounded to Josh like it was as much an art form as it was a science, but Lester seemed to have it down pretty well. He knew a lot about gold and how to get it out of the ground. "So Lester," began Josh in a naïve tone of voice, "ya'll ever come across any iron pyrite?"

Lester snickered. "You mean fool's gold. Sure, ever' now and again."

Sarah's eyes widened as she looked up from her plate towards Josh. What was he doing? Peripherally, Josh sensed Sarah looking at him but he didn't allow his eyes to go there, focusing instead on Lester. "I've heard that it's hard to tell apart from real gold, is that right?"

"Well that depends," said Lester, "on who's tryin' to do the tellin'. If a fellar has handled a lotta gold in his life he'll get a feel for the real thing, it's heavier than fool's gold and if the light's just right he can see that it's got a little different color to it. But if a guy don't know what he's a-lookin' for he could get the wool pulled over his eyes." Lester paused and then said with a laugh: "You got some fool's gold ya want to pawn off on somebody?"

Josh laughed. He didn't like being less than totally honest with Lester, but he had given the marshal his word that he'd keep his plan confidential. "Oh no," he said in a tone that suggested it would be ridiculous to even think that he had some fool's gold. "I've just heard different folks talk about fool's gold in the past but I never knew what it was for sure."

"Well, now ya know," said Lester as he placed his knife and fork on his empty plate.

"Yeah," said Josh, "thanks for settin' me straight on that." Josh was skeptical of the marshal's scheme; but at least now he had another opinion of its one key element.

Chapter Six

Daylight came early in the summertime, but that was of little consequence to Josh as he'd been awake for a good while looking at the stars and waiting for the new day. The sun was not yet visible, but there was an awareness of light in the east and the birds were singing. Dawn in the mountains makes a man appreciate being alive, thought Josh. It was kind of like as the darkness retreated, God had wiped your slate clean for one more day; what you did with that day was up to you. It could be a day that would make God proud or maybe not. Josh wasn't sure about today. He intended to go to Seth's claim and see for himself who was on it and how they came to get it. It'd be a touchy proposition, but it was something he couldn't walk away from. In his mind it was a wrong that needed to be righted.

It was not long after a pine squirrel's high-pitched chatter punctuated the symphony being put on by the birds that Josh became aware of Sarah's eyes upon him. Try as he might, Lester was unable to convince Sarah to take his bed for the night. She instead slept on the ground outside the cabin near Josh. "Good morning," she offered.

"Mornin'," said Josh. "Did ya manage to flatten any ah them rocks last night?" he added good-naturedly.

The friendliness of Josh's words sent a surge of feel-good through Sarah's body; it was akin almost to the warming effects of a hot cup of coffee in the crisp morning air. Sarah frowned in a playful manner. "I'm not sure but I think the rocks won."

Josh had been the perfect gentleman throughout the night, as Sarah knew that he would be when she insisted on no special treatment. Separated by only a few feet, it was difficult for each of them to not fantasize about the possibilities of a relationship had the circumstances been different. But the situation was what it was, and thinking about it only led to more frustration. After a time, Sarah succumbed to fatigue while Josh continued on, analyzing the events of the past few days and attempting to suppress from his mind what the rhythmic breathing lying a short distance away represented.

Josh sat upright. He could hear Lester moving about in the cabin. A light bluish white smoke was drifting from the stovepipe. "Shouldn't be too long before the coffee's done," he said matter-of-factly.

There was a sense in the air of politeness and superficiality. Josh and Sarah were both aware of yesterday's events and why Josh had come to Lester's camp. They were like white elephants before them that neither wanted to admit were there. Sarah was the first to take them on. "So are you going to kill the men on your friend's claim?" she said with concern in her voice.

Josh's gaze was fixed across the canyon. There were several mule deer making their way down the slope towards the creek for water. "These guys are late," he said, purposely ignoring her question. "I woulda thought, being this close to Lester's cabin that they'd have come for water in the dark."

Sarah stared at Josh in silence; finally after what seemed like a long time, Josh turned towards her. "It'll be their call. If I know for certain that one or the other of 'em killed Seth, then I aim to use my authority as a deputy marshal and arrest them. If they go along peacefully then nobody'll get hurt. The choice will be theirs. But at this point I don't even know if they had a hand in killin' Seth."

"Won't you be going against what the marshal wanted you to do, at least for now anyway?" asked Sarah.

Josh tossed his blanket back and reached for one of his boots. "As far as I'm concerned riffraff is riffraff," he said as he pulled on his boot. "A man's gotta deal with it 'fore it spreads. Besides, I ain't all that certain that the marshal's harebrained plan is gonna work."

"Maybe you should give it a chance before you tip your hand," replied Sarah.

Josh glanced over at Sarah as he reached for his other boot. He had an annoyed look on his face. "You know, ya'll sure do seem like you're sidin' pretty heavy with the marshal," and then he added: "Maybe ya'll are spreadin' your bedroll in the wrong camp." The words weren't even completely out of his mouth and he was regretting them. But they were like an avalanche; once it starts there was no stopping it until it reaches flat ground. The energy for it had begun to build yesterday when they'd met the marshal on the trail and he'd seen the way the two of them had looked at one another. It was a telling, unmistakable look that only two people who have shared the ultimate physical intimacy have. Josh had done well to suppress his anger and disappointment up until now, but it was inevitable that he was going to say what he had at some point. It was as if the emotion that spawned his words had been continuously poised, just waiting for the slightest provocation.

Sarah had a hurt look in her eyes. She hadn't meant to be argumentative, and she certainly didn't want to give the impression that she cared for the marshal; in fact, her intent was just the opposite. She was concerned that Josh might get killed going after his friend's killer. She just wanted to go someplace else and start over in life, but now she had jeopardized the one glimmer of a chance that she had of doing that. "Josh," she began apologetically, "I didn't mean…"

"Sarah," interrupted Josh. "Just let it go. I didn't mean to speak out the way I did. We can talk later." He paused with a frustrated look. "I don't need my mind all cluttered today." And with that he turned and walked towards the cabin.

Chapter Seven

Most of Bear Creek's residents were still asleep or just now disengaging from the night. The sun as yet was still a faint promise of what it would be later in the day. Sheriff Hollis, however, was up noisily sipping his first cup of hot coffee. He had no prisoners in the one cell at the sheriff's office, but he had told his wife that he did and needed to go in early to relieve one of his deputies. It was a small white lie to perpetuate a much bigger one—that being he was there to protect and serve the good citizens of Bear Creek. Hollis had made himself comfortable. He had his feet up on his desk and was tilted back slightly in his chair. He hadn't wanted to get up this early and leave the comfort of his bed and wife, but he also didn't want the person he was going to meet coming to his house. The person that he was meeting was an informant—a reliable one that he had used in the past. For a price he could be counted on to keep his mouth shut. Hollis harbored no illusions that his informant's loyalty was due to any other reason save for the money and the possibility of a well-placed bullet. He wasn't totally certain what information the man had for him other than it had to do with Ben Stevenson, the merchant from Boise. Hollis had met the man in passing on the street yesterday; neither had spoken except the informant, who nodded his head as a greeting of respect to the sheriff and mumbled two words that were barely audible: "Dawn tomorrow." The sheriff's office had a front door that most everyone used and a back door that provided access to the privy behind the office. There was a shallow draw that originated near the privy and ran away from the sheriff's office for several hundred yards before curving back towards the creek bottom. Both the draw and creek bottom were heavily vegetated with willows, sagebrush that in places was as tall as a man, and rye grass that was the equal of the sage in height. Between the poor morning light, the topography, and the vegetation, it made for an almost ideal situation for someone to enter and leave the sheriff's office by way of the back door totally undetected.

Hollis had already unlocked the back door, so it did not alarm him when he heard the doorknob being worked and the slight squeak of the hinges as the door opened and then slowly closed. And then it became quiet—too quiet. A short hallway ran from the back door to the front of the office, where the sheriff's desk was located. Hollis could not see down the hall. Slowly, he drew his pistol and pointed it at the hallway. "Come out and show yourself," he commanded.

"Sheriff, it's me, Rudy," came the response in a hushed tone.

Hollis recognized the voice immediately. It was the man he'd been waiting for, Rudolph Holchek—or Rudy as he was generally called. He sighed in exasperation and laid his pistol on the desk. "Well, get your ass on in here," he said, somewhat perturbed.

Shortly, Rudy presented himself before the sheriff. He was of average height with a well-developed paunch, attributable in large part to his fondness for beer. He had a full beard, red in color, that did little to hide his jowls and ruddy complexion. His crumpled slouch hat complemented his overall scruffy-looking appearance. He carried no sidearm, preferring a rifle instead, which he had left back at the merchant's camp. "Mornin'," he said, seemingly oblivious to the sheriff's aggravation with him.

Totally ignoring Rudy's greeting, Hollis said curtly: "What the hell are ya doin' sneakin' up on me like that. I coulda shot ya."

"Sorry, Sheriff," said Rudy. "Just wanted to make sure I wasn't walkin' in on some stranger. All this secret meetin' stuff makes me nervous."

Hollis looked Rudy in the eye and said sternly: "Ain't nobody but me or my deputies gonna be in here at this time ah day, and you can trust them."

"OK," said Rudy meekly.

The sheriff eased off a little in his tone with Rudy. "Well, I suppose a man's gotta be careful," he said, just wanting to put the incident behind them. Changing his demeanor to one of business, Hollis continued: "So when's Stevenson leaving?"

"Tomorrow morning," replied Rudy, "but there's something you otta know." Rudy paused almost like some schoolgirl who had some juicy gossip that she'd be willing to share but only after the proper amount of envy had been demonstrated by the potential recipient.

Hollis looked at Rudy. He was almost gleeful. "So what is it, Rudy?" he asked curiously.

"Stevenson has been ridin' outa camp ever' day in the late afternoon. He always goes to the west, up Chokecherry Creek, and comes back just about dusk. Said he's just talkin' to potential customers and takin' orders for next time we come back, but I wasn't buyin' it so I followed him yesterday." Seeing the anticipation in the sheriff's eyes, Rudy deliberately paused, knowing that he was about to come to the good part. Rudy smiled. "Old man Stevenson has been meetin' a United States marshal outa Boise. I wasn't anywhere close enough to hear what they was sayin', but I seen Stevenson give the marshal some small bags that sure looked like what he's been keepin' gold in."

The look on Hollis' face was initially concern that was quickly giving way to an angry excitement. *How dare the damned feds meddle in my jurisdiction*, he said to himself. It was an insult that one of them would come to Bear Creek and not check in with him. It could mean only one thing: they were on to him. Hollis looked Rudy hard in the eyes: "Are you certain the guy you saw was a U.S. marshal?"

"Sheriff, I'm tellin' ya as sure as there's fish in the creek the guy I saw was the same guy I seen in Boise, and that fellar had a star on his chest," replied Rudy emphatically. "I seen his horse too. Same big ole gray. No doubt about it."

Hollis eyed Rudy for a moment. His candle didn't burn

too bright, but he was making a pretty convincing argument about Stevenson meeting this marshal. As ludicrous as it was, Hollis felt offended that the citizenry had found it necessary to call in a federal marshal. But no matter—he would have the last say in this matter.

"You done good, Rudy," said Hollis.

"Figured you'd wanna know 'bout that marshal," replied Rudy.

Hollis took another sip of his coffee. "So how much gold and money you figure Stevenson will be takin' back to Boise?"

Rudy shrugged his shoulders. "Don't know. Stevenson's bein' purty tight-lipped 'bout that. I heard once from one of the other mule skinners that we was bringin' 'bout thirty thousand dollars' worth of goods from Boise, and since we been here business has been good."

Hollis could only speculate on the amount, but based upon the price of manufactured goods in Bear Creek, he supposed it could be around forty-five thousand. It'd be a nice haul.

Rudy was hesitant to ask the sheriff for his money as he was intimidated by him. He saw Hollis as a man that was quick to anger with little patience for most folks. He was unpredictable. He was arrogant and felt that he was superior to most men—certainly Rudy. "It's startin' to get light outside," said Rudy somewhat nervously. "I best be gettin' back to camp."

Under other circumstances Hollis might have quibbled with Rudy over the value of the information, but not today.

He was as anxious for Rudy to go as was Rudy. The presence of the marshal from Boise could be a complicating factor in his current plans, and he needed to act quickly to correct this problem. Taking a key from an inside pocket in his vest, Hollis unlocked a drawer on the right side of his desk and removed a small metal box. He opened it, revealing a considerable amount of cash, and counted out a hundred dollars. Tossing the money on the desk towards Rudy, he said: "Here ya go."

Rudy stepped forward and picked up the cash. He didn't dare risk counting it in front of Hollis for fear of antagonizing him. Nonetheless, it didn't seem right to him that Hollis and his cronies stood to make a lot of money while he walked away with pennies by comparison. It bothered him too that Hollis treated him with such contempt. In all of their dealings, at some point, there was always that look, that tone of the conversation that it was an effort for Hollis to tolerate his presence. But in the end, Rudy always took the money and agreed to do the bidding of Hollis for a few dollars more. At times he felt guilty about having sold his integrity and self-respect for such a paltry amount, but at least he could say that he hadn't sold his soul. He may have betrayed his employer but he hadn't killed anyone. Perhaps it was a fine line, but in his mind it allowed him to continue to take Hollis' money. Rudy nodded in appreciation of the money. "Thanks, Sheriff."

Hollis stood up with his coffee cup and moved towards the pot on the stove to refill it. It was an action that didn't go unnoticed by Rudy. It was early and a cool morning. A cup of hot coffee would've tasted good, but did this uppity sonovabitch offer one? Hollis poured himself another cup of coffee. "Rudy," he said, turning from the stove, "you be sure and keep a close ear to the ground between now and when Stevenson leaves. Let me know if you hear anything different. I especially want to know what's going on with this marshal from Boise."

Rudy wished he could just go now but he forced himself to say: "You can count on me."

Hollis took a noisy sip of his second cup of coffee. "Damn, that's hot," he exclaimed, "but that's the way I like it." And then he added: "Rudy, on the second night try to convince Stevenson to camp at Sheep Springs. You can probably expect some guests for supper."

Rudy nodded. "I'll try but sometimes you never know about Stevenson. He gets something in his head and he can be as cantankerous as an old bull."

Hollis looked sternly at Rudy. "Make it happen, Rudy. I'm sure you can find a way."

"I'll do what I can," replied Rudy, and then he turned to leave.

"One other thing, Rudy," said Hollis. "No heroes this time."

Rudy's mind flashed back to the last trip when one of the other mule skinners had gotten killed during the robbery. Sam had been his name. He'd been a friend to Rudy when a lot of other people treated him with indifference, or as sometimes happened in saloons, mocked him because of his weight and being a little slow. Rudy had hollered at

Sam to not fight back, but his friend died in a hail of bullets just as he shouted, "It ain't right, Rudy." Rudy wasn't a particularly brave man; he'd come west to avoid the big war back east. He'd rationalized, perhaps correctly, that it wasn't good common sense to shoot it out with the robbers. Still, it gnawed at his conscience—especially when he was by himself and he had lots of time to think—how he had betrayed his employer and one of the few people in his life that he could actually call a friend. He was learning the hard way that there were some things that money couldn't buy. And yet here he was taking Hollis' money again. Rudy turned to respond to the sheriff. Hollis had that arrogant smirk on his face and there was evil in his eyes. He really didn't care if Stevenson and his men died or not, but if they didn't resist it would make it easier for his men. Rudy felt disgust, even a little shame. "I best be gettin' back," he said in a voice lacking energy, and with that he turned and left by way of the back door.

Hollis watched Rudy's departure. He didn't have a good feeling about their meeting. There was something about the fat guy's demeanor that seemed off. He couldn't put his finger on it; maybe a little disrespectful? He didn't know—he would have to think on it.

Chapter Eight

Sarah knelt down beside the creek to wash her face and hands. She could've done that at the cabin, but she felt it best to give Josh some time alone with Lester to discuss today's events. She was beginning to feel like her presence just complicated things. Sarah tested the water with her hand; it was frigid. Nonetheless, she looked for a place where the water flowed quickly over the multicolored gravel. There were shades of orange, red, white, purple, and black rocks intermixed with fine sand and, for some fortunate few, yellow gold. Sarah scooped up two handfuls of the icy cold water and brought it to her face; it took her breath away. "Oh my goodness," she exclaimed aloud.

There was brief laughter behind her. "That crik water'll darn sure get your attention at this time of the day," said Lester.

Sarah gasped and turned quickly to see Lester standing there with a side of bacon in his hands. "Ya like bacon?" he asked in a rhetorical manner, as if who in their right mind wouldn't like bacon.

Sarah blinked her eyes to shed the water from them and bring Lester into focus. He was smiling, and for a brief moment she wondered if he could see her nipples that had become erect in the cool morning air. But then she discarded this thought, almost as quickly as it had come, due to the heaviness of her shirt and Lester being a gentleman. Nonetheless, her upbringing dictated that she fold her arms in front of her as if to preserve her body's warmth. "It's chilly this morning, Lester."

"Yes ma'am, it is. I just been up to my ice house and fetched this here side ah bacon. Figured we'd have bacon and biscuits and gravy for breakfast." It was obvious to Sarah that Lester was proud of the hospitality that he was able to afford her and Josh. He'd worked hard for what he had, but he didn't mind sharing with people that he cared about. What she didn't understand, though, was how he could be so seemingly unconcerned about what was on tap for the day. People could die and there was no telling who that might be. And now as the glow of the sun became visible on the eastern horizon, that reality was tying her stomach into a knot.

"You've missed your calling, Lester," said Sarah teasingly. "You shoulda been a cook in one of them fancy San Francisco restaurants."

Lester accepted this for the compliment that it was intended to be, but then humility caused him to reply with a laugh: "Well I ain't poisoned anybody yet, but I reckon me and them snooty city folks wouldn't get along too well so I suspect I'm better off where I'm at."

Sarah smiled. She liked Lester and felt comfortable around him. She didn't get the feeling that he was judging her. In a way he reminded her of one of her uncles back in Boston. He was a fisherman, a little rough around the edges but a good man. He'd worked hard to get what little he had in life but he didn't mind sharing with those in need. "So you have an icehouse?" said Sarah.

"Yes, ma'am," said Lester proudly. "Ya wanna see it? It's just around the bend up this here path," he said, gesturing towards the path that he was standing on.

Sarah paused briefly. It occurred to her that maybe she should go to the cabin—not to engage Josh in any more discussion about what he was going to do today, as he'd already made it pretty clear where he stood on that, but maybe just as moral support. On the other hand, maybe just giving him time to process things would be best, and so she said: "Sure, lead the way." Sarah had noticed the path earlier on her way to the creek. It appeared to go up the canyon parallel to the creek, but since it disappeared into the ponderosa pines she didn't know where it led to.

Lester, and now Rufus who had come down from the cabin, started up the path. They'd gone only a short distance into where the trees got thicker and the path curved away from the creek and went about thirty yards up a side drainage. The entrance to the icehouse appeared to be more like a mine shaft that extended into the side hill for about six feet. At this point there was a heavy log door hung on big metal hinges from a large upright log beam. The door was secured by a crossbar that extended across it and rested in supports on either side. However, what was not visible or perhaps expected by a person on the outside was this same locking device was on the inside of the door. The intent being that a person could take refuge in the icehouse if need be. Lester lifted the crossbar from the door and opened it. He stepped inside and lit a match, which he put to a candle that rested on a stool in the corner. "Shut the door, if you don't mind," he said to Sarah. "Need to keep the cold in." Sarah did as Lester asked. The silence was eerie and the images illuminated by the candle were, for her, a close second. The room, which was about six feet wide and eight feet deep and just tall enough for Lester to stand upright in, had the front and hind quarters of a deer suspended from meat hooks in the log ceiling. The rib cage was also hanging there, as Lester didn't like to waste any of the deer. All around the room were blocks of ice stacked about chest high. Lester had cut these from a beaver pond a short ways upstream from his cabin last winter and hauled them on a makeshift sled that his mules towed to the icehouse.

"This is impressive, Lester," said Sarah, somewhat in awe. "You've put in a lot of work here."

Lester nodded in acknowledgement. "Yeah, me an' Rufus and the mules. Not much else a fellar can do in the winter when ever' thing is froze up, but come summertime it sure pays off."

"I suppose so," said Sarah, who was beginning to visibly shiver. She could see that Lester was aware that she was uncomfortably cold, but it was also apparent that he was hesitant to leave just yet.

Lester turned to face the wall behind him and Sarah. Coming out of winter, there had been six tiers of ice blocks stacked against the wall; there were now four. Lester turned and looked at Sarah. It was one of those looks that was pensive yet foretelling of a change in the course of the conversation. "Sarah," he began, "I think I'm a fair judge of character and I think that I can trust you and Josh." Lester paused. A slight look of apprehension came over Sarah's face. She had no idea what he was leading up to. Lester extended the candle towards her. "Hold this, will you?" Sarah nodded and took the candle. Lester stepped next to the ice wall, near the center, and grasped the top ice block on the back side and slid it towards him so that it fell to the ground. He then pushed it to the side and repeated the process for the rest of the blocks until he had removed them all. There, hidden behind the ice wall at ground level, was another small door about two feet by two feet. It was also hung on heavy hinges, but it had a hasp with a small iron rod to prevent the door from being opened from the other side. Lester removed the rod and opened the small door. There was more darkness, but Sarah could see well enough in the candlelight that it was the entrance to a tunnel. "This," said Lester solemnly, "is my go-to-hell place."

"Your go-to-hell place?" repeated Sarah naively.

Lester smiled shrewdly. "I don't have to tell you, Sarah, that there's lots ah bad folks in these parts. I figure it's only a matter a time 'fore they get around to try and take what little I got here, and when that day comes I aim to put up a fight. But if things go to hell on me, I figure my best chance of survivin' is to get to the icehouse, lock them out, and then escape out this here tunnel."

Sarah peered into the darkness. It looked scary to her. "Where does it come out?" she asked.

Lester tilted his head to the left, even though beyond the penetration of the candlelight, the darkness was as thick as molasses and there was no reference for direction. "Thataway 'bout a hundert feet. Comes up in the next little draw just behind some alder bushes. Got a flat piece ah shale rock over it."

Sarah knelt down at the entrance and extended the candle into the tunnel. It was small; a person would have to be on their hands and knees to move through it, and unlike the icehouse its sides were not lined with logs—it was just bare dirt, rock, and roots. To say that it was foreboding would be an understatement, as just looking in it seized Sarah with claustrophobia to the point that she felt panicky. She needed to leave, but as she carefully withdrew the candle from the tunnel, a long piece of canvas lying on the floor of the tunnel caught her eye. She paused with the light to get a better look.

Anticipating her question, Lester said: "That's my emergency gun. Double-barrel 12-gauge shotgun." He paused briefly. It was fortunate that the light conditions were poor, as the reservations that he had about saying anything more were undoubtedly written on his face. A flurry of mental debate ensued within him. He was no spring chicken and besides, these were rough times. It'd be akin to a last will and testament, except not on paper. He reasoned he could be buckin' for dumbass of the year, but he doubted it. And so he said: "I keep my gold in here too. You're the only person I ever told about this tunnel or my gold."

Sarah was not only taken aback by Lester's confession, she was flattered. "Your secret is safe with me, Lester," she said sincerely.

Lester looked into Sarah's face. "I know," he said simply. Deep down, he knew that she was good people. It flashed through his mind that if he'd ever married and had kids that he would've wanted a daughter like her. Whatever the reason, he trusted her.

"We best be gittin' back," said Lester as he reached past Sarah and pulled the small door shut and latched it.

"Yeah, I imagine Josh'll be wonderin' what happened to his breakfast," replied Sarah as she petted Rufus' head. And then to Rufus, she cooed: "Good dog, Rufus. What a good boy you are."

Sarah stood and held the candle while Lester restacked the blocks of ice. Once things were back in place, they left the icehouse and headed back down the trail. As they neared the cabin Rufus ran ahead alerting Josh, who now stepped into the doorway with coffee cup in hand. "Thought maybe a bear got you two," he said jokingly.

"Naw, bears 'round here are smarter than that," replied Lester with a sly grin. "They'd wait 'til after breakfast. Git more for their trouble that way."

Josh laughed politely. "Speakin' ah breakfast, do ya'll need some help?" he asked as he stepped out of the doorway to allow Lester to pass.

"No, sir," replied Lester. "Believe I got it handled. Why don't you and Sarah just take a load off. Have another cup of coffee. Vittles'll be ready in just a bit."

Josh looked at Sarah. He could tell by her demeanor that she would not be the one initiating any conversation between the two of them. He didn't blame her after the way their early morning discussion had gone. He was on edge over going after Seth's killer and he'd taken it out on her. But even more, as he stood outside Lester's cabin and looked around at what Lester had made for himself amidst the peace and tranquility of this little canyon, he felt guilty for having brought the ugliness of his problem into Lester's life. It didn't seem right.

Sarah glanced at Josh as she walked past him. They made eye contact. It was brief and not inviting. "I think I'm gonna take Lester up on his coffee," she said, and then she disappeared into the cabin.

Josh was torn. At that moment he'd wanted to talk to her—about what, he wasn't even certain. He couldn't explain it; he just felt a need to be near her and to talk. Yet only a short while ago, their conversation had ended abruptly because of him. He could feel himself knotting up inside. *Damned women,* he said to himself. He took a deep breath and exhaled noisily. And then it came to him: None of this would be happening if Seth woulda just came straight to the ranch over on the Salmon River, but he always had that wanderlust in his eye. Maybe he wouldn't have been happy being a simple rancher. His mind was spinning and not in a good way. *To hell with breakfast*, he said to himself. *Maybe it's best if I just get underway. Just frustratin' myself here.* And with that Josh set his coffee cup on a stump by the cabin door and headed down to the pasture by the creek to fetch Thunder.

He had just finished saddling Thunder when he sensed someone behind him. "Breakfast is ready," said Sarah.

Josh pretended to be busy adjusting the cinch on his saddle and he didn't turn to face Sarah. "I think I'm gonna pass on breakfast," he said stoically. He'd made a decision, or at least he thought he had, and talking to her could possibly undo that. He just needed to tend to business. "I figure it'd be best if I visit them two hombres on Seth's claim the first rattle outa the box," he added in a casual, businesslike tone.

"Lester will be disappointed if you don't stay for breakfast," replied Sarah in a friendly but mockingly pleading voice. And then she added: "So will I."

Josh turned to face Sarah. Her last words had touched his inner core; it was an instant good feeling that immediately gave way to the prospect of delaying his departure and having breakfast. But then he stopped himself. "I need to tend to business. It could be a messy affair, and the sooner I put it behind me the sooner I can get back to my life."

There was a look of concern on Sarah's face. "I know you don't want to hear it and I know you cared a lot about Seth, but he's gone. And quite honestly, I don't see this bein' your fight. Nothing is going to bring him back."

The image of the Comanche warrior kneeling over him preparing to take his scalp flooded Josh's mind. If it hadn't been for Seth, that brave would've added Josh's scalp to his collection. He couldn't turn his back on that fact.

"It's a man thing, Sarah," interjected Lester, who had quietly walked up from the side.

"It must be 'cause I don't understand it," she said as she raised both her hands in an exasperated gesture while looking at Josh.

Josh looked at Sarah and paused briefly to select just the right words so as to hopefully not totally offend her, as both she and her dead husband had chosen, albeit out of desperation, to not travel the moral high road. "Aside from the fact that I owe my life to Seth, there just comes a point when decent, law-abiding folks have got to stand up to those who ain't," said Josh in as much of a nonjudgmental voice as he could muster.

Josh's words had struck a raw nerve within Sarah. "Sometimes people do things just to survive," she said somewhat defensively. "But don't get me wrong, I'm not saying killing is right."

"Maybe we just need to take this pot outa the fire 'fore it boils over," said Lester. "Ain't no good end gonna come of this arguin'." Lester paused and then looked at Josh. "You're welcome to set to breakfast, but if you feel the need to head out now I take no offense. I know you already said no but my offer to go with you still stands."

"Appreciate it, Lester, but this is my fight and no one else's."

Lester stepped closer to Josh and extended his hand. "Besta luck to ya," he said warmly as he and Josh shook hands.

"Thanks, Lester," replied Josh. "I appreciate your hospitality. You're a good man."

Sensing that Josh and Sarah might want a minute alone, Lester extended his right hand towards Rufus and snapped his fingers. "C'mon, Rufus. Let's go to the house and get you some breakfast."

For a moment Josh and Sarah watched Lester and Rufus walk towards the cabin, and then they turned their attention to one another. It was awkward, neither of them certain about where they stood with the other—or for that matter certain of where they wanted to be. So much had happened in the past two days. The events of that night in the Gold Strike Saloon replayed themselves endlessly in Josh's mind. They were like the blades of a windmill on a West Texas prairie—tirelessly spinning, bringing more water to the trough, except Josh's trough was overflowing. Sarah's eyes were moist. "I bet you regret buying me that drink at the Gold Strike," she said with a hopeful smile.

"Sometimes," said Josh truthfully, "and sometimes not."

Sarah's eyes were nervous. They searched Josh's face for an expression of anything more, but it was not forthcoming. She wanted to reach out to him, to touch him, but she didn't know how it would be received, so instead she gathered her hands in front of her to steady them. "Please be careful," she said.

"You can count on that," replied Josh airily. And then he added with a laugh: "I'm still mendin' from where the Swede winged me. I can't afford any more bullet holes."

Josh is like a poker player, thought Sarah. He's not going to tip his hand when it comes to his feelings, at least not for a whore anyway. The life went out of her face as this thought resonated in her mind. "Well, I reckon I'll just see you when you get back," she said flatly.

"I reckon so," said Josh as he gathered Thunder's reins and swung up into the saddle. "By then I'll probably be wishin' I'd ate breakfast," he added, continuing the façade of casual indifference towards the task at hand and his feelings for Sarah. And with that Josh started up the ridge away from Lester's cabin.

Sarah stood in front of the cabin and watched Josh's departure until he and Thunder disappeared in a patch of ponderosa not far from the top of the ridge. She hoped with all her being that he would return. But why? After all, she reasoned, I've only known him for two days.

Chapter Nine

Bullwhacker Creek was situated about ten miles north-west of Bear Creek in a relatively short but deep canyon whose bottom was thick with quaking aspen and willows. The side of the canyon that faced north had a dense stand of Douglas fir trees, which made for good escape cover for critters that had come to drink at the creek or folks up to no good on Sheriff Hollis' mining claim. Those folks were in the form of Buster Kregg and his gang. Buster had made a nuisance of himself in the California goldfields around Placerville to the point that he'd been invited to a necktie party by a lynch mob. Ironically, the local sheriff had intervened to save him so that a judge and jury could hang him legally. Unfortunately, Kregg was sprung from jail and the good citizens of Placerville were denied justice as Kregg and his men vacated the area in search of new opportunities. That quest landed them in Bear Creek, Idaho Territory. In addition to Kregg, there was Sean O'Fallon, a mean-spirited half-breed of Irish and Bannock Indian blood who was no stranger to killing folks. He was a quiet type that people didn't mess with. And then there were the Menagher brothers, Billy and Jethro, who just straight up didn't like working for a living, for as they were fond of saying, "It didn't make any sense for a fellar to bust his ass all day when he could just take it from someone else who had." And then they laughed as only the Menagher boys could with that cavalier indifference to other people's loss. These were the occupants of Sheriff Hollis' mining claim.

It was about a three-hour ride from Bear Creek to the claim. The summer sun seemed particularly unmerciful today as it bore down on the sheriff, and to make matters worse, there wasn't a single cloud in the sky to intercept its wrath. Large sweat stains on the underarms of the sheriff's shirt provided proof of its intensity. And so it was when he started on the game trail that weaved amongst the quaking aspen trees in the bottom of Bullwhacker Creek, he was appreciative of their shade and bitched only a little when the branches raked him in the face. It was close to midafternoon when he reached the edge of the clearing where the cabin on his claim was located. Past experience had taught him that it was a wise man who exercised caution when entering situations unannounced. This could be good advice when it came to Kregg's bunch, especially if they'd been drinking. Hollis leaned slightly forward, resting his forearms on the pommel of his saddle, and surveyed the clearing. There was no one in sight, and all was quiet save for the babbling waters of Bullwhacker Creek and the raven's harsh cawing that had just spied his presence. The cabin door was open, probably to allow access to whatever breeze that might come up in the stifling heat. The corral beyond the cabin and closer to the creek was empty; its gate stood wide open. Saddles, however, straddled the top rail on the corral. "These lazy idiots are asleep," whispered Hollis aloud. He sighed angrily. Hollis nudged the sides of his horse and rode slowly into the clearing. There was movement in the trees beyond the cabin. A horse nickered in a contented tone. Hollis stopped. It was one of the gang's horses; it had been hobbled to reduce its potential to roam very far. Nonetheless, it was the only horse in sight. Hollis was about to ride on when he caught movement out of the corner of his left eye. The door to the privy, which was located behind the cabin in a small opening in the trees, swung open. Billy Menagher, oblivious to the sheriff's presence, stepped out still pulling up his pants. Hollis said nothing but instead stared in disbelief as Billy ambled back towards the cabin, yawning as he went. "What a dimwit," mumbled Hollis to himself. And then, finally, Billy saw the sheriff. His head did a double take and instinctively he started to run. He'd taken maybe four or five steps when it clicked who he was looking at and he stopped. He watched as the sheriff rode slowly towards him. He could tell by the look on Hollis' face that he wasn't particularly happy. Billy knew that if it had been a situation where it had been someone other than Hollis that was wise to them, they could've all been either dead or in handcuffs.

"Afternoon," said Billy as Hollis drew near him.

"It damned sure is," replied Hollis coldly. "And pretty soon it'll be nighttime and then it'll eventually be daytime again and I'd be willin' to bet that sluice box down by the creek will still be in the same place as it is right now. In fact,

I'm pretty certain that it ain't moved since the last time I was out here."

"What's gotcha so fired up, Sheriff?" came a voice over near the corner of the cabin. It was Buster Kregg followed by the half-breed and the other Menagher brother.

Hollis got off of his horse and dropped the reins. He took several steps towards Buster before speaking. He knew that he'd gotten their attention, but he also knew better than to press his luck with violent men like these who required little provocation to kill. And so he said in a serious but more respectful tone: "Buster, don't you all remember what I said about we got to make like this here is a producin' claim?"

Buster was a big man, well over six feet tall with shoulder-length black hair. Except for a big walrus mustache that hid his upper lip he was clean shaven, when he got around to it, which was usually about once a week. "Seems like I do recall that conversation, Sheriff," drawled Buster.

"Well, Buster, the sun's high in the sky and you and your boys is shaded up. I know it's hot, but it just seems right peculiar to me that ever' claim I went by on the way up here there was folks out ah-workin'."

"Maybe you should get your sorry ass out here and lend a hand, Sheriff," said O'Fallon before Buster could reply.

Hollis glanced at O'Fallon, ignoring the comment, and then shifted his eyes to Buster, hoping that he would get a more rational response before the half-breed's anger infected the Menaghers and the whole situation went to hell. With the exception of Billy Menagher, they were all armed.

Hollis knew that he couldn't show any fear to Buster and his gang. And so Hollis said in a calm voice: "Buster, folks is gettin' suspicious. They see you and your boys come to town and pay with gold dust or currency, but they don't ever see much work up here. So you can paint that picture for yourself."

"Well, Sheriff, I can see your point but you need to go easy on the boys and me," whined Buster. "It's a hot son of a bitch out here ah-digging and totin' gravel and workin' that sluice box."

"I don't doubt what you say," replied Hollis. "But the fires of hell will be hotter, and that's where we all could end up sooner than we was hopin' for if our little business arrangement is discovered."

"As long as you're the sheriff, what do we care?" interjected Jethro Menagher.

Hollis looked at Jethro. He was living the same fantasy that the sheriff had been so naively living until this morning when he'd talked to Rudy. It was time for everybody involved to undergo a reality check; the only problem being, there was something about what Rudy had said concerning Stevenson giving bags of what looked like gold to this marshal from Boise. If that were true and the marshal was taking gold to Boise, it could make for some easy pickings. It had occurred to Hollis on the ride up from Bear Creek that the intrusion of the marshal might not be a bad thing if he was transporting a lot of gold. This could be especially true if the marshal ended up in a shallow grave and Hollis didn't have to split the gold with anyone. Add this to what he already had in the bank in Boise and he'd have a nice grubstake to start over somewhere else. Obviously, the only problem with this scheme would be if Kregg's gang found out about the gold, they'd kill him for sure.

"Jethro, the jig's up," said Hollis.

"What are you talkin' about?" asked Buster in a concerned voice.

Hollis looked Buster straight in the eyes. "There's a United States marshal from Boise up here pokin' around."

Buster was taken aback a bit. His first thought was that the law from California had caught wind of him. "Whaddya mean 'pokin' around'? Does he know anything?"

"Don't know for sure," replied Hollis. "I been told that he visited Stevenson's camp several times since he's been in Bear Creek, but I don't know what went on between the two of 'em." Hollis had gotten good at lying over the years, and he was fairly confident that Buster had not detected these half-truths.

Buster took a plug of chewing tobacco from his shirt pocket and bit off a piece. He chewed on it several times to a point where he could use his tongue to shove it over into his right cheek. It made his cheek on that side bulge out like a squirrel carrying nuts. "Ya know, Hollis," said Buster, deliberately addressing the sheriff by his last name, "them two is no doubt up to something but it ain't gonna do 'em no good. We got the element of surprise on our side. We'll find us a spot where we can watch Stevenson and his bunch ah wagon drivers for a spell, and if things don't look right, we won't hit 'em."

Hollis was caught off-guard by Buster's response. He'd never expected him to show any caution, especially knowing that the Menaghers probably wouldn't be supportive. It wouldn't pay to have Buster and his gang unoccupied if he went after the marshal and the possible gold that he might be carrying. "I got one of Stevenson's mule skinners on my payroll," said Hollis sternly. "He ain't aware of any special precautions for Stevenson's trip back to Boise."

"Who is this guy?" sneered Billy Menagher.

"His name's Rudy Holchek, fat guy. Got a red beard. You probably seen'em in the Gold Strike, more an' likely half-drunk."

Buster scoffed. "So a drunk is your inside man?" Buster laughed along with the other gang members.

Hollis' facial expression remained sober. After the laughter subsided, he said: "This guy has never steered me wrong in the past. I got no reason to believe that this time is any different."

The afternoon sun was at Hollis' back and getting lower in the sky; the angle was such that it made Buster squint his right eye as he looked at Hollis. "Whaddaya aim to do about this here marshal? I mean I thought you law people talked to one another. Maybe you could just ask him straight up what the hell he's ah-doin' here?"

Hollis tossed his right hand in the air as if to emphasize the obvious course of action which Buster had just suggested. "I can't ask somebody something that I ain't never seen," he said irritably. "Apparently this guy's been here for some time, just skunkin' around in the shadows tryin' to dig up whatever dirt he can, I suspect. Besides, it don't take no genius to figure out he don't want me to know what he's up to."

Buster paused as if in thought, pursed his lips, and then spat a big stream of tobacco juice on the ground between him and Hollis. Some of the juice was intercepted by his moustache and hung there like morning dew on grass. Buster put his hands on his hips as if he was preparing to lecture a schoolboy. "The way I see it, Sheriff, is me and the boys here we do most all of the heavy lifting in this here arrangement of ours. We take all the risks and then we have to cut you and your deputies in for an equal share. It's a pretty sweet deal for ya if I do say so myself."

"It's about as sweet as a bucket of horse shit if you ask me," shouted O'Fallon.

Without thinking, Hollis blurted out: "Nobody asked you."

Instantly, the half-breed went for his gun; Hollis, however, was quicker and had his .44 Colt drawn, cocked, and leveled at O'Fallon's belly.

"Let it go, Sean!" shouted Buster.

O'Fallon's hand froze on the grip of his partially drawn pistol. There was dead silence and then Buster said in a calm voice: "It ain't worth it, Sean."

O'Fallon glared at the sheriff. His breathing was rapid and the hatred radiated from his eyes. He smiled in a devilish manner as he slowly lowered his pistol back into its holster. "There'll be another day, Hollis," he snarled.

"Maybe so," said Hollis as he carefully lowered the hammer on his pistol and holstered it. There was a moment of uneasy silence as Hollis continued to look at O'Fallon; then, satisfied that the half-breed had played his hand, Hollis turned to Buster: "Don't worry about this marshal. I'll take care of him."

"When?" replied Buster curtly.

"Maybe tomorrow. I don't know for sure. Gotta find him first." Hollis grinned inwardly. The fact that Kregg and his boys wanted nothing to do with killing the marshal suited him fine. He would be perceived by them as "lifting his share of the load," and if the marshal was carrying gold, as he suspected, it would be a bonus that he wouldn't be sharing with anyone.

"Well make sure that you do," said Buster emphatically. "We don't need no lawman snooping around here."

"I'll do my part," replied Hollis in a conciliatory tone, "but are you guys gonna do yours or not? I told Holchek to get Stevenson to camp at Sheep Springs the second night out from Bear Creek. Figured it'd be a good spot for you guys to take care of business, and then make a wide swing up through that Crooked Creek country to throw off any do-gooders from Bear Creek that might get it in their head to try and follow you."

Buster eyed the sheriff suspiciously. "I ain't so sure that I'm too skookum with the idy that this here Holchek guy knows when and where we're gonna hit'em."

"Rudy's alright," replied Hollis quickly. And without thinking, he added: "I'd bet my life on it."

Buster spat another stream of tobacco juice on the ground between him and Hollis—except this time it was closer to Hollis. "Well if things go south on this here deal," he said in an unfriendly tone, "that's exactly what you will be bettin'."

Buster's words as well as the entire meeting with his gang had angered Hollis, but he had little choice but to bite his tongue and endure it. Just a little longer and he'd have his grubstake and he could cut his ties with the likes of the Kregg gang and leave Bear Creek. But for now, he couldn't let anything upset their business arrangement. Ignoring Buster's threat, Hollis said: "Stevenson is leaving Bear Creek in the morning. I'll try to meet you back here in a week."

"Don't be late, Sheriff," said Buster in a sarcastic tone. "Wouldn't want you to miss out on your share of old man Stevenson's money." And then as if on cue the gang laughed, but not in a friendly way.

Hollis looked at Buster as he laughed. He was an oaf. The sun glistened on the tobacco juice that was imbedded in his droopy mustache. *These ungrateful sonsabitches'll get theirs one day*, said Hollis to himself. And then aloud he said: "Well, boys, I got me a marshal to find so I'll be seein' ya." Hollis walked to his horse and got on. His departure was met with silence. As he reined his horse around to head back across the clearing and down the trail, all of the gang except O'Fallon was walking towards the cabin. He stood where he'd been throughout the meeting, glaring at the sheriff. Hollis met his eyes briefly as he wheeled his horse around and then turned and slowly rode away, not knowing if he was going to get shot in the back.

Chapter Ten

Josh studied the map that Lester had drawn for him of how to get to Seth's claim. From Porcupine Creek, where Lester's claim was located, he had to go north on the wagon road about five miles and then turn up Moonshine Creek and go roughly another six miles. Along the wagon road, the terrain had been forgiving and relatively open. Rolling sagebrush-covered hills interspersed with pockets of quaking aspen and ponderosa pine dominated the lower lying country, but since starting up Moonshine Creek the terrain had gotten considerably steeper, causing Thunder to labor harder. Increasingly, there were more Douglas fir trees and dense cover on either side of the trail, providing more opportunity for an ambush. A throwback to his time in the cavalry, Josh always evaluated whatever terrain he was in for its military tactical advantages and disadvantages. "Gotta be gittin' close to Seth's claim," he said aloud as if it were for Thunder's benefit. He folded the map and put it back in his pocket. The trail that he was on was about a hundred yards up from the bottom of the canyon where Moonshine Creek ran. The creek bottom itself was so choked full of aspen, alders, willows, and rocks that in many places it was impossible to get a horse through it. Josh studied the terrain up ahead from atop Thunder. Lester had said that Seth's claim was just beyond the first big bend in the canyon, and that appeared to be coming right up as the canyon jogged sharply to the left. Josh nudged the sides of Thunder and they started again up the rocky trail. A pine squirrel stood upright on the branch of a big fir tree along the side of the trail and chattered loudly, announcing Josh's approach. And, as if to not be outdone by the squirrel, a raven circling overhead added its raspy call. *Well, I guess there's not gonna be any sneakin' up on these guys*, said Josh to himself. *But that'll be okay unless their intentions are bad from the git-go*.

As Josh rode along he tried to remain vigilant, constantly scanning the area on either side of the trail ahead, but he soon became aware that his eyes were looking and his mind was elsewhere, thinking about Sarah. From a physical standpoint he couldn't ask for more: she was a pretty girl. And he thought that she'd had some fetchin' up in life based on the way she conducted herself since leaving the Gold Strike, but facts were facts and he was having trouble getting beyond the fact that she'd been a whore. It'll always come down to that, he thought. But maybe if they got clean out of the area and started fresh somewhere else, things would be different. Josh inhaled deeply, as if he needed the air, and then exhaled more slowly. He was getting himself wrapped around a post, thinking about Sarah. There just didn't seem to be any good end to it. There were too many images that came to mind, not the least of which was the marshal and her. The uneasiness between the two of them on the road yesterday had been as heavy as the smoke from a wet wood fire. It'd be hard to get beyond that image, that near-for-certain fact that she'd been with the marshal.

It was not long after Josh passed the big bend in the canyon that he heard voices. He couldn't make out what they were saying but they didn't sound excited. They were coming from down by the creek about two hundred yards up the canyon. Josh pondered the situation for a moment. He reckoned that he might get more cooperation if he wasn't too heavy-handed with these guys, at least not to begin with. And, although he knew it to be good, he checked his pistol: six chambers loaded and the action working smoothly. Josh was confident of his abilities with a gun—not necessarily that he was the fastest but that he would make his first shot count. Too often, gunfighter types un-holstered their pistol with blazing speed only to miss with their first shot. Josh rode on and soon came to a wide, flat spot in the bottom of the canyon. It looked like lightning had started a fire there some years back, as there were only scattered big trees and a fair amount of grass. Tethered in the midst of this meadow appeared to be the same sorrel and palomino horses that he'd seen above Lester's cabin last night. To the left of them, down closer to the creek, was a wall tent. A stump with an axe buried in it was situated in front of the tent near a pile of chopped wood. No one was in sight, but then he heard the voices again. They were coming from beyond the tent and up the creek a little ways. Josh dismounted from Thunder, not far from the tent. He loosely tied Thunder's reins around a branch on a tree that had fallen over during the fire. He paused. He could still hear the voices, talking in normal tones down by the creek. Josh carefully surveyed the camp and the area surrounding it to make sure that he wasn't surprised by anyone else. It was quiet except for the wind blowing through the trees and the perpetual sound of a waterfall that didn't exist. Not wanting to make a foolish assumption, Josh moved quietly to the front of the tent. The flaps were down but not tied. Slowly, with his right hand he drew his pistol, keeping his thumb on the hammer but not risking the noise of cocking it, and with his left hand, he parted the tent flaps. There were a couple of bedrolls laid out and some personal effects. Immediately to the right and just inside the tent was a wooden grub box. It appeared to be about the size that would fit inside a pannier for easy packing, and on top of it sat a metal pan full of dishes and utensils. Not much of note, thought Josh. He was about to release the tent flap when his eye caught sight of a pocket watch hanging from the center tent pole near the back of the tent. It looked like one that he'd seen a thousand times before. Quickly looking over his shoulder, Josh turned and entered the tent. He untied the watch from the pole and took it outside to look at it in the light. He opened the watch and read the inscription on the inside cover: *Good Luck, Seth. Love, Mother & Father.* Reading the inscription brought a lump into Josh's throat. Seth had received this watch from his parents shortly after he had told them that he had enlisted in the army. It was one of his most valuable possessions. He was never without it, so to find it here could only mean one thing. Josh put the watch in his front pants pocket and turned towards the creek. The adrenalin surged within him. There was little doubt, at least in his mind, that one or both of these men were responsible for Seth's death.

The two men were busy working a sluice box at the edge of the stream and hadn't noticed Josh walk up. "How ya'll doin'?" he asked in a non-threatening tone.

Both men instantly turned and looked at Josh. It was obvious they were fearful. They were young, early twenties, and had a look about them that suggested they could be cocky when the advantage was theirs but they wisely perceived the current situation as a draw at best. Both of the men were of medium build with dark, short hair. One of them, however, had a full beard while the other had only a mustache. Both of them were wearing gun belts. "What can we do ya for, mister?" asked the man with the full beard.

"I'm lookin' for a guy named Leroy Bates," said Josh as he looked the bearded man square in the eyes. "Ever hear of 'em?"

"Who wants to know?" asked the bearded man.

"Deputy U.S. Marshal Josh Morrow, that's who." Josh could see the apprehension in the bearded man's face. He glanced over at his partner, who was equally as nervous.

"Why are ya lookin' for this guy?" asked the bearded man.

"Well accordin' to the records at the mining claim office in Bear Creek, he filed over a friend of mine that had originally filed on this very claim that we're standin' on. So if I was a bettin' man I'd say one of ya'll standin' right here is Leroy Bates."

"Well, Deputy," began the bearded man with some newfound courage, "if you been to the claim office, then you oughta know that the laws in this here mining district says that any claim abandoned for more 'an three days is fair game to whatever feller that comes on it."

"So that's what ya'll are sayin'," replied Josh in a disbelieving tone of voice, "this claim was abandoned and you two just happened upon it."

"That's pretty much it," said the bearded man. "We'd been pokin' around further upstream but hadn't found much." He paused, as if he wanted to be careful of what he said next. "And well, sir, we'd been by this claim a number of times and we'd seen some guy a-workin' it by himself. And then one day there was no horse here and nobody around here but the camp was still here. We kinda took note ah that, and by and by we says to ourselves it looks like this claim has been abandoned."

"And so ya'll rushed into town to take advantage of the fact that a dead man can't work his claim. Is that about it?" said Josh somewhat sarcastically.

The bearded man's demeanor changed. Josh could see anger in his eyes; his partner, on the other hand, seemed fearful. "You know, Deputy," said the bearded man in a surly voice, "I don't know that I care for your tone."

"Well, that's unfortunate," replied Josh calmly. "But ya know, Leroy, I don't much care for this little game of cat-and-mouse ya'll been playin'."

The bearded man laughed derisively. "I ain't broke no laws and you got no proof that I have."

Josh sensed that their conversation was about to go south. At present he didn't have a good angle on both men as the mustachioed one stood slightly behind and to the side of Leroy. "Well, I don't know if that's exactly true," said Josh as he took a couple of steps to the left. His movement instantly agitated Leroy.

"Ya know, Deputy," said Leroy in a somewhat threatening manner, "it might be best if you just stayed right where you're at. I ain't the fool that you think I am."

Josh shrugged. "All ridey then. Have it your way. It don't make no never mind to me." Josh paused. "I got something I wanna show you, though."

"What's that?" shot back Leroy.

"It's in my pants pocket so don't be gettin' all fidgety when I go to my pocket."

Leroy nodded in agreement. "Alright, let's see whatcha got."

And with that, Josh pulled Seth's watch out of his pocket. He held it up by the narrow, intricately braided lanyard that Seth had made for it. There was an immediate look of mild shock on both men's faces as they realized their privacy had been violated. But it was a situation where neither man wanted to protest very loudly. "Does this look familiar?" asked Josh coyly.

"You know it does," said Leroy contemptuously. "You took it out of our tent. Just 'cause you're a lawman it don't give you the right to go snoopin' through people's belongin's."

Hell, the tent probably belonged to Seth too, thought Josh, but he said aloud: "How'd you come by this watch?"

Leroy stammered a bit while he processed a response. "I bought it off a guy in Bear Creek."

Josh was almost certain that Leroy was lying. "You remember what this guy looked like?"

Leroy's response was immediate. "He was a big guy."

Josh laughed. "That's it, just a big guy. Ya'll don't remember anything else about him?"

"No," said Leroy bluntly, "I don't."

It was clear to Josh that Leroy wasn't about to admit to anything that was going to link him to Seth's murder. The circumstances looked pretty suspicious, but would it hold up in court? He didn't especially like the idea of goading Leroy, and probably his friend as well, into a gunfight to get justice for Seth, but maybe there was no other way. And then, almost as if it had been by some divine intervention, he saw just beyond the two men what might be the deciding proof that he needed. Standing upright and leaning slightly into a thicket of willows were two rifles; undoubtedly they were Leroy's and his partner's. One was a Sharps repeater and the other one—the one that had given away their location with its shiny brass receiver—was a .44-caliber Henry. A small patch of clouds had been obscuring the brightness of the sun when Josh first approached the men, but now they had dissipated and the sun was reflecting off of the Henry. Nodding towards the rifles, Josh said: "I suppose you just found those rifles over yonder there?"

"Them guns is ours," said Leroy's partner. "We brung'em from back home."

There was a naïve sincerity that was apparent to Josh about the way the mustached man had quickly claimed ownership of the guns. Might be the first truthful thing that's come outa these guys, he thought. "Nice rifles," said Josh innocently. "You don't see many of them Henrys around."

"No sir, you don't," said Leroy. "Cost me a pretty penny."

"I can imagine," replied Josh. "I'll bet them copper shells for it are pricey too. I can't recollect the last time I ever saw any for sale at a mercantile or such."

Leroy sensed something was amiss with the deputy being almost friendly-like, but he was like a wolf pup skittering around a hind quarter of a deer hanging in a tree that was being guarded by a well-disguised leg-hold trap. His instincts were telling him not to go there but he was already committed. And so Leroy said: "Yeah, whenever I find them copper shells I stock up on'em."

And with that the jaws of the trap snapped shut. "Leroy," said Josh, still friendly-like, "I got some things I wanna show ya'll." Leroy watched as Josh dug into his shirt pocket and pulled out a couple of objects. He held the first one up so Leroy and his partner could see. "This is my deputy marshal's badge," he said, pinning it on his shirt, "and this is a copper .44 Henry shell casing that I found where the man's claim that you're workin' was ambushed."

Leroy had a panicked look in his eyes; the quiet man began to back away from him.

"Stand easy there, pardner," said Josh to the quiet man.

"Ain't neither one ya'll going anywhere unless I say."

There was a look of overwhelming desperation and re-gret on the quiet man's face. "I told you this was a bad idea," he said to Leroy in a venomous tone.

"Shut your mouth, you dumb sonovabitch. That shell casing don't mean nuthin'," shouted Leroy angrily at the quiet man. "Besides, there's two of us and only one ah him."

"Don't ya'll do anything stupid," shouted Josh. But it was too late. The words had barely left his mouth when Leroy sent a bullet in his direction. Josh dived for cover behind some aspen trees. Leroy, on the other hand, jumped behind a ponderosa pine stump that had a wide base but narrowed some at about chest high where it had been whipsawed. The quiet man had run for the willows.

"It'll go better for ya'll if ya just give it up," shouted Josh to Leroy.

"I don't see that bein' a good way to go," replied Leroy. "Dancin' at the end of a rope ain't got no appeal to me at all."

"Ya never know," said Josh, "you might get a judge that'd just give ya jail time."

"No thanks, Deputy. I heard about that judge they got down there in Boise. He don't look favorably on my kind."

"Well ya'll's future don't look real good here 'cause I aim to kill ya if I can."

And with that Leroy popped up from behind the stump and fired two quick rounds at where he thought Josh was hiding. The bullets went slightly to the right of where Josh was. Josh had seen Leroy level his pistol over the top of the stump and fire quickly. If he tried that again he'd be a dead man. And then from behind the stump came Leroy's voice. "Edgar, gimme a hand here. We got'em in a cross-fire." There was no response. "Edgar," came the plea again. "Gimme a hand." Silence, save for the creek and a gentle breeze blowing through the trees. "You yellow sonovabitch, when I catch up to you you're gonna be sorry."

There was silence for several minutes. Josh knew that the quiet one, or Edgar, was undoubtedly working his way to the horses in the meadow. There was little he could do to prevent his escape unless he wanted to risk losing Leroy—and that wasn't an acceptable option as it was pretty clear to him that Leroy had murdered Seth.

"Hey, Deputy," shouted Leroy. "I gotta deal for ya."

Josh hesitated to answer as he didn't want to allow Leroy to get a better fix on his position, but then it came to him that he might be able to dig a little deeper and determine if the sheriff had any role in all of this. And so he said: "Oh yeah, what might that be?"

"We got a fair amount of gold stashed back at camp; it's yours if you just walk away."

"When my friend filed on this claim, he did it in both of our names." Josh paused and purposely laughed loudly. "And so now, after you've killed my friend ya'll want to give me something that shoulda been half mine anyway. You're gonna hafta do better'n that, Leroy."

"It's a good amount ah gold, Deputy." The desperation in Leroy's voice was clear. "You might want to give it some thought. It'd set ya up in life right nice."

"Naw, Leroy, I don't think I wanna even waste my time

ponderin' that," said Josh in a mocking tone. "The way I got it figured is Edgar probably grabbed that gold on his way outa camp, and if he didn't, it's mine anyway after I kill you. You gotta do better than that."

Leroy went silent again. He was frantic to come up with some way out of his predicament. He suspected the deputy wanted to know what the sheriff's involvement had been in all this, but he knew if he divulged that he would be a dead man; on the other hand it appeared he would be equally as dead if he didn't. After several minutes, Leroy shouted, "Hey, Deputy, you still there?"

What an idiot, thought Josh. "Yeah, I'm here," he shouted. "It ain't like I'm gonna take a walk."

"I just wanted to be sure that you can hear me good. I got information about the sheriff that I know you'd be interested in."

"OK," interrupted Josh, "what is it?"

"No, first you gotta promise me that I can ride outa here if I tell you what I know."

"No, your freedom isn't up to me," replied Josh. "You tell it to a judge and I'm sure he'll go easier on ya'll."

"I ain't gonna risk that. Either I tell you and you let me go or no deal."

Josh knew that his conscience would never allow him to let Seth's killer go free. He, as well as others, already suspected the sheriff was corrupt, so what Leroy had to say was probably no revelation except that if he were to testify to it in court, it could put a noose around the sheriff's neck. And so Josh shouted: "Tell it to the judge, Leroy, and take your chances. That's the best I can do."

There was no response from Leroy, and then like the proverbial mouse backed into the corner by the cat, he came from behind the stump running towards Josh, firing his pistol at where he assumed Josh to be in the aspen thicket. It was a desperate and foolhardy thing to do, thought Josh, as he took deliberate aim and shot Leroy dead before he had emptied his gun. Josh stood and walked slowly towards where Leroy lay. A tiny wisp of smoke rose from the barrel of his pistol. His legs twitched involuntarily a couple of times, as if the adrenalin that had driven them so furiously seconds earlier could not be stopped—even by death. Josh kicked Leroy's pistol to the side. As he stood over Leroy and looked at his lifeless body, he took no pride in having killed him. He hated this whole sordid mess that he had gotten into, but sometimes a man had no good choice. Just like Leroy's choice a moment earlier, you're damned if you do and damned if you don't, but judging by the wide-eyed look of surprise frozen on Leroy's face, he'd truly thought that he'd made the best choice.

Moonshine Creek was in a deep canyon that ran due west to its origin at the base of a tall mountain peak that intercepted the sun early on in the evening. Josh had just finished burying Leroy in a shallow grave not far from where he died as the last of the sun's outline sank behind the mountain peak. He'd made a simple cross out of two pieces of aspen and some rope he found at Leroy's camp. In the army somebody always said words over their fallen comrades, but Leroy was no comrade and Josh reckoned he was damned lucky he hadn't left him for the turkey vultures and coyotes; besides, it was better than Seth had gotten. Long shadows had fallen over Moonshine Creek. Edgar was long gone and so was any sign of the gold. He'd left behind a couple of their horses and Thunder, so either he was in a big hurry to leave or stupid. Josh gathered Thunder's reins and swung up into the saddle. He paused for a moment and looked back on what he was certain had been Seth's camp. He sighed; he couldn't help but wonder how things might have been different if only Seth were alive. The very top of the tall peak at the head of the canyon was now bathed in an orange glow; it would be a long ride back to Lester's.

Chapter Eleven

She never came right out and said it in so many words, but Lester could tell that Sarah was beside herself with worry about Josh; not that he wasn't concerned as well, but throughout the day she had probably asked him no less than a half dozen times how far it was to where Josh was going. And each time he had patiently described the route that Josh had to travel. And so, now as they sat down to supper he indulged her one more time. "About the first five miles is on the wagon route, that'll be the easy part."

And then she interrupted: "Well, how long do you think it'll take him to cover that much distance?"

"Well, that depends," said Lester, "on how hard Josh wants to push his horse. But the way I look at it, them two fellars ain't goin' nowhere, so if it was me I'd take it easy on my horse. So I reckon the wagon-road part over to where you head up Moonshine Creek ought not to take but a coupla hours. Now when he starts up that Moonshine trail," continued Lester in a more emphatic tone, "that'll be a whole 'nuther ball ah wax. It's rougher'n a bear's tongue, and it's a good ways back in the mountains to where this claim that Josh's wantin' to get to is at."

"So, that part might take quite a while," interjected Sarah.

"I 'spect so," said Lester in a reassuring voice. And then he added: "The way I got it figured it'll be right at twenty-two miles round trip for Josh. Hell, I wouldn't be surprised if he don't even come back tonight." And with that Lester helped himself to some boiled potatoes and then set them, still in the pot they'd been boiled in, near Sarah. "Better have some spuds," he said. "You worked hard today."

Sarah was hungry. She'd helped Lester operate his sluice box all day by carrying buckets of gravel and soil to be slowly poured into the sluice that was located in a shallow part of the creek where the current was still swift. Gold, being the heavier substance settled out and was caught in between the slats on the bottom of the sluice box. It was an ingenious process when it worked, but it did require gold and they'd found very little that day.

Sarah put some potatoes on her plate, and without encouragement from Lester she took a breast of fried blue grouse and passed the plate to him. For a moment there was near silence except for the occasional clinking of silverware and Rufus chomping his venison steak. And then, wanting to fill the awkward silence, Sarah said: "Kind of an off day for gold today, huh, Lester?"

Lester hesitated before answering. It was like he had been struck with a sadness that had momentarily incapacitated him, but then he said solemnly: "Been that way for quite a while now. I'm afraid this claim is kinda like me, it's 'bout played out." And then he forced a laugh in a vain attempt to hide his sadness.

Sarah had been so consumed by her own problems that she had become oblivious to the reality of Lester's situation. He was an old man and pretty much alone in the world except for Rufus and his mules. She knew that it would not be easy to put a convincing spin on countering these facts, and so she said: "You never know, Lester, you might get into some good paying dirt any day now. It might give you enough that you an' Rufus could go somewhere where it's warm all the time and just take life easy."

Lester smiled. He could see that Sarah was purposely trying to cheer him up. He felt embarrassed that he'd allowed himself to be the object of pity, if even for only a brief moment, but he had no family or friends and so when the temptation to toss that feeler out in the presence of Sarah had presented itself, he succumbed to it. And now he regretted it and so he said with false optimism: "Yeah, I suppose you could be right. A fellar never knows, why the next bucketful that you run through your sluice could have nuggets in it as big as your thumbnail."

"It could, Lester," added Sarah, continuing the ruse, "it could. From what I hear, the occurrence of gold can be fickle." And with that she paused, not wanting to tackle the inescapable reality confronting Lester of getting old and dying without dignity.

"Oh yeah, don't ya know it," replied Lester. "A fellar could get a big spring runoff and carry a bunch of new dirt and rock down the creek and you're in business again. Just like a new chunk ah country." He paused briefly, and then turning to the stove behind him he picked up the coffeepot. "Yes sir, just like new country," he chortled in a voice that trailed off. And then he extended the coffeepot towards Sarah: "Coffee?"

Sarah extended her cup. "Thanks," she said.

Lester appreciated what Sarah was trying to do for him. He'd been thinking about it all day, but he reckoned that he'd be proud to have a daughter like her even if she had been a whore. He'd only known a couple of women in his life that might have been marrying material, and one of those had took sick and died while the other had been killed by the Sioux over in Wyoming. After that he never seemed to cross paths with any decent women, and so now here he was an old man with no family. He could die tomorrow and no one other than Sarah and Josh would give a tinker's dam.

They'd pretty much finished eating and were sipping coffee at the table when Lester said: "Got something I wanna show you." And with that he reached into his shirt pocket and took out a folded piece of paper. He handed it to Sarah.

Sarah had a puzzled look on her face. "What's this?"

"Josh left it," said Lester simply.

Sarah unfolded the paper and began to read what was written there:

Dear Sarah and Lester,

If I do not return from my quest for justice I want the two of you to split my savings which Lester is holding.

Any of my other worldly goods that might be recovered are yours as well. Also, please write my father (William Morrow) in Galveston, Texas, and let him know what happened to me. Your friend, Josh Morrow

P.S. Sarah, you are a good woman. I wish you well in life.

Sarah began to tear up as she quietly read what amounted to Josh's will a second time. When she was finished she folded the paper and handed it back to Lester. She sighed heavily as a single tear rolled down her cheek. "I don't understand why he would do this for me, Lester."

"I do," said Lester in a kind voice. "You're a good person. Sure you hit a rough spot in Bear Creek, but that's in the past. Fair-minded folks'll judge you on who you are today and not for times gone by. Josh is one of those people; he's got a good heart."

"Oh, I know he does," said Sarah as she clasped her hands together and rested them on the table in front of her. "It's just that I've been nothing but trouble for him."

"Count your blessings, Sarah," admonished Lester. "Friends do for friends. Just look at what Josh is doin' right now for his friend Seth. If you ask me he's ah-dishin' up a big helpin' a bad times and he knows it, but he's ah-doin' it anyways. You should consider yourself lucky to have Josh Morrow as a friend."

"I do," said Sarah, "it's just that..." She paused, wondering if she should reveal any of her innermost feelings about Josh. She was embarrassed; here she was wanting to talk to Lester as if he were her father and she was seeking advice. The silence was deafening and then Lester said: "I ain't never had all that much experience when it comes to affairs of the heart, but what little I do know 'bout the subject tells me that if there's a spark there that by and by it'll become a fire."

Sarah blushed. She was so conflicted. Enough had been said. "It's getting dark," she said as she rose from her chair. "I best get these dishes done up."

For a brief moment Lester looked at Sarah; she avoided eye contact as she went about gathering the dirty dishes from the table. The single tear on her cheek had dissipated, but there appeared to be more in the making. Knowing that there was little he could do or say to hold them back, he rose from his chair and said: "Me an' Rufus is gonna go down and check on the mules. We'll be back in a bit."

"OK," said Sarah casually with her back to Lester, and then, when she could no longer hear the banter between Lester and Rufus, she sat down in the chair nearest the stove. For a moment she listened to the fire crackle and pop and the hum of the water in the big metal pot as it worked towards boiling. The solitude was overwhelming. She felt so alone; there was no point fighting it and so she allowed herself to cry. She wished that Josh would come back.

Chapter Twelve

Sheriff Hollis had arrived at the mouth of Chokecherry Creek at about dusk. He'd ridden a short ways up the trail and then made a cold camp in a shallow side canyon off the trail. If what Rudy had told him about Stevenson always riding out to Chokecherry Canyon to meet the marshal was correct, he hoped that he'd be lucky enough to intercept him somewhere down in the canyon.

After a cold breakfast of elk jerky and a couple of dry sourdough biscuits that his wife had made, Hollis saddled up and headed towards the main trail in the bottom of Chokecherry Canyon. He had no idea what the marshal looked like; his only clue was what Rudy had told him about the marshal riding a big gray horse. He'd been pondering this fact on the ride up to see Buster and his gang yesterday when it came to him that he'd seen a big gray horse tied to a hitching rail near the Gold Strike on several occasions during the past couple of weeks. In fact, if his memory served him correctly, there was a big gray hitched out front of the Gold Strike when the uppity Texan killed the Swede and walked out with the new whore. "That son-ovabitch's been comin' and goin' as he pleases right under my nose," grumbled Hollis aloud. "That's gonna end right soon." There was only one problem with that declaration: Hollis didn't know exactly where in Chokecherry Canyon the marshal would be, if at all. And so he started up the canyon on the trail that paralleled the creek looking for a man on a big gray horse, hopeful that he would be the marshal. Chokecherry Canyon was a fairly broad canyon in comparison to some of the other nearby drainages. There were, as its name implied, numerous chokecherry trees along the creek, but to either side of it there was good, rich soil that supported grassy meadows and scattered aspen and ponderosa pine. The canyon bottom had an abundance of forage for livestock and wildlife, making it a preferred route for pack trains going to Boise. Freight wagons, on the other hand, didn't go this way due to the lack of a road owing to the steep climb needed to get out of the head of the canyon.

It was shaping up to be another exceptionally hot day. Hollis had gone about two miles up the canyon when he came to a place where the creek meandered from one side of the canyon to the other. It was at this point that the trail crossed through the creek, which was no more than about fifteen feet wide and a foot deep. It made for a convenient place to water a horse due to the brush having been worn down over time from all of the traffic crossing the creek here. And so Hollis dismounted and allowed his horse to drink while he went just upstream and scooped water first onto his face and then up to his mouth to drink. And then came an unwanted voice. "Hot day, huh, Sheriff?"

Hollis looked up and across the creek; there stood the half-breed, Sean O'Fallon. He had an evil smile on his face and a swagger to his stance. Both of his thumbs were tucked just behind the center of his gun belt. He was staring intently at Hollis. "What are you doin' here, Sean? I thought you and Buster and the boys would be workin' your way over to Sheep Springs," said the sheriff cautiously from his kneeling position beside the creek.

O'Fallon laughed wickedly. "You think too much, Hollis," he said sarcastically.

Slowly and carefully, so as to not aggravate O'Fallon, the sheriff got to his feet. He felt more confident now that he was standing and facing the half-breed. It was almost like a replay of yesterday. "Does Buster know you're here?" asked Hollis.

"Oh, I reckon he's got a pretty good idea where I'm at. I didn't keep no secrets from 'im when I left."

"So you and Buster have parted company?" asked Hollis.

"Yeah, I'm done with those dumb bastards and you too," replied O'Fallon angrily. "We been buyin' you off way too long."

Hollis' demeanor became more tense. He watched O'Fallon's eyes carefully, as he knew that'd be the first indicator of when he was going for his gun. "Well, Sean, it's been over a year now and you boys have done alright and you've managed to stay outa jail and off the gallows. If you ask me, it sure as hell beats workin' for a livin'."

"Maybe that's the way you see it, Sheriff, but from where I stand we been havin' to slice the pie way too thin. And now with this marshal from Boise up here pokin' around, I figure you're about as useful as a bull with no balls."

"Sorry you feel that way, Sean," replied Hollis in a disingenuous tone of voice.

"Yeah, I'll just bet you are," snorted O'Fallon, and then he laughed. "But once I'm done with you, ain't none of this gonna matter 'cause you won't be feelin' a thing."

The half-breed's words didn't have the desired effect on the sheriff. His facial expression didn't change except for a slight smirk. It was like he welcomed O'Fallon's threat. "So you wanna try your hand again, do ya, Sean?"

O'Fallon stared back at Hollis. Both of his thumbs remained tucked behind the center of his gun belt. Yesterday at Hollis' cabin had been an embarrassment. He'd felt humiliated in front of his peers. And now it seemed like the courage that he had mustered to make the ride here and challenge the sheriff had been exhausted—now when he needed it most. But it was too late; his pride had committed him to a one-way trip. He couldn't back down now. His mind was spinning furiously. Second thoughts of what Buster and the boys were doing at that moment kept flashing through his mind like a bad lightning storm. His heart pounded in his ears so fast that he couldn't separate the beats. He was feeling sick to his stomach but he couldn't back down.

And then Hollis said calmly: "We gonna dance, Sean? I saved a spot on my card just for you."

The veins in O'Fallon's neck pulsated with anger, but it was apparent to him that his anger was no match for the sheriff's lack of fear; nonetheless, his pride was in charge and so he said in a hateful tone: "I'm gonna teach you some respect."

Hollis smiled derisively. He knew that he could beat O'Fallon in a gunfight and he intended to end it now rather than get bushwhacked later on, and so he said: "Sean, you're wastin' my time. Things didn't go good for ya yesterday so you went and got yourself all worked up about it and well, here ya are. So let's start the music."

Slowly, O'Fallon removed his thumbs from behind his gun belt and lowered his hands to his side. His hands were trembling, but this demon called pride was dictating his actions.

It was clear to Hollis that O'Fallon was scared, but he wasn't about to let him off of the hook and so he said: "Whenever you're ready, Sean, fill your hand. Course we know how that worked out." And then Hollis laughed.

Hollis' words had their intended effect. O'Fallon's eyes widened with intent and his pistol had just cleared its holster when the hammer of Hollis' .44 Remington dropped, sending a bullet into O'Fallon's wildly throbbing heart. The shock instantly registered on O'Fallon's face as his heart's rhythm stumbled to a halt. His pistol, still not cocked, eased from his hand and fell to the ground almost in unison to his knees slowly buckling. And then like the felling of a big tree when the last of the holding wood has been severed, O'Fallon tilted uncontrollably face first into the edge of Chokecherry Creek. Hollis stood on the opposite side of the creek, pistol in hand, staring down at O'Fallon's lifeless body. He was numb, almost indifferent to what he had just done. Within moments, a blood cloud had formed over the body that lingered in the shallow water at the creek's edge, and then little by little as it floated too near the current it was snatched away and sent on its way to obscurity.

The sheriff had come to savor the adrenalin rush that he got when killing a man, but this wasn't one of those times. He had a more important task at hand, albeit it involved killing a man, but it was a killing of importance; Sean O'Fallon was nothing more than an impediment to, ironically, the sheriff being able to disassociate himself from the O'Fallons, Kreggs, and Menaghers of the world. But this could only happen if he got rid of the marshal and got the gold that he was hopefully carrying.

Chapter Thirteen

There had been a full moon the night before and Edgar had taken advantage of it, riding throughout the night. His horse had thrown a shoe on the rocky Moonshine Creek trail and was now walking a little gimpy, making his progress a bit slower. He was a couple of miles from Bear Creek when his thoughts concerning the events at his and Leroy's camp had finally gelled into some sort of plan—or at least he hoped so. The first part of his plan called for him keeping all of the gold that he and Leroy had dug out of their claim since the last time the sheriff had been by demanding protection money. It had galled both he and Leroy that they had to make the sheriff a full partner, giving him a third of everything that they found; if not they were going to jail for murder. The inequity of this arrangement grated on them constantly, and there was seldom an hour of the waking day that they didn't bemoan the fact that they had to give the sheriff a cut for doing what they perceived as absolutely nothing to earn it. But now he had all of the gold that he and Leroy had recovered during the last ten days and he aimed to keep it. He'd worked too hard for it to do otherwise. They'd gotten into some rich dirt, even finding some decent-sized nuggets in the bottom of their sluice box instead of just flecks of gold. Edgar figured it was close to $10,000.00 worth; that was enough to lie for, maybe even kill for. And so it was that Edgar found himself riding by the light of the moon up a side canyon that intersected the Bear Creek road looking for a place to stash his gold. It was a dry canyon with mostly sagebrush and some scattered ponderosa pines. In his haste to abandon Leroy, he had grabbed only the saddlebags containing the gold and had not thought about bringing a shovel, but then, at that point, he just wanted to put distance between himself and the deputy marshal that had Leroy pinned down. He was riding slowly, looking for an opportune place to hide the saddlebags, when there it was. A huge ponderosa pine had been struck by lightning at some point in the past. The fire had hollowed out a good deal of the tree—so much so that it caused it to fall over during a big wind event. Edgar, who was riding bareback, pretty much slid down the side of his horse. He dropped the reins and walked over to the fallen tree; lying on its side, near the base it hit him at about waist high. A good deal of snowberry and some bitterbrush had grown up around the fallen giant. The entrance to the charcoal cavity was partially obscured. Edgar waded through the brush and knelt before the entrance to the cavity. In the poor light it was difficult to tell exactly how far back the cavity extended, but it was beyond the reach of his arm. "This'll have to do," he said aloud. "Won't be long term anyway," he further reasoned with himself. "Soon as things settle down I'll come back for this." And so

Edgar shoved the saddlebags up into the hollow tree close to five feet, he reckoned.

The sun was just peeking over the horizon as Edgar rode into Bear Creek. Lanterns were visible through some windows and others not, with the dark windows probably winning out. That was good, thought Edgar. Me ridin' in here bareback without no gear of any kind is bound to look peculiar to some folks. Don't need people runnin' their jaws about why I come to town without Leroy and such. They'll be doin' that soon enough.

Edgar's first stop was at the livery stable and blacksmith. A heavyset man with thinning brown hair that was graying around the temples stepped out to meet Edgar. "Mornin'," said the blacksmith as he eyed Edgar's appearance.

"Mornin'," replied Edgar in a businesslike tone as he slid down from his horse. "My horse threw its right front shoe. Do you suppose you can put a new one on for me this morning?"

The smithy, who had taken a Sioux arrow in his left hip some years back, walked with a limp. As he stepped closer to Edgar, he paused and looked at him in a bemused manner. "What the hell happened to you?"

Without thinking Edgar said: "Why?"

The smithy laughed. "Look at yourself. You look like you been sleepin' with the hogs."

It was only then that Edgar took in the full measure of himself. He had charcoal smudges and scuff marks the full length of his body. His appearance took him by surprise. His mind was frantic to process a suitable lie. And then it came to him so quickly that the words were there like he had no control over them. "I fell in the campfire."

"How come didn't ya get burnt?" replied the smithy disbelievingly.

"The fire was out. It was just ashes."

"Wuhl, were ya drunk? Ya look like ya musta wallered in it like an' ole sow hog."

Edgar was becoming irritated with the smithy's probing. He wasn't an experienced liar, having usually left that to Leroy in the past, but he was quickly learning that one lie usually led to another. "I was tryin' to get away from this fellar that bushwhacked me and Leroy. I was runnin' for my horse and I tripped on the fire ring at our camp. I was lucky to get away with my life."

The smithy's demeanor became more serious. "Well, what happened to your partner?"

"Dead, I reckon," replied Edgar with little emotion. "I aim to find the sheriff an' see if we can't track this fellar down that done the killin'."

The smithy shook his head. "Well, good luck with that." He paused. "Don't know about the sheriff, but you can probably find his deputies over at the Blue Bird Café havin' breakfast."

"Thanks," said Edgar, and with that he turned and headed towards the Blue Bird.

Bear Creek was not a big town and it took Edgar only a few minutes to walk to the café. As he entered the restaurant Edgar observed that there were patrons at three different tables; two of the occupied tables were along the wall on the street side of the room, and the other was a table along the opposite wall and towards the back. There was also a door there by which people could exit the restaurant if they'd tied their horse out back, or it was also the short-est route to the privy. It was at the table near the back door that Edgar saw the deputies. One of them, Edgar had never seen before. He appeared to be a little over six feet tall with a build that suggested he seldom missed a meal. His features were soft with a wispy blond moustache. He wore a Union cavalry slouch hat and carried a Walker Colt .44—not ex-actly a gunman's rig. His partner, on the other hand, was a familiar face. He was a wiry-looking guy with short black hair and a robust moustache and goatee. He wore a peaked Stetson hat and carried a Starr Army .44 in a cross-draw position on his left hip. It was obvious by his appearance that he fancied himself a pistoleer, and his demeanor did nothing to counter that image. He had accompanied Hollis to Edgar and Leroy's claim to collect payment not too long ago. Hollis hadn't introduced the man, and he didn't speak the entire time that he and Hollis were at Edgar and Leroy's camp. Hollis had made it pretty clear that his call wasn't social and to think otherwise would have been a mistake. From Edgar and Leroy's perspective, it was as if he thought he was better than they were and he was doing them a favor by even associating with them. The hypocrisy of it all was something that Edgar and Leroy had analyzed with the aid of some cheap whiskey around their campfire that night af-ter Hollis and his stone-faced deputy had left. Edgar could hear Leroy now. "There'll come a day when that high and mighty sonovabitch will get his comeuppance, and I'll be the one to give it to him," he'd boasted when he was about four sheets to the wind. As Edgar neared the deputy's table, the smaller one turned his head and made eye contact with him. It was obvious that the deputy recognized him but he said nothing.

"Mind if I sit down?" asked Edgar.

The deputy frowned but nodded towards the empty chair in front of Edgar. "Have a seat."

Edgar pulled the chair out from the table and sat down. The portly deputy, not knowing who Edgar was, looked on, somewhat puzzled at the cold reception his partner was giving him.

"What are you doing here?" asked the smaller deputy in a low and agitated voice that had a ring of incredulity to it.

Edgar didn't like the deputy and he couldn't help being somewhat obnoxious. "So you do remember who I am?"

"Course I do. You and your partner are workin' that claim out on Moonshine Creek." The deputy paused, and then added in a voice loud enough so that if anyone across the room cared they could hear: "Too bad about the original owner of that claim gettin' himself bushwhacked. We been workin' that case but so far ain't nothin' turned up. But you never know, just takes that one missin' piece of the puzzle and somebody will be meetin' their maker."

Edgar watched the deputy's expression as he spoke. He was arrogant and smug; it was like he was immune from any kind of retribution from the citizens of Bear Creek or any higher authority, but Edgar, on the other hand, could be going to "meet his maker" should that one critical piece of information turn up. Edgar realized there was little he could do, not if he wanted the deputy U.S. marshal off his back. He was no match for this guy; it would take the sheriff and his deputies to get rid of him. It was the only way that he would be able to spend any of the gold that he had hidden outside of town or, for that matter, work the claim anymore. And so, for the time being he was going to have to tolerate the deputy's veiled threats.

The arrogant deputy looked Edgar hard in the eyes and repeated his earlier question in a whispered voice: "What the hell you doin' here? Hollis won't be happy."

"Leroy's dead," replied Edgar in a low voice.

A look of surprise, then concern, came over the smaller deputy's face. "So how'd he get that way?" he asked irreverently.

Edgar looked over his shoulder to see if anyone was listening before speaking. The bigger deputy, the portly one, seemed oblivious to Edgar's announcement but nonetheless leaned forward to hear better, almost as if he were listening to a dirty joke being told in a hushed voice. "We had a deputy U.S. marshal visit us yesterday afternoon. He accused Leroy of being the one that killed the guy whose claim we're workin'. Said this guy was his friend."

At first the smaller deputy seemed perplexed, even confused as Hollis had confided in him that the marshal appeared to be camped somewhere in Chokecherry Canyon and that he was going out there to take care of him. But now Edgar was saying that this lawman was well south of there on Moonshine Creek. Something wasn't adding up. "What'd this guy look like?" asked the deputy.

Edgar got a pondering look in his eyes. "He was a young guy, kinda big. I'd say over six foot. He had dark hair and was clean shaven except for a moustache." Edgar paused, and then he exclaimed: "He had a southern accent. Maybe like he was from Texas or some such place."

Both deputies' faces instantly lit up. Their expressions were so telling that Edgar immediately asked rhetorically: "You guys know this guy?"

"Yeah," replied the smaller deputy. "He's the one that killed the big Swede over at the Gold Strike here a few days back. And then he skedaddled outa town with that young whore that was workin' there."

"Well, I don't know nuthin 'bout any whore," said Edgar. "This fellar was by himself."

"So how is it that Leroy gets killed and you're able to get clean away?" asked the smaller deputy in a suspicious tone.

"Well, we was workin' our sluice box and not expectin' any trouble, ya know, when the next thing we know this lawman is standin' there with his gun pointed at us. He says we was workin' his friend's claim and he wants all of our gold. Said if we didn't give it to him he'd kill one of us and then see if the other one would be more talkative. We thought he was bluffin', bein' a lawman and all, but he wasn't. He shot poor ole Leroy right twixt the eyes. He went down in a heap and I mean just right now. He didn't so much as twitch. But I'll tell you what, watching your best friend get it like that can change your attitude right quick. So fellars, long story short is I had to give him all of our gold or end up like Leroy."

"And he just let you go?" asked the smaller deputy disbelievingly.

"Not exactly," replied Edgar. "We was standin' right next to the crik. The gold was in saddlebags and when I went to hand it to him I just swung the bags hard and hit his gun hand. Knocked his pistol into the water. I took off runnin' and was goin' faster'n greased lightning until I tripped over our fire ring at camp. But I thrashed around for 'bout as long as it takes a lizard to eat ah ant and I was off again. Lucky for me my horse was grazing right near camp. I grabbed my bridle but didn't dare take time to put it on. I just hopped on bareback and took off. Didn't bridle my horse until I got on down the trail a ways."

"You're a lucky man," said the smaller deputy. "That guy took care of the Swede pretty handy-like."

"Well, what you fellars aim to do about him?" asked Edgar. "Me and Leroy gave the sheriff some hard-earned gold to—"

"Shut up, you fool," interrupted the smaller deputy. Nodding his head towards the back door, he said: "Let's go outside."

And with that the three men pushed their chairs back and got up; as they did, Mabel, the owner and only wait-ress, approached with coffeepot in hand. She'd overheard enough of their hushed conversation to know that they were talking about the young Texan that had been there a few days earlier. She liked him in spite of the apparent general consensus floating around town that he'd killed the big Swede in an argument over a whore. Neither the sheriff nor his deputies had attempted to clarify the rumors being circulated by the Swede's friends. Their version had the young Texan goading the Swede into a fight by taking up with his girl. And now, here was a miner claiming that the Texan had killed his partner in cold blood. The Texan's reputation in Bear Creek would be going downhill in a hurry when word of this got around. "You boys ain't had but barely one cup a coffee this morning," said Mabel in a jovial tone. "You gonna be able to make it through the day on that?"

The portly deputy smiled weakly at Mabel. "Guess it'll have to do," he said. "We got business to tend to."

Mabel looked on as the deputies dug in their pockets for money to pay for their breakfast. She was tempted to banter with the miner who had charcoal on his face, hands, and much of his clothing, but as her eyes briefly encountered those of the smaller deputy it was clear that this would not be welcome. And so she said nothing as she collected the coins placed on the table by the deputies and watched them file out the back door in silence.

The deputies and Edgar walked a short distance away from the restaurant to an area near a big ponderosa pine tree and almost within spitting distance of the privy whose door was open. The smaller deputy glared at Edgar. "Don't ever make mention of our agreement in public again," he said sternly. "It could go real bad for you if you do."

"Sorry," said Edgar meekly. "Guess I wasn't thinking." He paused. "It's just that I gotta get this guy off ah-me."

"Hollis is gone takin' care of some business right now," said the smaller deputy. "Not sure when he'll be back, but I reckon in the next day or so. When he does get back we'll see what he wants to do. In the meantime, you best lay low."

Edgar was taken aback a bit by the deputy's admonition. "Me, lay low?" he blurted. "This Texan is the one that killed Leroy and took our gold."

A sinister smile came over the smaller deputy's face. "Yeah, well he's the one with the deputy marshal's badge. And if we want to get right down to it—not to be splittin' hairs, mind ya—but Leroy did bushwhack the Texan's partner." The deputy paused and then said emphatically: "So, not knowing what cards this guy might be holding, I think it'd be best if you weren't paradin' around Bear Creek until the sheriff gets back and we decide what we're gonna do."

Edgar had an uneasy feeling about doing this. It was like the sheriff and his deputies wanted to wait and see how much heat the Texan could bring on them before deciding if they were going to help him or not. He was stuck—he had no choice but to do things their way; nonetheless he said: "A couple days back I'm pretty sure me an' Leroy saw this fellar over at old Lester Scoville's claim. It was 'bout dusk, but there was a horse there that looked like the one he was ridin' yesterday."

"Was the whore with'im?" asked the smaller deputy.

It wasn't anything that just jumped out at him, but Edgar sensed that the deputy had more than a casual interest in the whore. "Didn't see her," he said, "but we was pretty far up on the ridge and it was gettin' close to dark."

The deputy considered this for a moment and then adjusted his hat in a thoughtful manner. "That's good to know. I'll keep it in mind."

"I'll be in touch," said Edgar.

"See that you do," said the deputy. And with that the two deputies walked back inside to have another cup of coffee while Edgar was expected to make himself scarce.

Chapter Fourteen

It was about midmorning when Josh started down the ridge above Lester's cabin. It was sunny and the wind was dead calm. Here and there, yellow butterflies glided from plant to plant in search of nectar. The hobbled mules were downstream from the cabin a hundred or so yards, grazing on a small patch of bluegrass that they had somehow overlooked earlier in the summer. There was no one at the cabin, not even Rufus, but then that stood to reason as Lester never went anywhere without Rufus. Josh reined Thunder in near the cabin and got down. He was tired. The preceding twenty-four hours had been taxing. He didn't like having to kill a man. It never set well with him, and the events would continually play over and over in his mind. It was like a tug-of-war with a demon that one minute talked rationally saying that he had no choice and that he was justified in killing the men that he had, but then it turned on him saying that he took satisfaction in killing. It was the second demon that Josh feared the most. He'd known men in the army that had lost to it, or at least he suspected they had, as they spent a good deal of their pay on whiskey.

There could be but one other logical place for Lester and Sarah to be, and that was the sluice box down in the creek. Josh had taken only a few steps in that direction when he was met by Rufus, who was beside himself with excitement to see Josh. "Oh, what a good dog you are, Rufus," said Josh in a voice that one might use to praise a child. Rufus responded by jumping and rearing, placing his paws on Josh's chest.

"Well, lookie what the cat drug in." Josh looked up to see Lester approaching with Sarah close behind. "We's beginnin' to wunder 'bout ya," added Lester.

Trying his best to be nonchalant Josh replied: "I ran outa daylight 'fore I could get off that Moonshine Creek trail, so I decided to throw my bedroll out rather than push Thunder through that rock pile in the moonlight."

"That was probably a good call," said Lester. "Bet you're hungry."

"I am," replied Josh.

And then still not wanting to be the one to breech that awkward avoidance of what was on all their minds, Sarah interjected: "I could make you some hotcakes and eggs."

The fate of Seth's killer hung in the air before them like the stench of burning hair and hide of a calf being branded. It couldn't be ignored, and so Josh said matter-of-factly: "I settled the score with Seth's killer." There, he'd put it out in the open. It was there for Lester or Sarah to do with as they pleased. For a long moment there was no response, and then Lester said: "Ya did what ya had to do, Josh."

"I suppose," replied Josh. "This guy didn't give me much choice. He wasn't having any part of being arrested."

"Well, fellars like that gotta know," said Lester, "that if they take somebody's life for no good reason then they might just have to give up theirs. It's like the good book says: 'an eye for an eye and tooth for a tooth.'"

"I reckon so," said Josh somewhat forlornly. "But I think I just opened up a can of worms."

Lester turned his head to the side and spit a stream of tobacco juice and then wiped at his moustache with the back of his hand. "How's that?" he asked.

"There was two of these guys," replied Josh. "One of 'em got away. I really didn't give him much chase 'cause I figured I'd got Seth's killer and I figured I'd get the marshal involved in trying to recover the gold these two took from Seth's claim."

Lester shook his head and whistled softly. "That's a pretty tall order."

"I reckon it is," said Josh, "but it don't seem right to me that these two hombres should profit from stealing Seth's claim."

Sarah had hoped that by Josh confronting the men on Seth's claim that all of this violence would be over, and perhaps unrealistically that she and Josh could move on to a new life. It was apparent to her now that all of this was at best on hold, and so she said: "So what do you aim to do?" She paused and then knowingly she added: "Seems to me you've done about all that should be expected of a friend."

Josh gave Sarah a hard look. "I guess it all boils down to what you figure your life is worth? Or maybe what you figure a friend would do for you if the tables were turned."

Sarah regretted immediately saying what she had. She felt selfish, and truth be told, maybe she was. She had a chance, if things came together between her and Josh, to escape her misery as a prostitute, and now because of Josh's loyalty to his dead friend all of that might be lost. But she realized that it would probably be futile to question Josh on this issue, and it might even work against her if they were ever to have any kind of relationship beyond just being friends. And so she said: "I'm sorry, Josh. I didn't mean any disrespect to Seth or the friendship that you two had." She paused and then admitted reluctantly: "I've never had a friendship that strong, so I guess it's difficult for me to understand what you're doing."

Josh could see in Sarah's eyes the concern that she had for him. In some respects it was flattering, but it only fueled the conflict within him. While it was true he felt a sense of obligation to Seth, he nonetheless wished at times that he could just ride out of the Bear Creek country and not look back. It had treated him harshly; his conscience was now burdened with having killed two more men in his life. Their lifeless faces showed up far too often in his mind's image. It was during these moments that he had to tell himself that some men brought on their own early deaths. It helped a little, but it by no means took away the images. "There is a clear line, or at least I've always thought so, between right and wrong," said Josh to Sarah. "I've always tried to be on the right side of that line. Sometimes that ain't easy to do 'cause there can be a hefty price that comes with doin' the right thing. It would sure enough be simple to walk away from all this but knowin' how I am, it'd eat at me." Josh paused and laughed softly in a false gesture: "I guess I'm damned if I do and damned if I don't."

In their brief time together, Sarah had come to know that Josh was a man of principles. She respected him for it even though adhering to those principles might jeopardize everything she had hoped for. "So what's next?" she asked in a supportive tone.

Josh looked at Sarah and smiled purposefully, as if to convey friendliness. "Well, after I have me some of them hotcakes that ya'll said you'd make, I'll be headin' out for Boise."

"Boise," exclaimed Lester before Sarah could respond.

But then Sarah quickly added: "Why Boise?"

"That's where the marshal is headed to," replied Josh. "I aim to meet up with him and let 'im know where things stand here. This lawman stuff is totally new to me. I don't want to overstep my bounds, especially if I have to confront the sheriff. It'd be nice if the marshal was in attendance at that shindig."

Aside from her concern for Josh's safety, Sarah immediately wondered what was to become of her while he was in Boise. It didn't sound like she was invited to go along, which meant she was at the mercy of Lester's hospitality. She suspected that this wouldn't be a problem, but nonetheless, it bothered her that her well-being always seemed to be tied to the generosity of a man. At least with Lester she could earn her keep by carrying buckets of gravel to run through the sluice box. It was the first thing she had done in quite some time that allowed her to feel good about herself.

"How long ya reckon you'll be gone?" asked Lester.

"Well sir, I ain't sure," said Josh. "I'm hopin' not more an' four or five days but ya never know."

"Take what time ya need," said Lester. "We'll have the coffee on when ya get back."

Although Lester had just implied it, Josh didn't want to be so presumptive as to assume that Sarah could just stay on there, and so he said: "Lester, ya'll have treated me and Sarah like kinfolks and, well sir, I really hate askin' but—"

Lester interrupted Josh. "Sarah's more an' welcome," he said in a sincere tone. "She's been a big help in sluicin'. In fact, point of the matter is, I'd probably take offense if she wasn't stayin'."

"Much obliged," said Josh.

"Yes, thank you, Lester," added Sarah. "I appreciate it." And then it occurred to her that once again Josh had assumed responsibility for her well-being; the only problem with that was he seemed to be motivated by some sense of obligation to be a Good Samaritan and not much else.

In due time, Sarah had Josh's breakfast ready. She was a good cook, something that she hoped he took note of. She'd made hotcakes, scrambled eggs, and even fried up some bacon. And although Josh ate a lot, the inevitable time for his departure came much too soon for Sarah.

"I reckon I better be headin' out," announced Josh, and with that he pushed his chair back from the table. "That was some good vittles, Sarah."

Sarah was sitting at the table across from Josh. She knew it would do no good to try and talk him into delaying his departure, and so she said in a tone bordering on indifference: "Thank you."

Lester, who had been leaning against the wall near the open door so he could spit tobacco juice periodically, took the last sip of his coffee and approached Josh. Setting his coffee cup on the table with his left hand, he extended his right to Josh. "Watch your back," he said while firmly shaking Josh's hand.

"Thanks for everything, Lester," replied Josh.

Lester turned to leave; glancing briefly at Sarah he said: "I'll be down to the crik. Come on down when you're ready." And with that he and Rufus left.

Sarah took a cloth sack from a shelf above the stove and extended it towards Josh. "I fixed you some food for the trail."

Josh reached for the sack, causing their hands to briefly touch. It was casual, it was incidental, but it was tingly for both of them. "Please be careful," said Sarah.

Josh cared about Sarah but he wasn't sure in what way. At times he had himself convinced that he could ignore her past, but then it would come full circle and he wasn't so sure. Case in point would be working with the marshal and knowing, or at least pretty certain, that he'd been with Sarah for money. Josh couldn't bring himself to say words that he wasn't committed to, but perhaps, unwittingly, his actions spoke louder as he reached out and rested his hand on Sarah's shoulder. "Don't worry about me," he said.

Josh's touch had made her shiver. Sarah had wished that he would have wrapped his arms around her, but it wasn't to be. And so once again she stood and watched as he left her, not knowing if he would return or if he did, would it really matter in the long run?

Chapter Fifteen

It took time, valuable time for Hollis to dispose of the half-breed O'Fallon's body. From the stream crossing where he had killed him, he took O'Fallon, draped over the saddle on his own horse about a quarter mile down Chokecherry Creek. There, out of view of the main trail, he simply dumped O'Fallon's body for the dining pleasure of the turkey vultures, ravens, and coyotes. It'd only be a matter of days and O'Fallon would be unrecognizable—not that it mattered all that much as Hollis figured there was probably little love lost over O'Fallon's departure from the gang. Nonetheless, there was no point in possibly getting them riled up, he reasoned, by making a spectacle of the dead half-breed by leaving his body smack-dab in the middle of a well-used crossing on the Chokecherry Creek trail. After unsaddling O'Fallon's horse and setting it free, Hollis collected the dead man's weapons and tack and threw them in a beaver pond, where they sank in about four feet of water. "Well, the hell with it," said Hollis aloud as he watched O'Fallon's saddle sink out of sight. "That'll have to do. Besides, I'm the sheriff."

Hollis had little information to go on concerning the

marshal's plans. All he knew was what Rudy had said about the marshal camping in Chokecherry Canyon and Stevenson riding out to meet him. He'd assumed, since Stevenson had ridden out and back from town in what sounded like a few hours, that the marshal must have been camped somewhere near the mouth of the canyon. But, then he pondered that a smart man would move his campsite, maybe somewhere different every night. It's kinda like huntin' deer, thought Hollis; being a creature of habit can get you killed. He was assuming also that the marshal would be on the move today because today was when Stevenson was to leave Bear Creek for Boise. However, the bottom line was that he was doing a whole lot of assuming and supposing about what he thought the marshal was going to do, and now the sun had dropped below the western horizon and he hadn't seen hide nor hair of the guy. He'd pretty much run the course of Chokecherry Canyon, as he was now at the far end of it where the switchbacks began that would take you up out of the canyon and ultimately over onto the main wagon road to Boise. Hollis couldn't figure how he could have missed the marshal unless the marshal had left yesterday, got a late start today, or he'd rode on by while he was tending to the half-breed's body. "Be just my damned luck," mumbled Hollis aloud as he sat atop his horse and looked back down the trail coming up the canyon. As the shadows in the canyon grew longer and Hollis had still seen nothing, he reconciled himself to the reality that he'd probably missed the marshal and so he decided he was probably better off to make camp for the night. Hollis allowed his horse to have its head as it meandered to a place about seventy-five yards off the trail amongst some scattered trees, but where he still had a good view down the canyon. There was a good amount of grass for his horse and the place where he would lay out his bedroll afforded him some cover, but at the same time, he had relatively unobstructed views from at least three different approaches. Confident that this was a safe place for the night, Hollis unsaddled his horse and tethered it with a 50-foot rope tied to a young ponderosa pine. He then carried his saddle and saddle blanket into a more secluded area between several big trees and laid the saddle on the ground with the blanket folded and lying across it. He was in the process of untying his bedroll when he saw a wisp of light blue smoke drifting up from a stand of Douglas fir trees about a half mile down the canyon. As far as he knew, there'd been no lightning in a good while, so the smoke could mean only one thing and that was somebody was just setting up camp. His mind instantly went to the possibility that this could be the marshal. As thick as the trees are and as much as the trail snakes around through'em, thought Hollis, it could easy enough be him. He sighed heavily as he stood and watched the smoke. It'd been a long day; he was tired and hungry. Having to deal with O'Fallon hadn't helped matters. It felt good to be out of the saddle, and now it appeared that opportunity might be knocking. He was torn. Round trip, it'd be a decent hike for nothing if it wasn't the marshal. Be dark by the time he got down there, but if it was the marshal and he was carrying gold, it could be his ticket out of Bear Creek. There'd be no more O'Fallons or Kreggs or Menaghers or any of the other riffraff that he'd been dealing with in his life. He'd be a respectable gentleman someplace far from here. Hollis sighed again deeply. "Well, shit," he mumbled aloud. "Might as well get started." And so, in an effort to maintain the element of surprise, off he went on foot towards what he hoped was the marshal's camp.

The bottom of the canyon was fairly heavily wooded with mature pine, fir, and right along the creek, aspen trees. They were so tall and thick that Hollis could see clearly in only one direction, and that was straight up. He'd lost track of the smoke; he could neither see nor smell it. The light was fading fast amongst the big trees and it was to be a new moon tonight. The trail, in this part of Chokecherry Canyon, was not well defined at times due to the occasional blow-down tree that blocked the trail and caused a diversion around it. However, finding a way around an eighty- or hundred-foot downed tree often led to more entanglement and the need to extend the diversion in order to get back to the established trail. It was, in large part, these diversions that gave the trail its snakelike character that so frustrated Hollis. There were also numerous dry pine cones on the trail which Hollis took painstaking care to avoid—looking, analyzing each step that he took. It made the going slow but when stepped on, the cones crunched loudly. When that happened, a guy might as well just holler out, "Here I am." It was nearly dark now and Hollis still hadn't found the mystery camp. He reckoned that he'd come far enough but there was no sign of it. He couldn't afford to be stumbling around in the dark in this timber and get surprised by who-ever was camped here. His concern was growing rapidly and then his senses caught it: just a hint, but it was the smell of smoke. Hollis stood dead still, straining his senses to lo-cate the source of the smoke. And then he heard it—the soft, contented nicker of a horse. It was just one time, but he was pretty certain that it had come from down close to the creek. It was maybe a hundred yards off the trail. Hollis drew his pistol and cocked it. He wasn't taking any chances with this guy getting the drop on him. And so he stepped off the trail, pistol in hand, and started cautiously towards where he'd heard the horse; pine cones and twigs littered the ground. He'd taken about a half-dozen steps when he encountered a stronger smell of smoke. He paused and looked intently into the darkness and thick trees, unable to see a fire or anything that resembled a camp. It was deathly quiet except for an owl that had just started calling off to his left. He stood frozen in place for perhaps thirty seconds before continuing on, one carefully placed step at a time. The anticipation, and maybe a little fear too, had created a good amount of adrenalin within him. There was tension in the air such that he felt like he could just reach out and grab a handful of it. *Where is this sonovabitch,* said Hollis to himself. He sighed deeply. There were times when he ques-tioned how or why he had ended up where he was in life and this was one of those times. *Ought to be home in bed with the wife,* he said to himself and then his mind drifted to a kaleidoscope of the last time that he'd been with her in that way. But then in the next instant, the reality of what could happen to him if the marshal continued snooping around exploded onto his mind's stage in the form of him standing on the gallows. He'd seen men hang and it wasn't pretty. No, he'd go down fighting before that'd ever happen. Just the thought of being the one with a hood over your head hanging from the end of a rope with your neck clearly snapped sent shivers through him. He moved on and then within a couple of minutes he saw it: a faint flicker of open flame. He dropped to one knee. His heart rate quickened as he visually scanned what little he could see of the area next to the fire. He couldn't tell much other than there appeared to be a small clearing where the fire was located, but it was difficult to get an image of how the camp was laid out due to the tree cover. He had to get closer. Slowly, he got to his feet, not taking his eyes off of the campfire. He'd taken only a few steps when he saw movement near the fire. Hollis stopped dead in his tracks. He felt a surge of adrenalin that was almost painful. He'd heard this marshal fancied himself as a gunman. But then it came to him that he might be getting worked up for nothing. Maybe this wasn't the marshal; there was only one way to find out. From where he was standing, it was evident to Hollis that if he moved to his right about fifteen feet that he would have a better view of the fire and the man near it. And so with all of the stealth-like ability that he possessed he moved right, to the spot where his view was less obstructed; his efforts were rewarded. A man was kneeling beside the fire, tending, it appeared, to something that was cooking. His back faced outwards into the night. Hollis knew that he would have to confront the man to determine who he was, and so he began to slowly creep forward, one carefully placed step at a time. And then, when he was about thirty or forty feet away, it happened—he stepped on a pine cone. He realized it the instant that it happened, but there was no way that he could've prevented his weight from coming down short of just falling over sideways, which definitely wouldn't have been a good thing to do. Hollis had his pistol trained on the mystery man's back, expecting him to wheel with gun drawn, but that was not the case.

"Supper's 'bout ready," said the mystery man without moving. "C'mon in if you've a mind to."

Hollis was taken aback by the man's actions. He knew somebody had the drop on him, but he didn't panic and most likely get himself shot. The guy's not stupid, thought Hollis. He's gonna wait until the odds are in his favor. And so Hollis stepped into the shadowy light of the campfire with his pistol in hand, hammer back. The mystery man, still on his knees by the fire, turned to face him. "Evenin', name's Hank Burkin," he said far more calmly than one would expect from a man with a pistol pointed at him.

Hollis gave the stranger a quick size-up. He wasn't wearing a badge, but then Hollis didn't figure that the marshal would be. Still pointing his gun at the man, Hollis said: "My name's Tom Hollis. I'm the sheriff over at Bear Creek. Been lookin' for a fellar that I heard was in these parts."

The mystery man turned his head to the side and spit some tobacco juice. "And you think I'm that guy," he said with just a hint of irritation in his voice.

Hollis had never seen the marshal before, but some of the things that he'd been told about him fit this guy. For one thing, he wore his pistol in a cross-draw position. It was a double-action Starr .44 caliber, the kind of gun that a *pistolero* type might fancy. "Well, now that I see you up close I don't reckon you're that particular man. He was a half-breed with just a plum nasty disposition."

"That bein' the case then," said the mystery man, "I'd appreciate it if you'd point that pistol somewhere's else."

"Well, Mr. Burkin," said Hollis with some sarcasm, "I would, except this breed fella had some associates that were a little on the unsavory side. I ain't so sure that you're not one of 'em." Hollis paused to let this settle with the mystery man, and then in an effort to smoke out the man's true identity, he added: "In fact, I'm kinda leanin' towards thinkin' that you might just be this Buster Kregg fellar. From what I hear you look a lot like him."

Initially, there was mild shock that came to the mystery man's face, which quickly turned to anger. "No offense, Sheriff, but you're about as full of shit as a grain-fed goose."

Hollis continued his agitation of the mystery man. "Well, if you ain't Buster Kregg," he said, "you got some means of provin' otherwise."

The anger within the mystery man was growing, but he hadn't reached the point of folding his hand and revealing his true identity—not to the sheriff of Bear Creek, anyway. "I'm telling ya, Sheriff, I ain't this Kregg fella that you're lookin' for. Why hell, it don't even sound like to me that you know what this guy looks like and here ya are pokin' your gun in my face and callin' me a liar. If you ask me, it's a piss-poor way for a lawman to conduct himself."

Hollis took considerable offense at the mystery man's criticism of him, and so he said in a voice that made no attempt to disguise his anger: "You know, Mr. whoever-the-hell-you-are, you're about one dumb sonovabitch. In case you had't noticed I'm the one holding the gun here, so I'm thinkin' you might want to show me a little more respect."

The look of anger in the mystery man's eyes was immediately replaced with regret. He'd pushed the sheriff too far, but it seemed to him that the sheriff strongly suspected who he was already and was just playing a sick little game of cat-and-mouse with him. He wasn't about to apologize to the sheriff, but he said in a more subdued tone: "I didn't mean to rile ya but like I told ya my name's Hank Burkin and I'm headin' to Boise."

Hollis eyed the man for a moment. He was beginning to doubt himself. Maybe this wasn't the marshal after all. You'd think, he said to himself, that if he was a marshal he'd just own up to it 'cause he'd figure that lawman to lawman this conversation would be over. He didn't want to kill the guy unless there was good reason, but at this point it was beginning to look like he could be telling the truth, and if he had something of value it wasn't apparent by the light of the fire. And so Hollis slowly lowered the hammer on his pistol and holstered it.

The look of relief on the mystery man's face was obvious. "Much obliged," he said. "Got me a fool's hen this afternoon," he said, nodding to the grouse suspended over the fire by a green willow. "You're welcome to some of it."

Hollis was hungry. He eyed the grouse and the flames licking up around it. There was a small pot of coffee too, nestled in the coals at the edge of the fire. When the fire-light caught it just right, he could see the steam rolling out of the pour spout. And he could smell the coffee; its allure was the equal of a good chew or cigar. And there were preserves too, most likely strawberry judging from the unopened jar near a cloth sack that undoubtedly contained biscuits. Damn, it would taste good, he thought. And then it happened: the nicker of a contented but hobbled horse as it moved from the darkness of the trees into the shadowy light of the fire. Instinctively, Hollis' eyes moved from the mystery man to the horse in the shadows. His eyes widened as he recalled Rudy's words about the marshal's horse: "Same big ole gray." Standing just beyond the mystery man was a big gray horse. Its significance to Hollis was instantly apparent to the mystery man. Hollis knew it but it couldn't be helped. It was like touching your finger to a hot stove; how does one disguise that? His eyes had just met those of the mystery man when he recognized that terrified urgency, and in the next fraction of a second he had an awareness—not a tangible feeling, but an awareness because it was happening so fast—of drawing his pistol and firing. But his had not been the first shot. He'd felt a jolt on his left side, but this had become secondary to the image of the mystery man being rocked violently backwards, teetering momentarily on the backs of his legs and then still in the kneeling position falling over sideways away from the fire.

Hollis' heart was pounding wildly. It felt like it was in his throat. His grasp of the here and now was limited by the massive adrenaline rush that he was feeling. He took several deep breaths to calm himself. Little by little his sense of feeling returned. He had kind of a burning wet sensation on the outer edge of his left hip. The mystery man's bullet had grazed him. He was bleeding a fair amount, but he'd seen these types of wounds before. They tended to clot up if a guy put a bandage with some pressure on it. But first he needed to satisfy himself that he had in fact killed the marshal from Boise and that there might be a big payday awaiting him somewhere amongst the marshal's stuff. He walked, now with a limp on his left side, to where he was standing over the dead man. The flames of the campfire danced in the dead man's eyes, giving him almost the illusion of life. Hollis studied the man for a moment and then cautiously kicked the pistol away from his hand. Kneeling, he began rummaging through the man's shirt pockets; in the left was a sack of Bull Durham tobacco and cigarette papers, and in the right there was a plug of chewing tobacco and behind it something metallic. Hollis knew before he brought it into the light what it was. It wasn't a big badge but it clearly read: *U.S. Marshal*. Hollis looked at the badge for a moment, turning it over in his hand, and then he threw it as hard as he could into the night. And then looking down at the marshal, he said: "Ya shoulda showed me some respect." Hollis reached over and grabbed one of the marshal's lifeless arms, and rising to his feet began dragging the body to the darkness beyond the light of the fire; when

he reached that point he was breathing hard and his hip
was bleeding worse, and so he didn't just simply drop the
arm—he flung it forcefully back across the marshal's torso.
"Sleep tight," he said sarcastically to the dead man, and then
he began limping back towards the fire. By the light of the
fire Hollis could see that the blood trail from his hip wound
had now stained his left pant leg to just below the knee. He
was eager to look for the gold that he hoped the marshal
was carrying, but he was getting concerned at the amount
of blood that he was losing. He looked about for something
made of cloth that he could use for a bandage, and then he
saw the biscuit sack. It would work for a bandage, but he
intended to eat the biscuits so he didn't want to just dump
them on the ground. There was a wooden pack box further
into the shadows. He picked it up and brought it into the
light of the fire. It was deceptively heavy for no more than
it had in it, mostly some small bags of flour, sugar, beans,
and salt. Hollis became suspicious of what was really in the
box. He opened each of the bags and probed with his fingers to see if there was anything, like gold, hidden within
them but there was not. He hefted the box again; it was far
heavier than flour and sugar should weigh. He set the box
down and studied it for a moment. He must be missing
something, he thought. And then it came to him; he took
the bag of flour, which stood upright inside the box, and
placed it upright next to the box on the outside. The bag
was about three inches shorter than the top of the box, yet
when it was placed inside it was nearly flush with the top.
Hollis' discovery caused him to quickly remove the other

bags from the box. He thrust his hand into the darkness and searched for any kind of latch or knob that would allow him to lift its false bottom. He was almost gleeful as he ran his fingers along the seams of the box, but he could not find any means to pull the bottom out. Frantic, he turned the box upside down and began pounding on it with his fists until suddenly he heard it give way inside. He pushed the box over and there sitting atop a board, perfectly sized to fit flush within the box, were twelve small canvas bags. Hollis was beside himself with excitement. He opened one bag and then another to examine their contents: most contained gold but a few had currency or coins in them. There were thousands of dollars in the box, and there was another box just like it that rode in the pannier on the opposite side of the pack horse to balance the load. Hollis was ecstatic as he sat there on the ground next to all of the gold. Between that and what he had in the bank in Boise he was set—he could go somewhere new and live a life of leisure. He was almost to the point of fantasizing what that life would be like when reality set in. He was sitting not more than forty feet from the body of a United States marshal that he had just murdered and thousands in gold that belonged to Stevenson. In time, somebody would undoubtedly come looking for both, and they would not be friendly people. Hollis sighed aloud. There was little that he could do about any of that now. The adrenalin high of a short while ago had now given way to the fatigue and hunger that he had been feeling earlier. The food that the marshal had prepared was there for the taking. He'd even laid out his bedroll.

Hollis' hip throbbed and it continued to bleed. He needed to bandage it and just get off his feet for a while so that it would clot up. In Hollis' mind it all made for a convincing argument to spend the night in the dead marshal's camp, eat his supper, and sleep in his bed. After all, to the victor go the spoils.

Chapter Sixteen

It had taken Josh a couple of days of riding at a pretty steady pace to reach the point where he was at now, overlooking the town of Boise. The town was situated in the bottom of a broad basin on the banks of the Boise River. Foothills covered with juniper trees, sagebrush, and grass surrounded the town. Now that Idaho City had passed its boom days, Boise was the biggest settlement for maybe four or five days' ride, and along with nearby Fort Boise it represented stability and law and order in the area. The town was of such size that no one took particular note of Josh as he rode in on this hot summer afternoon. He had two immediate concerns and they both involved comfort. His first priority was Thunder, and having spotted a livery and blacksmith down a short side street, he headed for it. Reining Thunder in, he dismounted in front of the big open doors to the livery part of the business. A short man whose shirt sleeves were rolled up above the elbows, revealing incredibly muscular forearms, emerged from the livery. "Can I help ya?" he asked.

"Yeah, I reckon you can," replied Josh. "I'll be needin' to stable my horse here for a night or two."

"I charge two bits a day if that sits right with ya," said the short man, barely looking at Josh.

"Sounds fair," said Josh, "but if ya'll don't mind I'll tend to him today. We been on the trail for a coupla three days and I wanna brush him down good."

"Suit yourself," said the short man. "There's brushes in the back there," he added, nodding towards the open doors.

"Much obliged," said Josh as he started to go around the short man.

"Where ya comin' from?" asked the short man unexpectedly.

Josh paused and looked at the short man. "Bear Creek."

The short man shook his head. "From what I hear that's a bad place to be."

"Can't say as I disagree with ya'll," replied Josh in a somewhat disgusted tone. "So far it ain't done right by me."

"Well, I don't think you're alone there," said the short man. "There's been a number of folks that's passed through here on their way to Bear Creek—decent folks, ya know—and then the next thing you hear is that they got themselves kilt and robbed out here in the wilds somewhere."

"Yes sir, that's a fact," said Josh sternly. "I got firsthand knowledge of that."

"Sorry to hear that," said the short man.

"Thanks," said Josh, and then it came to him that the short man might be a good source of information. "Ya'll know the marshal in these parts?"

A mildly surprised look came over the short man's face. "You know Caleb?" he asked.

A BAD PLACE TO BE

Josh hesitated for a moment before answering. He usually didn't think of the marshal on a first-name basis. Their meeting had been brief, and his suspicions of the marshal and Sarah had left him with a feeling of indifference towards the marshal on a personal level, but then he said: "Yeah, I ran into him a little while back up at Bear Creek. I kinda figured he woulda got in here last night or today."

"Naw, I ain't seen him, and I reckon I would if he was back in town 'cause he usually keeps his horse here," said the short man, and then he added, "You might check at the boardin' house just around the corner—he has a room there."

And so after tending to Thunder, Josh headed for the boardinghouse where the marshal stayed. It was a relatively short walk on mostly dirt streets; the boardinghouse, however, had a board walkway in front of it. It was a two-story building with a total of eight rooms for rent. Meals for the guests were taken family style in a dining room off of the kitchen on the ground floor. A parlor room for socializing was adjacent to the dining area. The main-street entrance to the boardinghouse opened into the parlor, which was where Josh soon found himself. No one seemed to be around, and it was quiet except for the ticking of a big clock on the wall across the room. It was encased in what appeared to be oak wood with a glass face and a brass pendulum that tirelessly marked the time. Beneath the clock was a padded couch, and along the wall near the window looking out onto the street was a padded chair. A painting of some pastoral mountain setting hung on the wall near the padded chair. On the wall to Josh's right and opposite the entrance to the dining room was a big rock fireplace. Above the fireplace was the mount of a big buck deer that seemed to be looking back at you regardless of where you were at in the room. There were several books and newspapers neatly arranged on a small table in front of the couch. Beneath the coffee table was a large rug that could probably pass for a tapestry in most places. It depicted an intricate floral pattern of a variety of colors, but mostly a dark hue. There was an abundance of solitude in the room; it was soothing to the senses. Josh felt at peace there, kind of like when he was in the mountains above timber line on a sunny day and he had a commanding view of nothing but rugged beauty; it was an inviting place. He was studying the ornately carved flower designs in a wooden rocking chair near the big rock fireplace when he heard someone approaching from the dining area. "May I help you?" came the voice of a woman.

Josh turned around to see a young woman—a pretty woman about his age—looking at him. He felt an instant physical attraction to her. He couldn't help himself. She was tall for a girl, maybe five foot seven or eight with long red hair and shapely. She wore a plain blue gingham dress that only seemed to accentuate her natural beauty. Josh brought his right hand up to the brim of his hat in a gesture as to tip his hat in the presence of a lady. It was a courtesy that his father had instilled in him at an early age. "My name's Josh Morrow. I'm lookin' for the marshal. Ya'll wouldn't happen to know if he's in, would ya?"

The young woman hesitated a moment as if she was evaluating Josh's character, and then she asked: "Are you a friend or business associate of the marshal's?"

Josh looked at the woman. It was apparent that the marshal had likely cautioned her about giving out information on his coming and going, which was probably a wise thing to do. *Might as well just lay my cards on the table,* thought Josh, and so he dug into his shirt pocket and retrieved his Deputy United States Marshal badge. "I'm the marshal's deputy," said Josh, displaying the badge and looking squarely into the woman's blue eyes.

The surprise on the woman's face was obvious. "Oh," she said. "I didn't know Caleb had a deputy."

Caleb? said Josh to himself. *Sounds like they're on a first name basis.* And then he said aloud to the girl: "He didn't until a few days ago when he deputized me up at Bear Creek."

"So that's where he went to," replied the woman. "He was pretty tight-lipped about where he was going."

"So I take it he ain't come back yet," said Josh.

"If he has he ain't been here," said the woman. "This is usually one of his first stops when he does come into town after being gone awhile."

The woman's words had a tone of certainty about them. It seemed she knew the marshal fairly well, or at least that's what Josh's imagination was leading him to believe. More importantly, though, was the marshal. *He should've been here by now,* said Josh to himself. Trying not to show concern, Josh said to the woman: "Well, I ain't seen him in about a week so he might have got a late start.

He'll probably be here tomorrow or the next day."

There was now a hint of worry in the woman's expression. "If you're Caleb's deputy, how come the two of you aren't together?" she asked with some noticeable edge in her voice.

"Well, ma'am," said Josh patiently, "we was doing different things in different places at the same time."

"And of course you're not going to tell me what those things are, correct?" replied the woman.

"No, ma'am," said Josh respectfully. "I'm afraid I can't do that, but I think ya'll can be of some help to me."

"How's that?" asked the woman curiously.

"Well, I need to know where I can find Judge Higgins, and I'll be needin' a room for a couple a days if ya'll got one available."

"Oh," replied the woman in a somewhat deflated tone of voice, having expected Josh's request to be of more importance. "The judge's office is in the courthouse down at the far end of Main Street," she said, pointing to the north end of town. "As for the room we've got one on the second floor, with meals it's a dollar a day."

"That sounds good," said Josh.

"Fine, Mr.—I'm sorry I've forgotten your name," said the woman, slightly embarrassed.

"Morrow, Josh Morrow, and your name?"

The young woman extended her hand. "I'm Lisa Ambrose, my mother and I own this boardinghouse."

Josh shook Lisa's hand, enveloping it completely. It was, as one might expect, soft to the touch, but her grip was firm and confident as she looked Josh in the eye. "Pleased to meet you, Lisa."

Lisa smiled and nodded politely. "If you'll follow me, Mr. Morrow, I'll have you sign our guest register and give you your room key."

Josh followed a few steps behind Lisa as she led him into the dining area and a small desk in the corner of the room where the registration book was located. The smell of her bath soap or possibly a perfume seemed to be more evident to him now. It was an inviting, if not tantalizing, smell of femininity—something that he hadn't experienced in a long time.

Turning, Lisa handed Josh a pen. "Sign in here, if you don't mind," she said, gesturing towards the guestbook.

Josh took the pen and bent over the book.

"Supper's at six and here's your key, room number seven, up the stairs and to your right," said Lisa as Josh turned to face her.

Josh smiled and tipped his hat slightly. "Thank you, ma'am, I'll see you at suppertime."

As Josh walked towards the courthouse, his mind was awash with different thoughts and emotions. He'd been attracted to Lisa. It was just a feeling but it made him feel guilty. He knew that Sarah had feelings for him, and truth be told he did for her as well but she came with baggage, and try as he might he hadn't been able to set this aside—not yet anyway. And then just to add to it all there was the matter of the marshal. It appeared that Lisa had more than a casual interest in the marshal, but Josh wasn't certain this went both ways given his suspicions about the marshal and Sarah. Josh sighed. *Women, they ain't nothin' but trouble,* he said to himself.

The courthouse, an impressive-looking building, was three stories tall. It housed not only the court but the jail and some offices. Josh entered the building and asked for directions to the judge's office. Up until now he'd taken it for granted that he could just tell the judge what had happened when he killed Leroy and the judge would believe him and that would be that. But now as he was about to knock on the judge's door he had a major case of butterflies; after all, he reasoned, the judge doesn't know him from Adam and he's about to confess to killing a man. Sure, he had a deputy marshal's badge, but now who knows where the marshal is and he's the only one, except Sarah, that can say how he got the badge. Josh knocked firmly on the door.

"Come in," said a gravelly voice from inside.

Josh opened the door and stepped into the judge's office, careful to close the door behind him. For an office, it was a fairly large room. To Josh's left were a couple of padded chairs and a small table between them. A bottle of whiskey and several glasses sat on the table. The chairs were positioned such that their occupants wouldn't be facing one another but would only have to turn their heads slightly to make eye contact. On the wall behind the chairs were bookshelves. It was an impressive library, totaling in the several hundreds of books. To the right of it was a permanent wood box. It was about three feet tall by about five feet wide and three feet deep. Its relatively large size owed to the fact that the judge's office was on the third floor of the courthouse. In the wintertime, for two bits the judge could usually get a young guy to split firewood out back of the courthouse and then carry it up the three flights of stairs to fill the box. And then there were other times when the local sheriff, having jailed someone for being drunk and disorderly with no means to pay the fine, would allow him to work it off by filling the judge's wood box. A stove—not the pot-bellied kind, but rather a flat top designed for cooking and heating—sat next to the wood box. Always in the winter, but only sometimes in the summer due to the heat, the judge would have a pot of coffee or sometimes hot water for making tea on the stove. He spent a lot of time in his office and he aimed to be comfortable. To the right of the stove was a gun cabinet that appeared to have seven or eight rifles and shotguns in it. It was made of a light yellow-colored wood, probably ponderosa pine, and had two doors with long glass panes that met in the center. Hanging on the wall to Josh's right was a grizzly bear rug, and to the right of it was the head of a massive bighorn sheep ram. Tucked into the corner, not far from the judge's large oak desk, were two wooden filing cabinets. But as Josh walked across the creaky wood floor towards the judge seated behind his desk, it wasn't any of these things, not even the judge, that held his attention. On the wall behind the judge was a Mexican battle flag and a Mexican cavalry officer's saber. Seeing the tract that Josh's eyes were on, the judge said: "Souvenirs I picked up in '47 down near the border. Are you a military man?"

Somewhat embarrassed, Josh lowered his eyes to meet those of the judge. "Yes sir, I am. I spent five years in the 2nd Cavalry fightin' Comanches and Mexican bandits."

The judge, a medium-sized man with salt-and-pepper hair and a large moustache that mostly hid his lips and a goatee, nodded his head. "The Second, they did good work. Do I detect a Texas accent in your speech?"

"Yes sir," replied Josh humbly. "I'm from Galveston."

"Oh yes, yes I've been there a number of times," said the judge approvingly. "So do your people make their living from the sea?"

Josh wasn't sure how to take the judge's congenial behavior towards him. He'd heard that he was a hard man, giving little quarter to violent criminals. Outwardly, he didn't seem to be that kind of a guy, but the judge was wearing a black suit coat that was unbuttoned and there was no mistaking the butt of a pistol in a shoulder holster. "My folks run a mercantile," said Josh. "A lot of their goods come by ship, so I guess in a sense they make some of their living from the sea."

"I was always fascinated by the sea," said the judge sincerely. "I thought for a time that it might be my calling in life until I had occasion to be on a ship at sea for about a week. Never been so sick in my life." And then the judge slapped the desk and roared with laughter as if he had just told a great joke. Josh laughed politely. There was an awkwardness building in the room, but just as it did the judge became serious, leaning forward in his chair. "So, I figure you know what my name is or you wouldn't be here, but that leaves me at a disadvantage," said the judge in an almost flippant manner.

Josh hesitated before saying it as he knew the judge would be taken by surprise, but he figured, what the hell, why not? "I'm Deputy U.S. Marshal Josh Morrow."

The judge snorted. "What the hell are you talking about? I know all of the lawmen in these parts and you aren't one of them."

Josh reached into his shirt pocket and took out his badge. "Marshal Johnson deputized me 'bout a week ago up at Bear Creek."

The judge eyed the badge but didn't ask to look at it closer. "So what prompted the marshal to deputize you?"

"Well Judge Higgins, things has pretty much gone to hell around Bear Creek, least ways for decent folks it has. The law up there ain't no help. In fact they might be the problem."

The judge frowned. "I'd heard rumors to that effect but I didn't know if I should believe them or not, that's why Caleb went up there."

"I can tell you, Judge, that the marshal didn't trust the sheriff in Bear Creek, and he wasn't lettin' on to anybody who he was until I ran into him," replied Josh.

"So why did he tip his hand to you?" asked the judge.

Josh's heartbeat quickened. "I reckon 'cause I was lookin' for justice for a friend of mine from my army days that went to Bear Creek and struck a good-payin' claim and got bushwhacked for it. I couldn't get any help from the sheriff up there."

"Caleb didn't offer to help you?" asked the judge.

"Well sir, it appeared he had bigger fish to fry," said Josh. "He was workin' with this merchant name of Stevenson. He had a plan all cooked up with him."

The judge nodded. "Yes, I know. We talked about it before Caleb left."

"To tell you the truth, sir, I figured the marshal would be here by now," replied Josh.

The judge had a worried look on his face. "That being the case, Stevenson should be close behind." The judge paused. It was obvious to Josh that he was pondering his options. Momentarily, he looked Josh in the eye. It was almost like a hard stare intended to melt away any façade that Josh might be perpetrating. "So just how committed to being a lawman are you?" he asked in a tone of voice that was bordering on accusatorial—accusatorial in the sense that Josh had taken the deputy's badge only to facilitate his quest to avenge his friend's murder.

The question had caught Josh by surprise. He'd never given much thought to being a lawman long term. He'd been thinking pretty much that when Seth's affair was settled that he would move on to the Salmon River country and try and pick up where he had left off. But now the judge was putting it to him point-blank: where did he stand? It was a fair question. He'd stood behind the badge when confronting Leroy and Edgar. He'd pushed that confrontation to the limit, knowing that the law was on his side and that it would, hopefully, back his play. Maybe now it was time for some payback. "Sir, I gotta be straight up with ya'll," began Josh soberly. "All the time I was in the army I had this dream that when I got out I was gonna get me a ranch and settle down. But I kinda looked at the army as something that I had to do first, it was like I needed to do my share to help make the country safe for folks. And now..." Josh paused. "...well sir, it seems like that job is never done. And so, like it or not, if a man doesn't want the country to go straight to hell, there is gonna be times when he has to step up and make things right, and I reckon this is one of those times."

The judge appeared satisfied with Josh's answer. "Good," he said. "There's lots to be done and no one really to do it. Bear Creek is beyond the jurisdiction of the sheriff here, and the army is dealing with some Indian raids down along the Snake River. I've got a bad feeling about the marshal. If he doesn't show up tomorrow I want you to see if you can find him. He told me before he left that he intended to take the pack trail up Chokecherry Canyon, and then after he topped out of there he was gonna drop back down on the main wagon road. Finding the marshal and Stevenson's gold is our first priority. Are we in agreement on that?"

"Yes sir, we are." Josh had that uneasy feeling again. He was about to find out if the law had his back. "But there's something that you should know."

The judge's expression was more concern than curiosity. "What's that?" he said flatly.

"I found the man that murdered my friend. I confronted

him with the proof right there on my friend's claim. I tried to arrest him, to get him to come along peaceably, but he wouldn't have any part of it. He took a shot at me and then the fight was on. Long story short is I killed him in a gun battle that he started."

The judge was silent for a moment before reaching to an inside pocket of his coat and getting a plug of chewing tobacco. He bit off a decent-sized piece and then returned the plug to his pocket. "Any witnesses to this?" he asked as he made several exaggerated chewing motions before positioning the chaw in his left cheek.

"Yes, sir," replied Josh. "The dead man's partner was there when it started, but he took off as soon as the first shots was fired."

The judge smiled briefly. "So if he was willing to tell the truth it'd be that his partner fired first?"

"Yes, sir," replied Josh.

The judge slid his chair back slightly, and pursing his lips he leaned to the right and spit a stream of tobacco juice in the brass spittoon that sat on the floor next to his desk; most but not all of the juice made it. The judge wiped his moustache with the back of his hand as he sat erect. "Well, son, it don't sound like to me that you got a helluva lot to worry about. Appears to me that you gave this scoundrel a chance to come along peacefully and he chose not to. In my experience that's the behavior of a guilty man."

For Josh, hearing these words was a huge relief. He'd had to answer to the law for killing two men inside of about a week and both times the law had backed him—albeit reluctantly in the case of the Swede. "Thanks, Judge," said Josh humbly. "I appreciate your support."

The judge sighed. "Well, son, decent folks shouldn't have to stress over their welfare as a result of being dragged through the muck by the unsavory side of our society. You acted in self-defense and truth be told you saved this court the trouble of having to hang this varmint."

Josh stood before the judge. Here was the no-nonsense judge that he'd been told about. His mind flashed back to his negotiations with Leroy. Perhaps this was why Leroy was adamant about not surrendering. Regardless, Josh was just glad that he and the judge were on the same side.

Chapter Seventeen

It was a few minutes before six and the dining-room table was already set for supper. It was a long table with high-back wooden chairs sufficient to accommodate ten people if need be. Tonight, however, there were only seven place settings. This owed to the fact that of the eight rooms in the boardinghouse only seven were rented; this included the marshal's, and he, of course, wasn't coming. Still, a seventh plate was necessary due to a mining engineer from San Francisco having brought his wife along.

The moment that Josh stepped into the hallway outside his room, he could smell the food being prepared in the kitchen below. It reminded him of his mother's home cooking and it made him all the more hungry. As he descended the narrow wooden stairs, Josh could hear voices coming from the dining area. All of his fellow dining companions were already there—and Lisa. Lisa's voice was prominent among them; however, as Josh quietly entered the far end of the dining room, everyone's attention was fixated on a well-dressed, middle-aged man who was railing on about, as he put it, "the moral depravity that had gripped the area."

A BAD PLACE TO BE

"Why just up the road here in Idaho City half the population is Chinese and"—he paused to make eye contact with Lisa and the mining engineer's wife—"begging your pardon, ladies," and then turning to the men at the table he continued, "a large number of these Chinese are prostitutes. Purveyors of disease and misery catering to the carnal weaknesses of men, that's all they are."

Josh paused at the entrance to the dining room. *What is this,* he said to himself, *a church meetin' or supper?* He was having second thoughts about staying when the mining engineer's wife made eye contact with him, which soon alerted the others to his presence and caused a lull in the conversation. "Good evening, Mr. Morrow," said Lisa. "Please join us. We were just about to eat."

Somewhat reluctantly, Josh took a seat opposite the man doing all of the talking. He'd barely sat down when the talker opposite him noticed his badge and said: "Sir, I see by your badge that we share a common goal."

"How's that?" responded Josh somewhat sourly.

Sensing Josh's impatience, the talker said: "Forgive me, I'm Reverend Corneilus Hathcock. The area of commonality between us, as I see it, is that we are both trying to rid the country of evil and wickedness. Don't you agree?"

Josh did not want to get into a discussion with the reverend. He just wanted to have some supper and get a good night's sleep. Preacher men, as he saw it, were always passing judgment even though the good book said: "Judge not for ye shall be judged also." It seemed as if everyone's eyes were upon Josh waiting for a response to the reverend, and so he said: "Well, Reverend, I think you and I's take on things is probably a little different."

"In what way?" said the reverend, a little surprised.

Josh sighed. What a way to ruin a good meal, he thought. "Well, Reverend, I heard ya'll going on about the Chinese prostitutes and the disease and misery they was spreadin'." Now to my way ah thinkin'." Josh paused briefly as Sarah flashed through his mind. "I think, given a choice, that probably most all of them prostitutes would rather make a livin' doing something else. If you stop and think about it in these here times, one way or another, women are going to be at the beck and call of men."

Clearly, the reverend was taken aback. He'd expected a deputy marshal to be right there in lockstep with his condemnation of prostitution. "I hate to be disagreeable, Deputy," replied the reverend curtly, "but in my opinion most of these prostitutes have succumbed to weakness and taken the easy route."

Josh's pulse rate shot up. "Ya'll call a life of being beat, cheated out of their money, infected with social diseases, and most likely dying young an easy route?" Josh sighed disgustedly. "Sorry to offend you, Reverend, but I think you're a pompous idiot. You seem to have forgotten that Jesus forgave the prostitute."

The reverend's eyes widened and his face was turning red with embarrassment. It was clear to him from the expressions on the faces of the other people in the room that his position was not being favorably received. Still, the reverend glared at Josh. "How dare you speak to me in that manner," he said in as venomous a tone as he could muster. "If I was not a man of the cloth and adverse to violence I'd call you outside." And with that the reverend took the napkin from his lap and threw it down onto his still clean plate and stood.

Josh had not intended to say the things that he had but his emotions, perhaps newly formed since meeting Sarah, had gotten away from him and so he said: "My apologies, Reverend."

But it was too late and the reverend walked briskly from the room and out the front door, slamming it behind him.

There was dead silence in the room except for the occasional clanking of a serving plate or cooking pot in the kitchen where the cook, Lisa's mother Annabel, was busy getting the food ready to be served. And then just as the uneasy smiles in the room were about to demand commentary from someone, Annabel backed through the swinging door that separated the dining room and kitchen. She had a platter of roast beef in one hand and mashed potatoes in the other. Within seconds she sensed something was amiss from the silence, which was confirmed by the expression on Lisa's face and the absence of the reverend, but she didn't let on to these observations as she said cheerfully: "Supper is served." And then she said, looking directly at Lisa: "Could you help me bring the rest of the food out?" Lisa nodded and followed her mother into the kitchen.

"Smells delicious," said the mining engineer.

"Most definitely," added a rotund little businessman opposite the engineer's wife.

But then not to be outdone in complimenting the host's food, a crusty little guy with a salt-and-pepper beard sitting next to Josh said: "Ya'll better get what ya want when the plate comes 'round 'cause I'm so damned hungry I could eat fly-blowed mule and lick the plate."

Josh had to suppress a smile as he noticed from the corner of his eye the engineer's wife cringe. So far, supper—Boise for that matter—had made him appreciate the tranquility of staying with Sarah at Lester's place. He imagined that they and Rufus were sitting down to supper about now too.

It was just about simultaneous the opening of the door to the street and the door to the kitchen. Seeing a man standing in the parlor, Lisa quickly set the food that she had brought from the kitchen down on the dining-room table. Wiping her hands on her apron as she walked, she went to the man in the parlor and after a brief exchange returned with him. "Everyone, this is Mr. Perkins. He'll be joining us for supper," said Lisa as she guided the stranger to the reverend's vacant chair. And then seeing the crumpled napkin on the reverend's plate, Lisa quickly snatched it away. "I'll get you a fresh napkin."

It was Perkins himself who broke the social ice jam for free-flowing dialogue. He was a skinny man, not too tall with short blond hair, and a cherubic face which was consistent with his apparent inability to grow a beard as he had just a wisp of some chin whiskers. "I'll tell you," he said as the food began to be passed around the table, "I was torn if I should eat or just get good and drunk tonight. I don't know. I might just do both."

There was something about the young man that piqued Josh's curiosity, and so at the risk of being the target of Perkins' loquaciousness he asked: "Why's that?"

Perkins looked up from the plate of roast beef in his hand towards Josh. It was only then that he saw Josh's badge. "Why hell's fire, you're the man I need to be talkin' to anyway. I was gonna look up the sheriff after supper but you'll do."

"Well then spit it out, mister," said Josh impatiently.

By this time all eyes in the room were on Perkins. "Well, sir," began Perkins, "I come down from that Bear Creek country." And then it was as if just the mention of Bear Creek had sent him in another direction, and he said: "I'll tell you what, there ain't no more godless place than if you was dead and going straight down. I had my fill of it and decided I was just gonna get out with this little poke of dust that I scraped outa the ground and call it good."

"So is this what ya'll wanted to tell me?" interrupted Josh.

"Oh hell no," exclaimed Perkins. "Everybody knows what a vile place Bear Creek is. I was comin' to what I needed to tell you. Late yesterday, I came across some freight wagons up at Sheep Springs. All the drivers was dead. Appeared they'd stopped for the day and somebody just came into their camp and got the drop on'em and then just shot'em like they was being executed."

It's gotta be Stevenson's party, said Josh to himself. "Where was this at?" asked Josh.

"Sheep Springs," replied Perkins. "It's 'bout a good solid day's travel northeast of here."

"How many bodies were there?" asked Josh.

"Well sir, there was four wagons and four bodies," said Perkins. "I seen these fellars sellin' their goods up at Bear Creek. Looked like they was doin' a pretty lively business so I 'spect whoever robbed 'em made off with a good amount of gold."

"I reckon so," said Josh pensively. "What about the dead men's personal belongings, were they disturbed or taken?"

Perkins paused as if he were reconstructing the image of the dead men's camp in his mind before answering. "You know, Deputy, now that you ask, I don't believe that they was. Things looked liked they was in their proper place except them fellars was all laying together near their fire ring colder'n last week's coffee."

Josh pondered this information. It sounded to him that Stevenson was going along with the marshal's plan by not putting up any resistance and just handing over the fool's gold, but they got themselves killed anyway. The only question was if it was because the bandits detected the ruse or they just didn't want any witnesses. Regardless, Josh needed to let the judge know what had happened. Pushing his chair back from the table, Josh said: "Nice to have met you folks, but if ya'll will excuse me I got some business to tend to." And with that Josh started for the front door. He had just stepped outside when he heard someone behind him.

"Mr. Morrow," said Lisa. "Can't your business wait until after supper?"

"Probably," said Josh, "but I don't want to intrude on the judge at a late hour."

Lisa smiled. "I doubt the judge would take offense if you went over later in the evening."

Josh sighed. "I reckon ya'll's right but I pretty much steered that supper conversation in there in the wrong direction with the reverend, and I figure if I stay there'd be no gettin' around banterin' with Perkins and that could just end up chunkin' another log on the fire."

Lisa could see that Josh's mind was made up. "How about if I fix you a plate and put it in the oven to keep warm. You can eat when you get back."

"Much obliged," said Josh. "I'll see you in an hour or so." And with that he turned and walked away, wondering if there was any other meaning intended in Lisa's act of kindness.

After some asking around, Josh got directions to the judge's house. What should have been a simple matter of informing the judge as to his intentions concerning the marshal and Stevenson turned into a two-hour social call drinking whiskey on the judge's back porch. As the whiskey flowed so did the army stories. They were of different eras, but the bond of having risked their lives in service to the country was unmistakable. It was just getting dark when Josh left the judge's house, a little tipsy but with a profound respect for the man. He'd not intended to be gone so long and certainly had no expectations of having supper at the boardinghouse, but as he quietly opened the door, there sat Lisa in one of the big padded chairs reading by the light of a coal oil chimney lantern.

"Had I known you were going to be a night owl," she said in mock anger, "I would've told you to eat down the street before coming home." And then she smiled.

"I'm sorry," said Josh. "The judge is a hard man to break away from."

Lisa got up from the chair. She could see that Josh had been drinking. "Are you hungry?" she asked in a tone of uncertainty.

"Some," said Josh, "but I don't expect you to feed me."

"Well, your food is still in the oven. It might be kind of dry by now but it's up to you."

"Lead the way," said Josh. And then as if it had been a reflex, there was an instantaneous pang of guilt that flashed in his mind. He knew that his only motive was not just eating, and truth be told he was fairly certain that Lisa didn't go to these lengths for all her guests. But here he was following her and conjuring up indecent images of her in his mind. He could blame it on the judge's whiskey, but he knew that wasn't totally true either. His mind was awash with the images of first Lisa and then Sarah and then the big Swede and the blood pooled beneath his head on the floor of the Gold Strike Saloon. *Damn them all*, thought Josh, and then Lisa said: "Have a chair. I'll be back in a minute."

Josh took a seat at the big dining-room table. He was alone there. It felt good to be free of the incessant babble of the reverend or Perkins.

Momentarily, Lisa returned with Josh's food and a cup of hot coffee. She set it on the table before him. "Thank you, ma'am," said Josh. "I sure do appreciate this."

"You can call me Lisa. 'Ma'am' sounds like I'm an old lady."

"OK, Lisa," said Josh with a respectful emphasis on her name, "but that will mean that ya'll will have to call me Josh." They both smiled.

"Fair enough," replied Lisa as she sat down at the table two chairs away from Josh.

Josh felt awkward eating in front of Lisa, but shortly she initiated small talk to take the edge from this feeling.

"So where's home for you?" she asked.

Josh swallowed. "These days, I reckon it's wherever I happen to be, but originally it was Texas."

Lisa laughed softly. "I kinda figured the Texas part out," she said playfully.

Josh blushed. "So how long have ya'll lived in Boise?"

"Almost five years now," replied Lisa. "We came as a family but my older brother took sick and died and road agents robbed and killed my father. It's just been me and my mother running this place for the past year."

Josh paused from eating. "Sorry to hear that," he said. "This is a hard country. It don't seem to allow quarter to nobody."

Lisa nodded. "My mother and I are finding that out." And then she added with sarcasm, "You'd be amazed at how many good upstanding people will sneak out and not pay."

Josh shook his head. "Ain't much surprises me about people anymore."

There was a lull between them. The silence was accentuated by the stove in the kitchen popping periodically, having likely burned into some pine pitch. But the need for a fire on this warm summer night spoke volumes to Josh as he took a sip of his hot coffee and ate his still warm supper. And he felt even guiltier when he considered how difficult or expensive it had been for two women to get firewood from the distant hills.

"I take it you're leaving tomorrow," said Lisa solemnly.

"Yeah, I aim to get an early start," replied Josh.

"Are you going back to Bear Creek?"

Josh laughed derisively. "Not right away but eventually I got to."

A sudden knowing look of concern came over Lisa's face. "Have you got a girl there?"

Josh was uncertain how to answer. He didn't consider Sarah his girl, but on the other hand there was no denying that she meant more to him than just a casual acquaintance. Deep down he still didn't know if he could accept her past. And so he said: "No, not really."

Lisa forced a nervous laugh, and then looking Josh in the eye she asked: "What does 'not really' mean?"

Josh was temporarily speechless. "It means that I've been helpin' a girl out who was down on her luck and she has become my friend."

There was a look of disappointment in Lisa's face. "So your friend is waiting for you in Bear Creek."

A BAD PLACE TO BE

The conversation was beginning to make Josh uncomfortable—or it could be the judge's whiskey was beginning to wear off. "Close to there," he said cryptically.

The probing continued. "So how did you come to meet your friend?" asked Lisa.

And there it was. It was as if Lisa had been a mischievous little kid throwing rocks at a hornet's nest and had finally gauged her throw correctly. Josh's response would obviously dictate how many and how mad the hornets that emerged from the nest would be. Lying was certainly an option, but it seemed to Josh this usually created more problems than it solved, and so he said: "She was a saloon girl in Bear Creek."

The look on Lisa's face was mild shock. It was as if she was stunned, but then she said with some hesitation and somewhat disbelievingly, "A prostitute?" The words rolled off her lips like she needed to purge something nasty from her mouth.

Josh nodded. "Yup, for a while she did what she needed to do to survive."

Lisa shook her head. "I could never do that. I'd rather be dead."

Josh looked up from his plate as he finished his food. There was defiance in Lisa's eyes and perhaps resentment too of a girl she'd never met. "Ya'll need to be careful 'bout drawin' a line in the sand," said Josh calmly. "When it gets right down to it, lettin' go a life, it ain't all that easy."

Lisa's demeanor had become one of anger and embarrassment. The silence was growing and then she said without looking at Josh: "We got apple pie for dessert."

Josh pushed his chair back and stood. "I reckon I'll pass on the pie and just turn in. Thanks for supper. It was mighty good."

"You're welcome," said Lisa as she glanced at Josh and then turned quickly away to the task of clearing the table.

Josh left the dining room in silence and went upstairs to his room. He opened the window that overlooked the street below. He could hear music and raucous laughter from a saloon down the street, but he wasn't tempted by it. A dog was barking in the distance. The room was warm. He stripped down to his underwear and lay on top of the bedcovers. He had his hands clasped behind his head, which was turned slightly so he could see out the window and up at the stars in the night sky. An hour or so had passed and Josh was still awake, processing the day's events. He could hear the rhythmic snoring of a man in the next room. Nighttime was well underway when he heard faint footsteps in the hall outside his door. And then there was silence, save for the snoring man next door. It was close to a minute before the light knock on the door came. Josh's heart rate quickened. He was tempted to open the door but he reasoned, hadn't he already done that in Bear Creek? Again the knock came, but Josh turned over and tried to go to sleep. Soon the footsteps could be heard going away and down the stairs.

It was a long night and not particularly restful for Josh, but he was on time for breakfast. Lisa, however, was under the weather, said Annabel, and would not be helping to serve. After breakfast Josh paid his bill, giving Annabel, in spite of her objections, twice what he owed, saying that he wanted to make amends for Lisa having to get him a late supper. And he told her that he hoped Lisa was feeling better soon.

Chapter Eighteen

The sun had not yet totally exposed itself over the eastern horizon when Josh headed out of town on the road towards Idaho City. In its heyday Idaho City had been the most populous town in the area, but now the gold that had fueled its growth had been mostly extracted from the ground—at least the easy stuff had. Much of the town's dwindling population was now comprised of Chinese immigrants that applied the necessary labor and ingenuity to make the played-out claims pay. The town was also known for its Chinese prostitutes, and so it undoubtedly had other vices such as liquor and gambling available to separate men from their money. Since it was the first decent-sized town that a person came to after leaving Sheep Springs, Josh reasoned that the Stevenson party's killers might just come here to celebrate.

Idaho City was a good day's ride from Boise. It was located in the beginning of the mountains with ponderosa pine, but many of the trees around the town had been cut down to provide lumber to build the town. All of the mining activity had left the land scarred and tired looking.

It was late afternoon when Josh reined Thunder in at

the livery on the edge of town. A fat man with black greasy hair and beard to match emerged from the stable. He was humming something nondescript much in the way a cat purrs due to being content with life as it is at that moment. "Afternoon," said the fat man as he shuffled towards Josh in no particular hurry.

Josh nodded his head. "Howdy," he said, purposely trying to keep his eyes from the enormity of the fat man's belly. But it was near impossible as its size begged for a peek. It covered the fat man's belt buckle—assuming he was wearing one—and all but one of the buttons in the fly of his pants.

"Ya lookin' to board your horse?" wheezed the fat man.

"Yes sir, I am," said Josh as he stepped down from Thunder.

It was only then that the fat man noticed Josh's badge. It was obvious by the big-eyed double take that he gave Josh. "You partners with that other marshal that was through here a week or so ago?"

"I reckon so," said Josh. "Ain't that many lawmen in these parts." Josh paused briefly. "Speakin' of the marshal, ya'll ain't seen him in the last day or two, have ya?"

"Can't say as I have," replied the fat man.

"Any strangers come to town in the last day or two, maybe wantin' to sell some mules or horses?" asked Josh.

The fat man smiled. "There's always strangers coming to town, not like the boom days but we still get some folks most days. But as far as trying to sell me some stock, it's been a good while since I had any propositions to do that."

Josh frowned. "Nobody suspicious-lookin'?" he prodded.

The fat man ran the fingers of his right hand through his hair and then he scratched his scalp in apparent contemplation. "Ya know," he began slowly, "there was a coupla fellas in here late yesterday, kinda full of themselves. You know the type—pretty proud of the fact that they was wearin' six-shooters."

"What'd they look like?" asked Josh somewhat eagerly.

"Well, lemmee see," said the fat man as he tried to recall the men's images. "They had short brown hair, the both of 'em, and one had a full beard but the other only had a moustache. Not a thick moustache either. It was the kind that if ya poured some cream on it and turned your cat loose, he'd probably lick the whole thing right off."

"These guys tall or short?" asked Josh.

"I'd say average build, maybe five eight. They both had fairly new Stetsons that was crowned to a peak like ya see some folks do," replied the fat man.

"Anything else about them that stands out?" asked Josh.

The fat man shook his head. "No, like I said, they was kinda smart-alecky. Just being 'round 'em ya got the feeling that ya better not look at 'em the wrong way or you'd be lookin' down the barrel of a gun."

"That's good to know," said Josh. "I appreciate your help."

"Ya know, Deputy, there was one other thing," said the fat man, extending the index finger on his right hand and poking the air in front of him. "I just remembered, they was talkin' 'bout going to the assay office. It kinda struck me funny 'cause these two hooligans didn't look like miners."

The fat man's words were like a bugler had sounded off in Josh's mind. Maybe the marshal's plan was working after all. "So where is the assay office?" asked Josh.

"Well sir, there is two, three places that'll coin a fellar's gold, but the assay office is two blocks thataway on the right," said the fat man, pointing up the main street.

Josh turned and looked in the direction that the fat man was pointing. He couldn't see the assay office but assumed it wouldn't be a problem to find it.

"What'd these fellars do?" asked the fat man.

Josh paused before answering. Probably don't need to be totally tipping my hand at this point, he thought, and so he said: "I'm not sure, maybe nothing but I need to talk to'em to figure that out."

After personally tending to Thunder, Josh started up the street in search of the assay office. In its heyday there had been several hundred businesses in Idaho City, with the bulk of those being saloons. But now the town was struggling to survive, and it was clear by the number of empty buildings that it would never be its former self. It was going the same route that so many other gold-rush towns already had; in the end only the hardy would remain. The assay office was as the fat man said it would be. A sign in the window stated the high points of what they had to offer. A person could get his gold dust turned into coin within six to twelve hours or he could sell it and be paid by a bank draft drawn on a bank in San Francisco; either way it had to be assayed first to determine its purity. This would be a logical place for someone to convert gold dust into a more spendable form, thought Josh, but would anyone be so stupid as to rob and kill four people and then go directly to the closest big town to cash in their spoils? It was this thought that hung in Josh's mind as he entered the assay office. Almost immediately inside the door was a wooden counter that extended across the room to within about two and a half feet of the walls on either side of the room. A desk and chair and several large wooden cabinets were behind the counter. A set of scales for weighing gold sat on the counter. The front part of the office was unoccupied, but Josh could hear voices through an open door leading to the rear of the building. "Hello," said Josh in a voice louder than normal conversation. There was an instant pause in the voices beyond the open door. Soon a prematurely bald, middle-aged man appeared. His demeanor in the brief interval that it took him to spot Josh's badge went from relaxed and friendly to serious and guarded. It was something that did not go unnoticed by Josh.

"What can I do for you, Deputy?" said the bald man haltingly as he read Josh's badge.

"My name's Josh Morrow. I'm workin' for Judge Higgins down in Boise. I was wonderin' if ya'll had anybody come in here within the last day or so wantin' to sell or coin some gold dust except what they had turned out to be iron pyrite."

Josh could see the fear in the bald man's eyes as he placed both his hands on the countertop as if he were leaning there in a relaxed, cordial manner—or, Josh thought, maybe to steady his shaking hands. The bald man laughed nervously. "It's been a while since I've had some greenhorn come in here and try to sell me fool's gold." He laughed again. "No sir, it's been quite some time since I've had that happen."

It was at this point that the second voice in the back room appeared briefly in the form of an old, gray-haired man. He stood about six or eight feet inside the back room but was clearly visible from the front counter. Josh could feel the man's eyes upon him to the point that it caused him to glance away from the bald man and make eye contact with the old man through the doorway. However, no sooner had he done this than the bald man turned—not casually but quickly as if angry. "Get back to work, Ira. I'll tend to this gentleman." And with that the old man abruptly averted his eyes from Josh and walked away, further into the back room and out of sight. Turning to face Josh, the bald man asked: "So what's this all about?"

Josh sensed that the bald man was lying, but getting at the truth might be difficult. Maybe he could smoke these guys out, thought Josh, if they thought they were in danger of being arrested, and so he said: "A merchant from Boise was robbed and killed along with his teamsters up at Sheep Springs a coupla days ago. He was carrying fool's gold instead of the real thing, so if anybody should happen to show up here with any sizeable amount of it, I wanna talk to'em." Josh paused and then added: "There's likely to be a noose waitin' for'em in Boise."

The color was largely gone from the bald man's face. "You can count on me, Deputy, I'll sure let ya know if these two fellars show up here," he said in a faltering voice.

Josh did not let on that he'd detected the bald man's mistake, but it was becoming rapidly apparent that the bald man had realized his error too late—much like a coyote steps into a steel trap and hears the snap but hasn't felt the full impact of the pain. He was caught.

"If ya'll hear of anything that might help me," said Josh calmly, "I'll be stayin' at the hotel just down the street."

The bald man barely parted his lips and took a deep breath to calm himself before speaking. "Sure, Deputy, I'll let you know if anything turns up here."

"Much obliged," replied Josh, and then turning he walked out. He was reasonably certain that the wheels had been set in motion by his visit. He could've called the bald man on his mention of "two fellars" but he didn't want him to wiggle out of it on the spot. It'd be better, thought Josh, to let this mistake work on the bald man and see if that didn't lead to an even bigger mistake. In the meantime, the aromas from a little café down the street were beckoning to Josh. His hands and his stomach were steady and supper sounded good; he doubted the bald man could say the same thing.

It wasn't long after Josh left the assayer's office that the bald man, whose name was Harold Jenkins, closed the office for the day. However, instead of going home to his wife, he headed for a boardinghouse on the far end of town in the direction opposite of the hotel where Josh was staying.

A BAD PLACE TO BE

The boardinghouse had two entrances—one at the front of the building for access from the street, and one at the rear to facilitate easy access to the privy behind the building. Jenkins stopped first at the privy and relieved himself and then entered through the rear of the building. It was suppertime and he knew that most of the guests would likely be in the dining room, but he didn't dare show his face there and risk any more than he already had being associated with the Menagher brothers. Fortunately for Jenkins, the Menaghers' room was the first one inside the back door. He knocked lightly on the door. No response. He knocked again, slightly louder. Still no response. They're either eating or God only knows what saloon or whorehouse they're in, thought Jenkins. He sighed deeply and was turning to leave when he heard familiar voices outside. Jenkins stepped to the back door. It was the Menaghers; they were drunk and playing grab-ass with one another. Jenkins stepped out the back door, which caused the Menaghers to instantly stop in their tracks. "What the hell are you doing here, Harold?" hissed Billy Menagher.

Jenkins put his finger to his lips and motioned for the brothers to follow him to a willow thicket behind the privy. The brothers followed Jenkins more out of curiosity than respect into the willows, where they were out of sight and, hopefully, hearing of anyone at the boardinghouse. "We got big trouble," said Jenkins in a hushed but excited voice.

"Why's that?" asked Jethro Menagher. "A deputy marshal from Boise was just in my office asking if I'd had anybody come in trying to sell fool's gold. He knew all about

Stevenson carrying fool's gold. You boys been had."

"That's bullshit," said Billy, sounding considerably more sober than he had been before coming into the willows. "What'd you tell him?"

Jenkins' voice was shaking and he was glad that he'd gone to the privy before confronting the Menaghers. "I told'im that it'd been a long time back since I'd had anyone come in with fool's gold."

"Well, did he believe you?" asked Billy, getting more angry.

"I don't know, maybe," said Jenkins. "He was hard to read."

"Long as you don't say anything he don't know shit," replied Billy.

Jenkins was clearly fearful. "Well, I..," he stammered, "I think I might have screwed up a little bit."

"What are you talking about?" asked Billy angrily.

"Well I happened to let on that if these two guys come in to sell fool's gold I'd let him know, just playing along with'im ya know."

"So, he still don't know anything," said Billy, a little per-plexed. Billy could see that Jenkins was hesitant to speak. "Alright, Jenkins, what's the problem here?"

"The deputy never said anything about two guys—I did. It just slipped out. So if he caught it, he knows I'm lying."

It took a moment for the Menaghers to process the consequences of this. "You dumbass," snarled Billy. "You can bet he's gonna be watching you like a hawk. And what's the first thing you do but come straight to us. You're dumber than a sack full of rocks."

"Well, I figured our problem would be solved if you guys just took care of this deputy," said Jenkins meekly.

Billy scoffed. "Why hell, Harold, why didn't I think ah that? All I gotta do is kill this here deputy U.S. marshal and everything will be okay."

"Well, it's better than waitin' for him to come knockin' on our door and arrest us," replied Jenkins in a surprisingly bold tone.

A devious smile came over Billy's face. "We got another option, Harold, that you ain't brought up."

Jenkins knew all too well what Billy was talking about. "You know, Harold, I might not have even considered this option if you hadn't of insisted on a third when we had real gold to sell to you."

Jenkins became defiant. "You're lucky that I even dealt with you what with all the robberies going on around here, and then you an' Jethro come walzin' in dressed like a coupla dandies and want to turn your hard-earned gold dust into coin—who do you think you're kiddin'? Anybody else woulda put the sheriff on ya. Besides, I think Ira is wise to you guys so I'm not the only one who knows about our arrangement."

Billy stepped close to Jenkins, face to face. Jenkins could smell the whiskey on his breath. A mean look came over Billy's face. "Well, Harold," he said in a mocking gay tone, "first things first."

Jenkins gasped, and his eyes bulged as the six-inch blade of Billy's knife entered his chest cavity just below the sternum. He began to sag as only a dying man would, his eyes begging Billy to release him from the hook that he seemed to be hanging from, and then just when there appeared to be not an ounce of compassion in Billy he quickly jerked the knife down and back, releasing Jenkins to fall to the ground in a lifeless heap. Billy stared at Jenkins for a moment, and then satisfied that he was dead, he bent over and wiped the blood from his knife and his hand on Jenkins' clothes. Standing, he said to Jethro: "C'mon, let's see if we can find Ira."

Ira Moyer was seventy years old. He'd been a prospector most all his adult life, which for him had started at the age of fourteen after Indians killed his folks. He'd never struck it rich; mostly he'd just made wages and enough to get by. Prospecting was in his blood, and he'd never been able to let go of it until this past year when his body rebelled at wading in the cold streams and packing gravel to run through his sluice box. He was lucky that his mother had schooled him some. He could read, write, and cipher numbers. It was these abilities that had gotten him the job at the assayer's office. It allowed him to make a living and still work on the periphery of the profession that he loved. He had a respect, almost a reverence for the determination and hard work that it took to dig out a good-sized poke of gold. It galled him that people like the Menaghers circumvented this entire process and just took other people's hard-earned gold. He'd had enough, and so after checking at the hotel where Josh said he would be staying, he went to the next most logical and closest place that he might be: the Blue Bird Café.

Josh was sitting across the room against the far wall. He'd purposely picked that table, as it afforded him a fairly clear view of anyone coming in the front door. And so it was when Ira stepped inside the Blue Bird Café, he was momentarily silhouetted in the door frame. Josh, having the advantage of looking in only one place, spotted Ira right away through the after-dinner cigar smoke and the heads and shoulders of the seven or eight other patrons seated at the tables between him and the door. It was obvious that the old man was looking for someone as he stood motion-less at the door and slowly scanned the room. Suddenly, that instant awareness of having found who he was looking for came over his face and he started in Josh's direction. As he neared the table Josh gestured towards an empty chair. "Have a seat, Ira," he said in a friendly tone. And then he added: "I thought I might be seein' ya'll tonight."

As he sat down, Ira looked once more at the people on either side of him. If he recognized anyone he didn't let on.

"Buy ya'll ah cup ah coffee?" offered Josh.

Ira shook his head. "I can't stay long. I'll lose my job if Jenkins was to see me talkin' to ya."

Playing along, Josh replied: "Why's that?"

Ira glanced over at the door and the people in the room and then back to Josh. "Jenkins was lyin' to ya 'bout them boys that you was lookin' for."

"I figured as much," said Josh calmly.

"Them boys was in the office just yesterday," replied Ira. "The damn fools had a bunch ah iron pyrite all bagged up. You woulda thought they'd found the mother lode or something. They got right mad when Jenkins told'em they had fool's gold and that it was worthless. Course when they saw me sittin' at the back of the room, they went into some big production 'bout how hard they'd worked to get all that. I knew it was a lot of phooey. Why hell, a man can just look at them two dudes and see that they ain't never done a hard day's labor in their life."

"I suspect you're right," said Josh. "But tell me, why is your boss so willin' to lie for these guys?"

"He's pretty tight with them Menagher boys. They been comin' in ever since I worked there. I never waited on'em. Jenkins always took care of them his self."

"'Menagher' is what these two characters go by?" asked Josh rhetorically.

"Yeah, Billy and Jethro," replied Ira. "Least ways that's the names I heard."

Josh pondered Ira's words. It was all coming together. Jenkins had enabled the Menaghers to convert their stolen gold to coin or currency without drawing suspicion, undoubtedly for a cut of the proceeds. "Did ya'll ever hear these Menaghers mention Sheep Springs or the name Stevenson?" asked Josh.

Ira was thoughtful for a brief moment. "No, I never heard any of those names, but like I told ya they dealt strictly with Jenkins. There was even one time when them two varmints came in that Jenkins told me to go across the street and have a cup of coffee."

Josh took a sip of his coffee. "Ya know, Ira, I ain't so

sure it's a good idea for you to go home tonight," said Josh in a serious tone.

Ira looked at Josh a little fearfully. "Ya thinkin' these two hooligans would wanna do something to me?" he asked as if he couldn't believe it.

"Ya never know," said Josh. "I'm thinkin' my conversation with Jenkins this afternoon has probably gotten back to them guys by now. And the problem with hombres like this is when they feel threatened they get mean."

Ira became quiet for a moment and then he said: "I got a friend, Willy, lives in a shack at the south edge of town. Guess I could go there tonight."

Josh took some coins from his pocket and laid them on the table for his meal. "How 'bout I escort you out there?"

There was mixed emotion written on Ira's face. He didn't want to show fear to these young, cocky pups, but there was no denying reality: he was an old man and he was afraid.

It was about a fifteen-minute walk to Willy's cabin along the creek. "I'll see ya in the morning," said Josh to Ira. And with that Josh turned and began the short walk back to town.

Chapter Nineteen

Buster Kregg was not the fool that the Menagher brothers were. He'd sensed at Sheep Springs that something wasn't quite right with the gold—it just didn't have enough heft to it—but he'd kept quiet. And so when the Menaghers informed him they were going to Idaho City to sell their share of the gold dust, he declined to go. It was time to part company with the brothers. They were out of control; they had slaughtered Stevenson and his men even as they begged for their lives. Kregg knew that common, decent people would tolerate only so much before they would come together and take matters into their own hands. He'd seen vigilante justice before and it was not forgiving. The Menaghers had become truly evil; it was time, Kregg reasoned, to put distance between himself and the brothers. Besides, he had a pretty good idea where the real gold was at.

It was early evening when Kregg rode into Bear Creek. He intended to have a talk with Hollis, but it'd been a long day and he was in need of a drink. Hollis can wait a little while, he told himself as he reined in his horse at the hitching rail in front of the Gold Strike Saloon. Somewhat stiff from the ride, Kregg stepped down gingerly from his horse. He stood still for a moment while his walking legs came back and then he proceeded into the Gold Strike. It was a busy evening; tobacco smoke hung in the air like it belonged there, and there was a steady babbling of mostly indiscernible voices save for a word or two now and again. Occasionally, laughter or profanity rose above it all, causing only a few heads to turn.

"What'll it be?" asked the bartender as Kregg stepped up to the bar.

"Beer," replied Kregg.

The bartender drew a beer and set it in front of Kregg. "That'll be a nickel," he said.

Kregg tossed a nickel on the bar without speaking or even looking at the bartender. He then raised the mug and drank about half the beer without stopping. As he took the mug away from his mouth, he exhaled and inhaled noisily in rapid succession like a diver coming up for air might. "Damn, that tasted good," he said to no one in particular. Momentarily, he belched loudly. The miners standing at the bar to either side of Kregg appeared to not notice his indiscretion—or if they did they had the good sense to ignore it. Kregg raised the mug to his lips once again and tilted his head back, finishing off the beer. He did not even set the mug on the bar before gesturing with it to the bartender for another.

In short order the bartender had refilled Kregg's mug and set it in front of him, saying nothing. He stood with both hands on the bar looking at Kregg.

"I suppose you want another damned nickel," said Kregg, half joking.

The bartender was not amused. "That's the price a drinkin', mister," he said flatly.

Kregg gave the bartender a dirty look and tossed another nickel on the bar. He then took a long drink of his beer, and seeing an empty table at the back of the room he started towards it. He hadn't eaten since early this morning and the beer was already giving him a bit of a buzz. But he didn't care—hell, that's why he'd gone into the Gold Strike in the first place.

Kregg had been drinking one beer after another for close to an hour and a half when Sheriff Hollis walked into the saloon. As drunk as he was, Kregg spotted Hollis first. There was that instant surge of drunken courage—something that he'd never been good at controlling. And then it was clear by the shocked expression on Hollis' face that he'd seen Kregg. Hollis started slowly towards Kregg's table, not knowing what kind of reception he would get. As he came next to the table, Kregg looked up at him. His eyes were watery and bloodshot, and his facial muscles lacked the rigor to form much of an expression. "Sit your ass down, Hollis," slurred Kregg. "We need to talk."

Hollis sat down only because he didn't want his voice to project any further into the room than it was already likely to. "Don't say anything," whispered Hollis through clenched teeth. "We'll go someplace else and talk."

"What, so you can back-shoot me, you cheatin' bastard," hissed Kregg.

"Keep your voice down," commanded Hollis. "We can talk but not here."

Kregg paused a moment as if considering his options, and then he leaned toward Hollis. "Alright, we'll do it your way, Hollis, but if you try an' cross me up I'll shoot you deader 'an buffaler shit. And you know I can do it."

Hollis looked Kregg in the eyes. He could tell even beyond the drunken façade that Kregg's anger was genuine; something had set him off. "I'm gonna leave. Wait about five minutes and then come over to my office."

As Hollis walked to his office his anger grew. Buster Kregg showing up in Bear Creek drunk and mad was the last thing that he needed right now. He felt like the proverbial child that despite being warned, goes out onto the frozen pond to play and now the ice has cracked all around him; there are even places of open water. His survival is definitely in question. "Dammit," said Hollis to himself, "I'm too close now to let some lowlife like Buster Kregg screw things up." But what to do? He'd already left two bodies out in Chokecherry Canyon.

Hollis entered the sheriff's office; it was empty as he knew it would be with both his deputies having the night off. He was in a quandary as to how to proceed; he was even undecided as to whether he should remain standing or sit behind his desk. "If this comes down to gunplay," he reasoned, "I'll be at a disadvantage sitting down, but if I'm standing—"

Suddenly the door opened and Kregg walked in, slamming the door behind him. He briefly took in his surroundings and laughed. "This is the first time I ever been in one ah these places and not been in irons of some sort." He laughed again. "Yes siree, it sure helps to be partners with the sheriff," he said in a sarcastic tone.

"Alright, Buster," said Hollis in a deliberately calm voice, "what's this all about?"

"Like you don't know, you lyin' sonovabitch," snapped Kregg.

"I don't. I just heard this afternoon that you boys saw fit to kill Stevenson and all his teamsters."

"That wasn't my doin'," countered Kregg angrily. "Them damned Menagher boys was the ones that done up that little piece ah handiwork. Those dumb shits are outa control."

Not wanting any surprises, Hollis asked: "So where are they now?"

"Hard tellin'," said Kregg in an evasive tone. "When they figure out what I have they'll probably come huntin' your sorry ass."

It was as Hollis had thought: the marshal had been carrying Stevenson's gold. The only question now was, had Kregg and his boys figured that out too? And so Hollis said: "You wanna let me in on this big secret of yours?"

As drunk as he was, or should have been after drinking as much beer as he had, Kregg swayed only slightly from side to side as he looked Hollis hard in the eyes. He was looking for a hint that Hollis was the liar that he suspected him to be. But that evidence was not forthcoming and so Kregg suddenly blurted out: "He didn't have nuthin' but fool's gold. And the Menaghers killed 'em all for it." So that was their plan, said Hollis to himself. Playing along, Hollis did his best to express surprise. "Fool's gold! The hell you say. Woulda been a clever trick had they lived to tell about it."

"Yeah, I reckon that was what they was ah-thinkin' alright," said Kregg in a sinister tone, "but it kinda backfired on'em." He paused and then he smiled in an evil way, looking directly at Hollis. "You woulda thought that as clever as these boys was tryin' to be that they woulda had someone else carry the real gold for 'em. Somebody that wouldn't attract attention..." Kregg paused briefly, and then he said in a louder voice: "...say like a United States marshal."

"Well Buster, I hear what you're saying and you're dead wrong," replied Hollis in a stern voice. "I never saw hide nor hair of that fellar."

"Is that a fact?" said Kregg in a doubting voice.

"It is," said Hollis. "I rode the full length of Chokecherry Canyon and never saw any sign of this guy."

Kregg lowered his hand to where it rested alongside of his pistol. "You're a lyin' bastard."

Hollis opened his mouth to speak but Kregg interrupted him. "Stop, don't say a word unless it's the truth. You tell me one more lie and I swear as sure as there's a sun in the sky I'll kill ya right here and now. So think about it. I'm not shittin' ya in the least. I'll kill ya dead if the words coming from your lips ain't the truth. So, tell me about the marshal."

Hollis' mind was racing. Kregg was drunk but maybe not as drunk as he had thought. There was doubt in his mind. If the beer hadn't slowed Kregg's reflexes, could he beat him? Would Kregg try to kill him anyway once he found out about the gold?

"Let me prime the pump a little bit," said Kregg in an evil tone. "I came down Chokecherry on my way back from Sheep Springs. Turkey vultures make a mess outa a man's face after they peck out his eyes and strip the meat off his cheekbones. Ya can't really tell who a fellar is at that point but ya know, the hell of it is them damned vultures don't much care to eat badges. Like I say, Hollis, nothing but the truth or you're gonna be bleedin' all over your nice clean floor here."

"Alright, Kregg, I killed the marshal," said Hollis, feeling like he was a schoolboy being disciplined. It galled him to tell Kregg what he wanted to know, but to kill him— and he was reasonably certain that he could—right here in his office would raise a lot of suspicion, especially amongst his two deputies. As far as they knew, Kregg was an ally. Obviously, they'd want to know why he had killed Kregg. They knew that he'd gone to kill the marshal but they didn't know about the gold, and supposedly they were to share everything as part of their business arrangement. That damned fool's gold is fouling everything up, said Hollis to himself. Eventually the guys will find out about it and want to know where the real gold went to.

"Ain't you forgettin' something?" said Kregg with a devious look on his face.

Hollis looked intently at Kregg. He didn't have any good choices.

Kregg laughed purposefully, as if to show his bravado. "Thinkin' about it, ain't ya, Sheriff?" he said almost tauntingly.

Hollis stared back at Kregg. He hated him and his sick little cat-and-mouse game that he was playing. There was little doubt in his mind that Kregg intended to try and kill him once he found out where the gold was. "OK," said Hollis bitterly. "I'll cut you in for a fourth. I gotta split with my deputies."

"Bullshit," replied Kregg quickly. "I want half, and if that doesn't suit ya it'd be worth it to me to just shoot your sorry ass right now and walk away with nuthin' but satisfaction."

To hell with it, thought Hollis. Might as well just get this little shindig over with 'cause there's no negotiatin' with this dumb sonovabitch. I woulda gave him a quarter and he coulda rode off into the sunset with money in his pockets, but no sir he's gotta be greedy and dish out all his blow and go at the same time. And so Hollis said: "Alright, Kregg, you win. Half it is but that's a shit pot full a gold for nothing."

Kregg laughed with an arrogant satisfaction. "Well now you know how me and the boys felt ever' time you came around with your hand out wantin' your share for doin' nuthin' but turning your head."

"You keep forgetin', Kregg," said Hollis smugly. "I'm the law and I coulda saw to it that you and your boys did a little jig on the gallows. So you might wanna figure out how much avoidin' that little affair was worth to ya 'fore you go spoutin' off."

Kregg shot Hollis an angry look. "So where's the gold?"

"I buried it a little ways outside of town."

"Well, we got 'bout an hour or so a daylight left today," said Kregg. "Can we get there 'fore dark?"

"I reckon," said Hollis, "if we get started here right shortly."

"I gotta fetch my horse," replied Kregg. "It's over in front of the Gold Strike."

"I don't think it'll do for us to be seen ridin' outa town together," said Hollis. "I'll meet you at the mouth of Spring Creek. It won't take long to get to the gold from there."

Kregg gave Hollis a dirty look. "I'm warning ya, Sheriff. You better be on the up and up here or it's gonna go real bad for ya."

Hollis shot Kregg a look of total indifference. He was fed up with his threats. "I gotta saddle my horse." And with that he turned his back on Kregg and walked towards the back door and the corral behind the sheriff's office.

It was dusk. The sun was but a faint orange glow beyond the western horizon when Hollis arrived at the mouth of Spring Creek. The landscape was enveloped in shadow—nightfall was not far away. Hollis reined his horse in and looked for Kregg. He was nowhere in sight, and the image of Kregg lining up his rifle sights on Hollis' chest flashed through his mind, but then momentarily Kregg stepped out from the aspen trees that lined the creek. "Where to?" he said.

Hollis gestured with his free hand. "Up the creek a ways," he said as he nudged the sides of his horse. Hollis continued on, the rhythmic squeaking of his saddle leather being the most dominant sound in his mind. He was in no mood to listen to any more of Kregg's bullshit. And so on they went, single file in virtual silence, each wondering what the outcome would be once they reached the gold. Day was rapidly giving way to night and each man, deep down, feared that he might not be alive to see the return of the day. But a man had to believe in himself and his abilities, especially men like these, and so each of them was confident that he would see the sunrise. Finally, Hollis turned up a short draw that was crowded with ponderosa pine and dismounted.

"This the spot?" asked Kregg rhetorically.

"Right over yonder," said Hollis, nodding his head towards a small rock outcrop.

Kregg got off his horse. He eyed Hollis suspiciously. "Lead the way," he said.

The adrenalin pulsated through both men, neither trusting the other. Neither wanted to be the one to remove the rocks covering the small opening hiding the gold. There was no trust between the two—not now nor would there ever be. Still, the two of them moved on, side by side, each anticipating the move of the other. And then Hollis saw it—possibly his chance for survival. A small jack pine was directly ahead; it would separate the men for probably two steps—Kregg on one side of the tree, Hollis on the other. And then they were there. Kregg's gun cleared its holster first with Hollis' a split-second later. Kregg's pistol roared, and almost on top of its sound was the blast of Hollis' gun.

There were three echoes as the sound cascaded away from the men further into the mountains and then it was lost. Only Hollis had heard the echoes, but just barely above the pounding of his heart in his ears. He took a couple of deep breaths to calm himself, and then with his pistol still aimed at what he hoped was Kregg's lifeless body, he stepped to the other side of the tree. He'd been lucky: the bullet from his .44 had made its way through the morass of limbs and found its mark in Kregg's heart. Kregg, on the other hand, had not been so lucky. His .36-caliber Navy Colt bullet had entered the trunk of the small tree, and then after penetrating the three to four inches of wood it exhausted its remaining energy when it exited dead center into a branch. An uncontrollable but momentary trembling swept over Hollis' body as the realization of how close he had come to dying registered. It was a reality check: he hadn't been the fastest.

Chapter Twenty

It'd been a chance sighting and just some incredibly bad luck for Ira Moyer as he and Josh walked by the livery on the opposite side of the street at the same time that the Menaghers were there. The Menaghers had decided to not push their luck by staying in Idaho City looking for Ira and possibly run into the deputy marshal that had come to town asking about them. And so there they were quietly saddling their horses inside the livery. In the fading light of day, it made it difficult to see into the shadows of the livery. However, this was not true for the reverse, as the Menaghers had no trouble making out Ira in the better light of the open street. The only question now was what to do about Ira, for he had obviously confided in the law, but as Billy pointed out to Jethro, "It wasn't before a judge and jury." Still, Ira was the only one, now that Jenkins was dead, who could say in a court of law that they'd brought in a lot of fool's gold shortly after the Stevenson party was murdered. If they went before Judge Higgins in Boise, they'd get their necks stretched for sure. And so, keeping his distance, Billy shadowed Josh and Ira to see where it was they were going. As it turned out, it wasn't all that

difficult for Billy to get a fix on Willy's cabin before breaking off and going back to the livery. He was pretty smug
with his sleuthing abilities, and was going on about it to
Jethro, when they heard a commotion at the far end of the
street near the boardinghouse. A dog was barking and there
were several people shouting—some at the dog and others
at apparently someone else. Jethro was certain that he'd
heard the words "get the sheriff" from amongst the garbled
racket. The brothers looked at one another; they knew exactly what the commotion was about. "We best be makin'
tracks," said Jethro.

"I reckon you're right, little brother," replied Billy. And
with that they led their horses to the livery entrance, pausing
as they checked up and down the street for people. There
were some folks out and about, but most of these appeared
to be drifting up the street to see what all the fuss was about.
The livery man, having been paid earlier, had gone for a beer.
But most importantly, there was no sign of any lawmen.
It was getting to be on the dark side of dusk as the brothers casually rode out the south end of town and away from
the excitement to the north. They'd not gotten very far out
of town, however, when Billy reined in his paint horse. He
sighed heavily. "Ya know, little brother, it just ain't sittin' good
with me the fact that we're leavin' that old man in an upright
position when his word could send us to the gallows."

"I don't know, Billy," replied Jethro with concern in his
voice. "I say we just keep on ridin'. Get completely outa this
damned country, Billy. It's gone bad, we're pushin' our luck."

Billy pondered for a moment what Jethro had said.

He appeared to be someplace else in thought, just staring straight ahead. And then he said, without looking at Jethro: "Sometimes a man's just gotta make his own luck."

"Maybe so," replied Jethro, "but I'm thinkin' the deck is stacked against us this time. Ya can't make luck where there's none to be made."

"We'll see," said Billy.

"What are ya fixin' to do, Billy?" asked Jethro nervously.

"I can't let that old man run his mouth to some judge 'bout all the times he seen us in that assayer's office, and especially not about this fool's gold business," said Billy. "Sure, it'll be a risk to get rid of him, but the way I got it figured it'll be a bigger risk not to."

"I don't like it, Billy. This deputy marshal snoopin' around puts a whole different spin on it for me," replied Jethro. The fear was evident in his voice.

"I ain't askin' ya to help," said Billy. "In fact, it'd probably be better if ya rode out tonight and we meet up later. I figure one person can do better at throwin' a person off his trail than two people can."

Jethro remained quiet. In the near darkness Billy couldn't read his body language. He couldn't see the tears forming in his brother's eyes and the anguished look on his face. And then Jethro said: "Billy, I'm done in with this life. It don't set good with me at all anymore."

Billy was taken aback by Jethro's words. "So whaddaya sayin', little brother?"

It was hard for Jethro to say what he knew must come next. They'd been together their entire lives. They'd depended upon one another, especially after their folks had been killed by Indians when they were just kids. Billy, being the older and bigger of the two, had always seemed to be the one who decided where they were going and what they were doing. And for a long time Jethro had looked to his older brother to make these decisions, but now things were different. Now, there just didn't seem to be any common sense in Billy; even more, there wasn't a shred of good in him. He was just plain evil. Jethro took a deep breath to steady his voice before speaking, but it was to no avail. "Billy, I think it's time…"—and then the emotion welling up in his throat forced him to stop.

"Time to what?" asked Billy a little impatiently.

"It's time that we part company, Billy," said Jethro quickly.

"Ya mean for good?" asked Billy with just a hint of sadness in his voice.

Jethro nodded his head and said: "Yeah, I reckon so. I wanna take a new trail in life, Billy, and I just don't see you going there."

Billy felt anger, even betrayal. First it had been Kregg going his own way and now his own brother. Screw'em, he said to himself. Billy laughed. "Little brother, what you don't understand is that you're on the only trail in life that the good folks of this world is gonna let you be on. It's too late for you and me. We done what we done and we are what we are."

"Billy, I ain't ignorin' what we done in the past but I just can't do it anymore. I'm tired ah always having to be lookin' over my shoulder. I wanna settle down and have a family."

"Why sure, Jethro, I can see it now," said Billy in a mocking tone. "You and the missus and a bunch a kids livin' on some patch a dirt somewhere. The missus cookin' and sewin' all day whilst you're out on your dirt patch starin' at the ass end of a mule pullin' a plow. Yes siree, sounds like heaven to me." And then Billy laughed.

Jethro could see that it was pointless to try and explain himself to Billy. It'd taken him a long time to come to this decision—or maybe more correctly, it'd taken a long time for him to be able to ignore the guilt that he felt in abandoning his brother. But Billy had made that possible when he stabbed Harold Jenkins to death behind the boardinghouse. The look in Billy's eyes had scared him—not just because of the pure wickedness that he saw, but because he feared that he might one day become what Billy had. It had become quiet as the two brothers sat there on their horses in the early darkness. The moon was up, a new phase, just a sliver. Down the road to the west lay darkness; in the opposite direction were the lights of Idaho City. Jethro leaned in his saddle towards Billy and extended his hand. "Good luck to ya, Billy."

It didn't seem right to Billy to be shaking hands with his brother but he couldn't fathom exactly why that was, not even as he grasped Jethro's hand. "Hope ya find what it is you're lookin' for," said Billy solemnly.

"Me too," said Jethro.

And then once again silence filled the space between the

two brothers. Both knew that there was nothing that could be said that would change things. Billy's horse snorted and stomped its right front hoof several times. And then from the darkness came a sniffle from the direction of Jethro. "Be seein' ya," he said quietly. And with that Jethro nudged the sides of his horse and headed west into the darkness; Billy, on the other hand, went east towards the lights of Idaho City and some unfinished business with Ira Moyer.

Chapter Twenty-One

As Billy rode along in the dark, he pondered his decision to stay and kill the old man. On the surface it was a cold and callous thing to do, but what choice did he have—run and wait for the day when the law finally caught up to him? He could do like Jethro, he told himself, and hang up his gun to become a farmer. But there'd come a day when his neighbors, the good people, would discover his past, and they'd no doubt be right there in the crowd watching and waiting for him to drop through that trapdoor to hell. "No sir," he whispered defiantly, "when I leave this world it'll be with a gun in my hand."

It was a cloudless night and the sky overhead was filled with stars. They were of some help to Josh as he picked his way through the brush and rocks on the hillside above Willy's house in the early morning darkness. First light was still more than an hour away, but it was Josh's intention to hide himself well before then in a patch of quaking aspen that overlooked Willy's cabin. He wouldn't be more than about a hundred and fifty yards from the cabin, and three to four hundred yards from decent hiding and escape cover to the east. It was here that Josh reasoned a guy would want to hide himself if his intent was to ambush old Ira Moyer as he emerged from Willy's cabin to attend to his morning constitutional at the privy nearby. He knew from having visited the livery man late last night that the men who were likely the ones that had taken the fool's gold to the assayer's office had retrieved their horses and left town. But it made no sense, reasoned Josh, to risk killing Jenkins, whose murder was now common knowledge in town, when Ira could do you about as much harm. And so Josh found himself hidden in a small aspen grove above Willy's cabin, waiting for daylight. It was chilly in the darkness amongst the trees, and it caused him to periodically shiver uncontrollably for a moment and then it would go away. He kicked himself for not having dressed warmer, especially for what he might have to do. It would be even colder at first light, and shivering while trying to make a long shot would not be good. Add to this the fact that he would be shooting with a .50 caliber Sharps rifle that he'd borrowed from Lester and it made for the distinct possibility that if the need arose in about an hour, he could be just punching holes in the air. On the other hand, the guy who'd murdered Harold Jenkins might have lost his nerve. He's gotta know that Ira has probably talked to the law by now, but then again maybe not, thought Josh. With nothing but time on his hands, Josh's mind continued to analyze the possibilities, not the least of which was that no one would try to bushwhack Ira this morning. Josh shook his head. "That'll make me look pretty stupid to the sheriff in town," he whispered aloud. "But, I told 'im this was just a hunch I had." Josh yawned. And still the night dragged on, enveloping Willy's cabin and the town beyond it in silence, save for the occasional dog barking. There were two pale yellow lights visible in the town. Josh stared at the lights and tried to imagine why whoever had lit them had done so at such an early hour. Random images of these people and the room where the light came from flashed through his mind. He was unable to decide who was most likely to be up at this hour. He knew one thing though: it would be warm there. And then Sarah came into his mind; it was inevitable, he supposed, as she filtered in and out of his thoughts most all of the time. He wished that he was with her now, at Lester's, secure in one another's arms instead of here on this cold mountainside, waiting to possibly kill a man.

Finally, the night began to give way to the approaching day. It was before the sun was actually visible above the distant ridge above Willy's, but Josh was sure that he'd seen movement in the trees there. He estimated the range to be about five hundred yards from where he sat. It would be a decent shot from this distance, especially in this light. Josh strained his eyes to see what had moved, but whatever it was had disappeared. Nonetheless, he rested the Sharps rifle over a big downed log and adjusted the sights. The light conditions were still marginal for shooting. And then suddenly, there was a dull glow visible through the south window of Willy's cabin. Josh's heartbeat quickened. He searched even more intently the area where he had seen movement a few minutes before, but there was nothing. Maybe he was mistaken, or maybe it had been a deer or coyote that had moved on. Regardless, Ira and Willy were up; light blue smoke, just a wisp, was drifting up from the stovepipe that protruded from Willy's cabin. There was a gentle breeze from the northeast, causing the smoke to bend over in a loose column pointing southwest. Josh made a mental note of this in the event that he had to shoot. It wasn't a strong wind, but at this range any wind could be a factor. And then the back door to Willy's cabin opened and Ira stepped out. It was the hour of reckoning. Josh hadn't told Ira what he planned to do, that he would be the bait in the trap. Ira started slowly towards the privy, yawning and scratching the back of his head as he went along. He was nearly to the privy when the shot rang out. The bullet spun Ira around, causing him to stumble and fall. Josh quickly shifted his eyes from Ira to the trees beyond the privy, and there it was: a puff of rifle smoke drifting away from a small patch of skunk bush. Josh pointed his rifle towards the brush; as he did, Ira got to his knees, clutching his right arm. And then the rifleman in the brush patch fired again, his shot going astray. Ira was up now and running towards the cabin. Josh took aim to the right of the smoke concentration from the second shot and squeezed the trigger. The .50-caliber Sharps bucked and roared, causing Josh to momentarily lose sight of his target area. But then when he refocused he could see a body sprawled in the dirt slightly downslope from the brush. The big slug had literally hurled the would-be assassin to the side and spun him around. Josh kept his eye on the man for a short time to make sure that he wasn't going to do any more shooting. And then, satisfied that he was dead, Josh got to his feet. He stood for a moment with the Sharps cradled in his arms just staring at the dead man in the distance. The sun was barely peeking over the horizon, and there was a chorus of birds singing all around him to start the new day. Josh hated killing. It would've been a good morning to have a hot cup of coffee while watching the sun come up and listening to birds. But he knew that there'd be none of that pleasantness once he reached the cabin and the dead man beyond it. There'd be blood, anguish, and the finality of it all for the dead man. Josh sighed and started down the hill to Willy's cabin.

The hike down the hill took only a few minutes, and as Josh neared the cabin both Ira and Willy emerged to greet him. Ira was without his shirt. He had a rag tied around the upper part of his right arm, and there was a bloodstain that ran from there all the way down his arm and onto the back of his hand. Much of the blood had dried, but there was still some that oozed from beneath the rag and trickled down for three or four inches, giving that skin a brighter sheen than where the dried blood was. But now, confident that the danger had passed with the apparent death of the shooter up on the ridge, Ira said almost flippantly: "Boy, I'm damned glad you finally got a bead on that sonovabitch. I was beginning to think I was a gonner."

"I'm sorry ya got shot," said Josh soberly. "I just couldn't get on to 'im until he fired."

"Well, I'm much obliged, Deputy," replied Ira respectfully. "You made it so this old man can see another sunrise or two."

Josh nodded his head and then he said: "Ya'll feel good enough to hike up to this dead fellar? I'd like to know if he was one of the Menaghers."

Ira had no desire to look at the dead man, but given the circumstances he figured that it was the least he could do and so he said reluctantly: "Yeah, I reckon I can hobble up there."

It was about three hundred yards to where the body was on the ridge. As they neared the dead man and the immense damage done by the heavy slug from the buffalo gun became apparent, Ira stopped. The dead man had an enormous exit wound on the right side of his torso, and it was clear that he had bled out fairly quickly. Sensing that Ira was no longer close behind him, Josh stopped and turned around. Ira looked pale and was beginning to gag. Suddenly, he turned away from the body and Josh and threw up. He continued to retch until there was nothing left. There was no good way to salvage Ira's dignity except to leave, but Josh had to know if this was one of the Menaghers. "I'm sorry, Ira," said Josh, "but can you tell me if this is one of the guys who came in with the fool's gold?"

Ira was bent over at the waist, resting his hands on his knees. Long stringy spit hung from his mouth. He tried to spit but it wouldn't detach and he found himself sputtering, and so he wiped it away with the back of his bloody hand. And then standing erect, he took a deep breath to calm himself. "That's one a them Menaghers. Don't know which one, though."

"Thanks," said Josh. "Ya'll better head into town. See if

ya can get the doc to take a look at that wound. I'm gonna poke around here a bit."

Ira nodded and started down the hill while Josh turned and continued on up the ridge. It didn't take him long to top out and start down the other side, and there he found what he had been looking for: the dead man's horse. He went straightaway to the saddlebags. There were four bags of what was probably Stevenson's fool's gold. Menagher was no doubt hoping to scam some unsuspecting person with it. Whether or not this had come from the Stevenson party would be easy enough to verify once Josh caught up with the marshal—assuming of course that he was still alive.

Chapter Twenty-Two

The letter had arrived with the mail on the stage yester-day afternoon but wasn't picked up until this morning. It was postmarked Bear Creek and addressed to Sheriff Zeke Willet, Idaho City. There was no return address and no signature. It read:

> The marshal from Boise is dead somewheres in Chokecherry Canyon.
> Sheriff Hollis is the one that kilt him.

The intent of the letter was obvious; the why and who were not. Nonetheless, Sheriff Willet gave the letter credibility, especially in light of the conversation that he had had with the deputy marshal earlier that morning on the ridge overlooking Willy Randolph's place. He knew the deputy was making arrangements for the dead man's burial and disposition of his personal effects, but after that he didn't know. And so he took the letter and went in search of the deputy starting with the undertaker's place. It wasn't far from the sheriff's office to the undertaker's—maybe five minutes walking—but it was sufficient time for the sheriff to consider the ramifications of tangling with Hollis and his deputies. He'd heard rumors of how things were done up in that Bear Creek country and he wanted no part of it. He'd already had two men killed and one wounded in his town in less than twelve hours, and the one thing that they appeared to have in common was the Stevenson party and the marshal—and they, if this letter was true, were all dead. Zeke Willet was not a coward, but he had a pretty wife and two small kids and Chokecherry Canyon was out of his jurisdiction.

Josh had just stepped out of the undertaker's front door when he heard his name being called. "Deputy Morrow, hold up a second." Josh turned around to see the sheriff, a man in his mid-thirties with an average build, approaching at a brisk walk.

"Glad I caught you before you left town," he said, extending the letter. "Got something I think you'll be interested in."

Josh took the letter and read it twice. He said nothing for a moment, as his attention was on the condition of the letter and the envelope that it had come in; they were both creased from being folded in half and the outside of the envelope was soiled. It had smudges of dirt on it. "Did this come this way?" asked Josh, pointing to the dirt on the envelope.

"Yeah, that's the way it was when I picked it up this morning at the post office," replied Willet.

Josh shook his head, a little perplexed. "Looks like whoever wrote this stuck it in his pocket for a while, kinda like he had to think on it before he mailed it."

"Yeah, he wasn't too clean either," said the sheriff.

"Ya'll mind if I hang on to this?" asked Josh.

"Help yourself," replied the sheriff. "You think the marshal is dead?"

Josh sighed. "Well sir, right now it ain't lookin' good for it to turn out otherwise."

"Whaddaya aimin' to do?" asked the sheriff.

Josh couldn't help but smile to himself. There wasn't the slightest hint in the sheriff's demeanor that suggested finding the marshal was his problem, and truth be told, maybe it wasn't. "I guess I'm gonna head for Chokecherry Canyon and see what I can turn up," replied Josh as he put the letter back in its envelope and stuffed it into his shirt pocket.

"Well, good luck to ya," said the sheriff as he extended his hand towards Josh.

Josh shook the sheriff's hand. "Much obliged," he said, and with that he turned and headed for the livery to retrieve Thunder.

Chapter Twenty-Three

Sheep Springs was located in a relatively small basin, about a half-mile wide, along the wagon road to Boise. It owed its name to a cluster of several good-producing springs that originated in a large aspen stand on a north-facing slope. The output from the springs meandered individually down through the trees until due to the topography, they had no choice but to come together and form Sheep Springs Creek. Even then it was just a spit of a creek barely five feet wide but ample enough to water stock or catch a cutthroat trout for supper. Add to this the bluegrass and fescue meadows that occupied much of the basin's floor and Josh could see why it was a favored stop-over place on the road to Boise.

It was early evening as Josh dropped off the ridge on the west side of the basin and started down the road towards the springs. He could see smoke—about the amount you'd expect from a campfire—drifting upwards out of the trees near the creek. However, as yet he could not see any people or horses, but it was suppertime. Maybe I'll have company tonight, he said to himself, or maybe I'll want to ride on. Passing the time of day with a total stranger was one thing, but laying out your bedroll in close proximity to theirs was another. And so it was when Josh rounded a slight curve in the rutted wagon road and came into a small clearing where the campfire was, he saw a solitary man tending a skillet on the fire. The man glanced over at Josh but made no attempt to get up. Josh rode on, and when he had closed the distance between him and the stranger to about thirty feet, he stopped. "Evenin'," said Josh.

The stranger was frying fish and he had just begun to turn them with a fork; some of them were sticking to the bottom of the skillet, and so he said without taking his eyes off of what he was doing: "Step down if you've a mind to."

"Much obliged," replied Josh. Dropping Thunder's reins where he stood, Josh moved towards the fire. He could see that the man carried no sidearm but had a Spencer repeater lying across a pack saddle which was within arm's reach. The man was middle aged, of average build with a red beard and short hair. He had on a wool felt hat that was well worn, having acquired several small tears in it, and his shirt and pants, which also had a few holes, were dirty. From all appearances he was your typical down-on-his-luck prospector.

As Josh got to within a few feet of the fire, the prospector looked up at him. There was an almost instantaneous change in his expression as his eyes settled on Josh's badge. "Have a seat, Deputy," said the stranger.

Josh knelt down near the fire. "Name's Josh Morrow."

The stranger looked up from his skillet of fish. "Jim Holchek's mine."

"Pleased to meet ya," said Josh.

"Do ya like trout?" asked Holchek with the implication that Josh was invited for supper.

"Yes sir, I do," replied Josh. "Ain't nothin' better than fresh-caught trout out of a mountain stream."

"There's some plates and forks in that pannier behind you there," said Holchek. "If you'll dig 'em out we'll give these fish a try. There's another tin cup in there if ya want some coffee or water outa the crik."

Josh retrieved the utensils that Holchek had asked for, and then excusing himself went to the creek for a cup of water. It was only then that he noticed the four new graves. He wasn't a superstitious person, but given a choice he wouldn't necessarily camp this close to four fresh graves; it made him wonder why Holchek had. And so returning to the fire and Holchek he said: "Did ya'll see them fresh graves right over yonder?"

A somber look came over Holchek's face. He was silent for a moment and Josh began to wonder if he'd heard him, but then he said: "Yeah, I did. The second one from the right is my brother, Rudy Holchek."

"Oh, I'm sorry," said Josh.

"It's alright, Deputy," replied Holchek. "I tried to warn Rudy that he was playing with fire but he just wouldn't listen."

"How's that?" asked Josh.

Holchek had an anguished look on his face. Josh could tell that he was conflicted about something. And then feeling guilty for opening such a fresh emotional wound, Josh said: "I didn't mean to pry."

Holchek sighed deeply. "No, all this killin' and robbin' has got to come to an end. My brother's dead now. Ain't nothin' gonna hurt him now. In fact, I think that he'd want me to say something or else he wouldn't have told me what he did."

Josh made eye contact with Holchek but remained silent, waiting for him to speak when he was ready. Holchek looked away and removed the pan with the fish in it from the fire. He stuck a fork in one of the larger trout and set it on one of the plates that Josh had fetched. Handing the plate to Josh, he said: "There's biscuits in that cloth bag on the ground there and blackberry jam and some apples too in the pannier. You're welcome to take what suits ya."

"Much obliged," said Josh, figuring that Holchek would tell him about his brother when he was ready.

And so they ate supper with the more normal mundane conversation about the weather and the quality of the fish interspersed with periods of silence. As trail standards go the meal had been good; Josh was comfortably full. He was mostly at ease with Holchek and so he said: "Ya'll mind if I throw out my bedroll here tonight?"

Holchek was in the process of rolling a Bull Durham cigarette and was just licking the paper to seal it; he paused and lowered the cigarette slightly from his lips. "Help yourself," he said and then resumed sealing his after-supper smoke.

It wasn't until after Josh had tended to Thunder and he and Holchek were sitting next to the fire that Holchek just out of the blue says: "Ya know most people looked at my brother as a fat, sloppy drunk. They was too many folks that disrespected him 'cause a that. But ya know, Deputy, he had feelings. It wasn't right the way folks treated him."

Josh had seen examples of that in the army. Invariably, there always seemed to be one or two guys in the company that because of some physical or personality trait, they became the constant target for harassment from many of the other guys. It never seemed right to him just from the standpoint of human decency, let alone the cohesiveness of the company, but the NCOs or officers never saw fit to correct it—not even after one man who had been the target of harassment had blown his brains out while in a drunken stupor. And still, there were those that were so obtuse to the reality of what had really happened that they had simply laughed and said: "Ole Charlie got drunk one too many times." And so Josh said with some conviction: "People can be pretty mean-spirited sometimes."

Holchek nodded his head. "They damn sure can." He paused and took a drag off his cigarette and then began talking as he exhaled the smoke. "Rudy didn't used to drink the way he did. It wasn't until he got so beat down by folks that he took to drinkin'."

Josh had been listening to Holchek as he fashioned himself a toothpick out of a bluegrass stem. It worked for some of his teeth but not all. "Sounds like your brother was basically a good man, Jim," said Josh.

Anger came to Holchek's eyes. "He was, he was an honest man until that crooked damned Hollis tempted him with some easy money."

"Ya'll talkin' 'bout Sheriff Hollis over at Bear Creek?" asked Josh.

"Yes sir, I am," replied Holchek defiantly. "The sonov-abitch led Rudy astray. Got to 'im after he'd been drinkin'. Paid him to spy on old man Stevenson."

"Well, from what I been hearin' 'bout Hollis that don't surprise me none," said Josh. And then he asked: "Was this just a one-time deal or do ya know?"

Holchek paused as if he was reluctant to speak, but then he said in a subdued tone: "I'm ashamed to admit it, Deputy, but no, it wasn't." Holchek sighed. "Not that it means much now, but Rudy said after this time he was done with Hollis."

The sadness and frustration in Jim Holchek's voice was obvious to Josh, but there was little in the way of consola-tion that he could say to him. The circumstances were what they were, and there was little solace that could be derived from them. Rudy had fallen in with a bad man for money, a feeling of importance, self-esteem—who knows, but it most likely had something to do with acceptance for who he was. It was a gamble that clearly hadn't worked. "Ya know, Jim," began Josh, "it appears to me that Hollis might have double-crossed your brother."

"I know," replied Holchek. "Why kill Rudy unless you don't want him ever tellin' anybody about the sheriff's part in this?"

"That coulda been it," said Josh. "But, tell me, Jim, did Rudy ever say anything about a marshal from over at Boise workin' with Stevenson?"

Jim nodded his head. "Yeah, he did. About all he said, though, was that old man Stevenson was meetin' this marshal out in Chokecherry Canyon, and it appeared to him that he was giving this guy bags of gold. But he said that as far as he knew Stevenson still had the same amount of gold in camp. He said Stevenson always kept his cards pretty close to his chest when it came to matters of gold or money, so he wasn't sure what these meetings with this marshal was all about."

Josh briefly considered telling Jim about the fool's gold but then thought better of it. Playing along, he said: "Yes sir, that is a bit peculiar." Josh paused for a moment as if thinking. "Did Rudy ever say if Hollis said anything about wanting to kill the marshal?"

Jim was fairly quick to shake his head. "No, he never said anything 'bout that."

Josh was surprised by Jim's response. Up until now he was fairly confident that he had discovered the mystery letter writer. He could see no reason why Jim would lie about Hollis killing the marshal. "Well sir, the marshal's overdue down to Boise. That's why I'm up here is to see if I can find 'im."

"What about the guys that killed my brother and the rest of 'em over yonder," said Jim, nodding towards the graves. "Ya lookin' for their killers?"

"Already located a couple of 'em down in Idaho City," said Josh. "Brothers named Menagher. One of 'em skeedaddled, and the other one I reckon by now is planted in the cemetery down there."

"Menaghers," said Jim thoughtfully. "I've heard of those guys before. A fellar pointed 'em out to me in a saloon in Bear Creek one time. They was sittin' at a table with a big guy named Kregg and a mean-lookin' half-breed. I don't remember what his name was but I was advised to steer clear of the whole lot of 'em. Rudy was no match for men like that. He wouldn't have stood a chance, especially if he wasn't expectin' to be killed."

"I suspect you're right," said Josh. "Men like that are unpredictable. They're just plain evil. Sounds like the marshal could have run into a real hornet's nest if he came across that bunch."

"Well, hopefully, if he tangled with them same guys that killed Rudy he fared a little better," said Jim pragmatically. "But ya never know, he could be worm food somewhere."

"Well sir, I'm hopin' to find out one way or another here pretty soon," replied Josh.

"I wish ya luck," said Jim. "But I'm movin' on. Gonna see if I can't find a more regular line a work. I've had enough of scratchin' the dirt lookin' for that big payday, and at the same time lookin' over my shoulder to see if somebody is plottin' to take it from me if I do." Jim paused and then he said sarcastically: "I reckon I'll just leave that dream for someone else." And then he laughed.

The irony of his dead brother having played a small role in causing Jim to abandon his dream was apparently something that he didn't want to recognize.

Chapter Twenty-Four

J osh was up before sunrise the next morning, as was Jim.
They would be headed in opposite directions today—
Jim in search of a livelihood more reliable and safer than
the goldfields, and Josh seeking justice for what seemed to
be a growing list of victims. For Jim it would be a dream
abandoned; for Josh it would be a dream interrupted by the
lawlessness of the goldfields and a commitment to a friend.

It was midmorning when Josh reached the head of
Chokecherry Canyon. He was at the beginning of the
switchbacks that zigzagged down the face of the mountain
to the bottom of the canyon. From this vantage point he
could see a long ways. In the distance, almost to the point
that he couldn't make them out, were two large birds circling in the sky. He assumed that they were probably turkey
vultures, which suggested there might be something dead
or about to die on the ground below them. Josh nudged
Thunder and they began the descent down the switchbacks
into the canyon. As he rode along Josh reflected on what it
was he was trying to do. Essentially, he was going to Bear
Creek to do what, confront the sheriff? He had no solid
proof that Hollis had done anything wrong other than what

Jim Holchek had told him and an anonymous letter. And besides that, if he tried to arrest Hollis it would be him against not only Hollis but his deputies as well. As far as he knew there wouldn't be anyone to back his play. Josh shook his head slightly and laughed. "What the heck am I gettin' myself into?" he said aloud. "Ever since I came to this country my life has been turned upside down."

It was about half an hour before Josh was close enough to the circling vultures that he could see a way to get through the trees beneath the birds. A fairly well-defined game trail, which intersected the main path that he was on, headed in that direction. Within a few minutes he could see a small clearing through the trees up ahead. There was movement there, ravens for sure…and then he saw it: a large black bear. It appeared to be feeding on a dead animal. Thunder became a little skittish at the sight of the bear so Josh reined him to a stop. "Hey, bear," yelled Josh as loudly as he could. The bear stood on its hind legs to see better, and then recognizing potential danger he turned and ran in the opposite direction. Josh gave the bear a minute or so to leave the area before riding on into the clearing. He was still a hundred feet or so from the dead animal when he suddenly realized what it was that he was looking at.

A helpless, angry feeling came over him: it was the marshal's gray horse. Josh rode closer before dismounting. A good number of opportunistic feeders had been working on the horse, but one thing that was still discernable was a bullet hole in its head. It appeared to Josh that someone had led it off of the main trail up this draw to a more secluded place and killed it so hopefully anyone looking for the marshal wouldn't see his horse wandering loose in Chokecherry Canyon. As far as Josh was concerned it was a despicable thing to do. The bear, ravens, coyotes, and undoubtedly the turkey vultures had all been there feeding on the remains of the horse. Josh circled the carcass slowly, looking for any possible clues as to who might have killed the horse. The stench in the hot sun was overwhelming, causing him to widen his orbit of the dead horse and at times even hold his breath. And then he spotted the partial outline of something lying in the tall grass beneath the aspen trees outside of the clearing. Quickly, Josh walked towards the object to investigate. As he neared it he could see that it was a saddle—most likely from the marshal's horse. Josh knelt and pulled the saddle around to where he could see the back of the cantle; there, stamped into the leather, were the marshal's initials: CJ for Caleb Johnson. The saddle, bridle, saddle blanket, even the saddlebags with nothing apparently taken, were all there. But then as Josh struggled to re-create the image of the marshal and his horse that day he met him on the road, it came to him—just a flash at first, but then it came and stuck in his mind. The marshal had been carrying a Sharps repeater in a saddle scabbard. Both the rifle and scabbard were missing. The scabbard had been nothing special, but the rifle had a light, honey-colored stock that had a deep scratch on the left side, beginning at the cheek piece and extending towards the butt of the stock for eight or nine inches. The image of the gun had stayed in Josh's mind as he had never seen a stock that color before.

After thoroughly searching the area surrounding the dead horse and finding nothing more, Josh decided to move on. He reasoned that it was a safe bet that the marshal was, as the anonymous letter had said, dead somewhere in Chokecherry Canyon. He needed to get word to Judge Higgins confirming that the marshal had likely been murdered. Who knows, thought Josh, maybe he'll send me some help to deal with Hollis and his deputies. There was no telegraph to Bear Creek, only the mail which went on the stage twice a week, so even if the judge could send someone it'd be a while before they came.

It was early evening when Josh rode into Bear Creek. He knew that Hollis wouldn't be happy to see him, but he was not certain what kind of a reception he would get— especially if he were to probe the sheriff about the marshal. One thing he knew for sure was that he wasn't going to be leaving Bear Creek this time under the same circumstances that he had the last time he was here. He was a deputy marshal and Hollis needed to respect that fact. And so Josh rode first to the livery and secured lodging for Thunder, and then on to the hotel where he got a room and then on to the café. He made no attempt to hide the fact that he was in town, and so he figured it wouldn't be long before Hollis would come looking for him.

Josh took a seat at a table on the far side of the café, where he could see both the front and back doors and have his back facing the wall. He'd barely sat down when the motherly-looking woman who ran the place emerged from the kitchen. Josh could tell by the look in her eyes that she remembered him, and then, as had others in town that he had encountered since arriving, she did a double take when she noticed his badge.

"Well, young man, I see you've added some decorations to the front of your shirt since the last time I saw you," said the woman with a smile.

Josh laughed. "Yes ma'am, I figured I better have the law on my side if I ever came back here again."

The woman laughed briefly and then she became more serious. "Where's your little sidekick?"

Josh knew right away that the waitress was referring to Sarah. His assessment of her was that she was a kind woman and that she'd inquired about Sarah not to have the latest gossip but because she just cared about people. And so Josh was straight up with her: "Sarah's stayin' with a friend up Porcupine Creek till I get some things settled."

The waitress stepped closer to Josh's table. There was a look of concern on her face as she leaned forward towards him. "Just so ya know, there's some fellar in town claiming that you murdered his partner and stole their gold. The sheriff and his deputies been going 'round like little banty roosters crowin' about how they're gonna get you."

The waitress' words were truly a surprise to Josh. He didn't think Edgar, a man who'd abandoned his partner in a gunfight, had the nerve to go to the sheriff and tell him such a lie. Josh knew how Leroy died was of no concern to the sheriff, but what had happened to the gold that Leroy and Edgar had stolen from Seth was, and now Edgar had apparently convinced him that Josh had taken it. Josh had the feeling that he'd just stepped into quicksand, but short of turning tail and running there was little he could do but play the cards he was dealt, and so he said: "I appreciate the heads-up, ma'am."

A feisty look came to the woman's eyes. "It's the least I can do. The way I see it anything that comes out of either Hollis' or his cronies' mouths has a pretty good chance of being a lie. By the way my name is Mabel, Mabel Oakley. Some folks just call me Ma, though. Whichever one of those works for you works for me."

Josh managed a smile for his new friend. "My name's Josh Morrow. Pleased to make your acquaintance, Ma."

The woman seemed flattered that Josh had chosen to address her in a more familiar manner. "If ya don't mind me askin'," said Ma, "what is it you aim to do here in Bear Creek?"

Josh was about to answer when the front door opened suddenly. There stood Hollis, gun drawn and flanked by one of his deputies, who had his pistol drawn as well. No sooner had this registered with Josh and the back door to the café opened. Hollis' other deputy stepped inside. He had a double-barreled shotgun leveled at Josh; both of the hammers were cocked. It was the smaller, more sinister of the two deputies. He had an evil, hateful smile on his face. His body language radiated an urgent desire to pull the triggers on the scattergun. It was almost like he was a bloodhound straining against his leash, and the only thing stopping him were multiple witnesses in the café. Josh kept his hands on the table. "Ma, ya'll better step to the side but do it slow-like. Appears these boys has got themselves all worked up."

Ma did as Josh asked, leaving a clearer path should either Hollis or his deputies decide to just shoot Josh where he sat. She had no sooner done this than Hollis, moving slowly towards Josh with his pistol aimed at his chest, said: "Well, lookie here if it ain't our Texas boy back again. I see what I heard about you masqueradin' as a deputy U.S. marshal is a fact."

"It ain't no masquerade, Hollis," said Josh angrily. "You and your boys best put them guns down 'fore ya'll get yourselves in any more trouble than you already are."

Hollis and his deputies laughed. It was a nervous, manufactured laugh owing to the tension and danger in the air. "How 'bout we do this?" said Hollis sarcastically. He paused and laughed again, and then said, mocking Josh's Texas accent, "Why don't ya'll just stand up real slow-like and with your left hand put your pistol on the table and then step back."

Josh studied Hollis' face for a moment. He was taking pleasure from this. There was nothing that he could do. They had him cold and they were just looking for the slightest provocation so they could gun him down. Nonetheless, Josh remained seated. It would take some real moxie or stupidity to gun him down in front of the other café patrons. And so he said: "What's this little charade all about anyway?"

"Murder and robbery," replied Hollis smugly. "Ya got away with goadin' that big dumb Swede into a fight and killin' him, but this time it's different. I got an eyewitness that says you just plain executed his partner."

Josh knew exactly what Hollis was talking about. It was his turn to laugh. "You're a prize, Hollis," said Josh angrily. "I'm doing your job by tryin' to arrest the guy who bushwhacked Seth Jacobs and jumped his claim. I tried to get him to come along peaceably but he came at me with his gun a-blazin'. He didn't give me any choice. You've got some nerve."

"We're done talkin' here," snapped Hollis. "Now take out your gun and lay it on the table like I already asked you to. You best do it before I shoot you for resisting arrest."

Josh could see the fear in the faces of the other patrons and even Ma, as feisty as she was. There was no point in arguing anymore with Hollis—to do so would mean certain death for him, but also the possibility that an innocent bystander could get killed as well. And so reluctantly, Josh slowly removed his pistol from its holster and placed it on the table; as he did he said: "You know, Hollis, the word's out on you. You're a crooked sonovabitch and that fact is known in high places in Boise. Your days are numbered."

"Shut your lyin' mouth, you whore-lovin' reb," snarled Hollis as he maneuvered behind Josh. "Keep your pistol on 'im," said Hollis to the chubby deputy that had come in the front door with him. "OK, Tex, now real slow-like put one hand at a time behind your back. Got a matching set of bracelets for ya'll to wear."

Seeing that Josh was going to be compliant, Hollis holstered his pistol and began putting the manacles on him. "Ya know, Hollis," began Josh. "There's too many good people around here to let ya'll get away with what you're doing. There's gonna come a time when they'll have had a gut-full of your evil corruption and just do away with ya."

Hollis knew what Josh had said was true; he feared that day was close at hand, but he laughed in an attempt to feign a bravado that he was having difficulty maintaining. With the manacles securely on, Hollis grabbed the now defenseless Josh and jerked him in the direction of the door. "Let's go, Tex, I gotta room waitin' for ya'll."

There had been enough people see Hollis and his deputies go into the Blue Bird Café with their guns drawn that a small crowd had now gathered outside. As Hollis and his deputies emerged with Josh, the speculative buzz of the crowd went silent. There were no shouts of outrage. No one was questioning the fact that Hollis was arresting a deputy United States marshal. They parted and made way for the sheriff as if they were a bunch of sheep and the sheriff was that mean sheep dog that they feared. It was what Josh had hoped would not happen—that the people would be intimidated and that they would say or do nothing. And then it was as if he had lost control of his thoughts and he blurted out: "Hollis is corrupt. How long are you going—" Suddenly, his head was jolted violently. There were flashes of light and then came the pain. And then through this rapid onset of pain and confusion, he became aware that he was no longer standing. Slowly it came to him that he was laying on his side. His senses recovered gradually—first the dirt in his mouth and then the dampness of the blood in his scalp, and finally he could hear Hollis shouting at him. "Get your sorry ass up and if you know what's good for ya, you'll keep your mouth shut."

With his hands behind his back, Josh struggled to get to his feet. He was dizzy and his head throbbed terribly. All eyes were on him to see if he could get up on his own, but not a word from the crowd. This was a fact not lost on Hollis or his deputies. The crowd's reaction, or lack of, had restored a feeling of security in Hollis—at least for the moment anyway. Finally, Josh regained his feet. He was wobbly but standing. "Let's go, Tex," said Hollis impatiently. "I reckon you know the way."

And so Josh staggered down the main street of Bear Creek flanked by the sheriff and his deputies. People on the street stopped to stare, and those inside hearing of the procession came out to gawk as well. There was finger pointing and cringes from those on the side of the street favored with a view of the blood on the right side of Josh's face. While on the ground the dried horse manure and dirt in front of the Blue Bird had adhered to the blood, making it look worse than it was. Finally, after what seemed like an eternity to Josh, the shameful little parade ended at the jail. The manacles were removed and he was shoved into the one and only cell. Josh collapsed on the bed; the pain in his head was excruciating. He closed his eyes tightly and clenched his teeth in an effort to ward it off, but it did little good. And then, as if things couldn't get any worse, Hollis said: "Tex, I wanna know what you did with the gold that you stole from Leroy and Edgar. And I'm ah-tellin' ya right now I ain't a patient man, so you best be tellin' me here pretty damned quick what you did with it."

Josh managed to sit up on the bed. "You're an idiot, Hollis," said Josh with as much anger in his voice as he could muster. "I ain't got any gold. You need to be talkin' to your friend Edgar about that. He's double-crossing you and your deputies kinda the same way you're doing them with the gold that ya'll stole from Marshal Johnson. I got a letter right here in my pocket that says you killed the marshal out in Chokecherry Canyon."

"You're full of shit," snapped Hollis. "That marshal didn't have no gold with 'im."

Josh could see the doubt and the early beginnings of anger in the deputies' eyes. "You're a liar, Hollis," replied Josh. "That was the plan all along, that the marshal would carry the real gold for Stevenson and Stevenson would re-place it with fool's gold. Your boys robbed the wrong man but you didn't."

"Alright, Hollis," said the smaller, more hotheaded deputy. "I'm not likin' what I'm hearing. What's the real story here?"

In between the throbs of pain, Josh was taking some satisfaction in seeing the focus shift to Hollis. Maybe, thought Josh, Hollis will turn out to be so rotten and cor-rupt that his own men will do him in. However, it soon became evident that this wasn't going to be the case. Hollis could see that he'd been discovered and lying would only cause more anger and doubt.

"OK, Jake," said Hollis reluctantly to the smaller deputy, and then with some defiance in his voice he continued. "Yeah, the marshal had some gold with him."

"How much?" interrupted Jake.

"I don't know, a lot," said Hollis. "But here's the deal. I know we said that we'd split everything that came our way, but it was me that had to kill a United States marshal to get this, not you guys. I'm the one that'll swing for this. And besides that, Buster Kregg figured out what went on here and he tried to kill me for this gold. So, I figured since I was taking all of the risk, that all of the gold should be mine."

Jake was not impressed. "Sorry, Hollis, but it don't work that way. We had an agreement, so unless you divvy up with me an' Eddy you could find yourself on the wrong side of the dirt come mornin'."

"Just remember, Jake," countered Hollis quickly, "you don't know where the gold is at."

"Well, I'm thinkin' that you're gonna take me there right quick," replied Jake in a threatening tone.

"Be dark 'fore we get there," said Hollis. "It'll have to wait 'til mornin'."

Jake pondered this for a moment. It was nearly dark and not knowing where the gold was at, he had little choice but to do the things the sheriff's way. Jake sighed heavily. "Alright, Hollis, we'll go in the morning. But I promise you, if you try and cross me in any way, you'll be sorry. Just remember, I know where that pretty wife of yours lives."

"Don't push your luck, Jake," snarled Hollis.

Jake flashed a devilish smile, but then his expression changed to one of mutual concern. He nodded towards the jail cell and Josh. "What are we gonna do with him?"

Hollis was quiet for a moment and then he said: "After we get back tomorrow we'll see if we can't persuade him to be a little more talkative about the gold he stole. How bad he hurts will be up to him, but if he thinks he's hurtin' now, that ain't nothin' compared to what it could be. Today was just a little warm-up, but I'm thinkin' we'll get him and Edgar in the same room and we'll see who's tellin' tall tales." And then Hollis laughed.

Jake turned to face the cell where Josh sat on the bed. There was no sign of compassion or doubt of any kind in his expression. "You know, we could do him like he done that poor ole Leroy fellar. An eye for an eye and a tooth for a tooth, huh? Yes sir, we could save the court the trouble of havin' to try this scoundrel and just dispense some justice our own damned selves." And then he laughed in a demented sort of way, but stopped abruptly as if he were once again considering the brilliance of Hollis' plan. "Yes sir," he said as he slapped his leg gleefully, "it'd be cheap justice at that." And then he laughed again.

"First things first," said Hollis.

Josh closed his eyes and lay back on the bed. It was pointless to argue with these men. Jake's moral depravity was the equal of Hollis', and Eddy, the big pudgy deputy, seemed oblivious to the caliber of men that he had aligned himself with.

"Alright then," said Jake in a tone that suggested he had usurped control of the situation from the sheriff. "We leave at first light. Thataway most of these pilgrims here in town won't be any wiser that we're gone, just in case some of 'em get the urge to break the deputy out."

Hollis had a stern if not angry look on his face. "First light it is, Jake, but just remember who's in charge here."

Jake looked at Hollis contemptuously. It was obvious that he was having to restrain himself when he said simply: "Sure, Sheriff."

And then Eddy, who had been left out of the discussion as he so often was, said with a twinge of resentment in his voice: "What about me?"

"You," said Hollis, quickly reassuming his leadership role, "will be guarding the prisoner tonight."

"Well, okay, Sheriff," he said in an almost whiny voice, "but I ain't had no supper."

Hollis sighed and then said: "Alright, I'll swing by the Bluebird on my way home and ask Mabel to fix you a plate and bring it over."

"Much obliged, Sheriff," replied Eddy.

"Not a problem, Eddy," said Hollis, "but just you re-member, I'm countin' on you to hold down the fort here."

"You can count on me," replied the pudgy deputy.

"I am," said Hollis in a serious tone. "I mean it ain't like anybody in this town gives two pinches a owl shit about this guy anyway, but ya never know."

It had been close to an hour since Hollis and Jake had left when there came a knock on the front door of the jail.

Eddy, who had been reading a dime novel with his feet propped up on the sheriff's desk, swung his feet to the floor and went to see who it was. There was an assortment of good smells coming from the other side of the door, but heeding the sheriff's admonishment he looked through the window to the side of the door before opening it.

"Hi Eddy," said Mabel cheerfully. "The sheriff said you was gettin' a mite gant over here."

"Yes ma'am, that'd be a fact," replied Eddy as he stepped to the side so Mabel could bring the tray of food in.

Mabel walked to the sheriff's desk and set the tray down. "I asked the sheriff if he wanted me to fix a plate for your prisoner but he was dead set against it so I didn't," said Mabel as she looked at Josh.

"Well, he's the boss," said Eddy casually as he sat down and began to cut into the steak on his plate. "You don't want to get crosswise with him."

"Oh, I know," replied Mabel. "I saw his mean side with this poor fellar ya got locked up in here, and I don't want any part of that. These old bones of mine break a lot easier than they mend."

Eddy slurped up a big mouthful of the hot coffee that Mabel had brought and then went back to eating.

"How's the coffee?" asked Mabel.

"Good," said Eddy.

"I'm glad you like it. I was afraid that I'd made it too strong," replied Mabel.

"Nope, just right," said Eddy as he slurped up another mouthful.

"Well, okay then, Eddy," replied Mabel as she turned to leave. "If you'll just leave the front door unlocked I'll drop back by in a little bit and pick up the dirty dishes. Maybe bring you a second piece of that apple cobbler."

"Oh, yes ma'am, that would be grand," replied Eddy in between bites of steak and potato.

And with that Mabel started for the door. "I'll see you in a little while, Eddy. Remember to save some space for that second piece of cobbler." And then she quickly added: "Don't bother getting up, Eddy. I'll let myself out."

Eddy's mouth was full and he mumbled something that was indiscernible to both Mabel and Josh. He swallowed, partially clearing his mouth, and then he had some coffee, drinking more liberally this time in an effort to clear his throat. He set the cup down and yawned heavily. "Oh man, gonna be a long night," he said quietly to himself. And then he took a few more bites of his food but paused again to have some more coffee, thinking the caffeine would help keep him awake. He finished that cup and was struggling to cut another bite of steak when the room began to spin. Eddy knew something was wrong. He attempted to push back from the desk and stand, but it was to no avail as he tumbled out of his chair onto the floor.

Josh had been lying quietly, watching the progression in Eddy's behavior, and now opportunity appeared to be knocking but he was helpless to take advantage of it. He stood and went to the cell door. He could see the keys lying on the corner of the sheriff's desk, but from where he was at they might as well have been hanging on Hollis' belt.

If only Ma would come back, maybe she would help him. Josh looked at Eddy; he was deathly still, but for how long? And then Josh caught his breath. There was someone at the front door. "Oh please God," he said to himself, "not Hollis." From where he was at he couldn't see the front door, but he heard its distinctive squeak as it opened and then quietly closed. Suddenly, as if she was an apparition, there stood Ma. She quickly assessed the situation and grabbed the keys off of the desk.

An overwhelming sense of relief swept over Josh. "I guess I don't need to tell you how glad I am to see you," he said.

"Laudanum works wonders," said Ma with a chuckle as she inserted the key into the cell door.

Josh gave Ma a sly but painful grin. "I kinda figured something was up with Eddy's supper when he was having trouble staying awake, but he wasn't about to quit eatin'."

Ma laughed. "No sir, that's Eddy alright. He'll probably be sleepin' for most of the night but you better skedaddle. The livery man's got your horse saddled and ready for you. You can trust him and probably a lot of other folks here that have had their fill of Hollis."

Josh stepped out of the cell and started across the room to a shelf where his gun belt was located. He moved gingerly, almost staggering at times; once there he had difficulty strapping his gun on.

Until then, Ma hadn't realized the seriousness of Josh's injury. "Are you sure you can ride?" she asked with concern in her voice.

Josh grimaced as a wave of pain and dizziness came over him. "To be right honest, Ma, I'm havin' a little trouble gettin' my legs and eyes to work the way they're supposed to."

"Maybe it'd be best if I just hid you out here until you get your wits about you," said Ma.

"No, Ma," replied Josh, "you've done enough already. Besides, if Hollis can't find me here he'll go where he figures I'll be, and that's where Sarah is at. I'm thinkin' he might threaten to kill her if I don't tell him where this gold is that he thinks I have." Josh paused as another surge of dizziness and nausea hit him, causing him to grab hold of the corner of Hollis' desk to steady himself. "I got no choice, Ma. But I'll be alright if I can get to my horse—he'll get me there."

Ma shook her head and heaved a sigh filled with doubt. "Well, boy, I don't see how you're gonna do this, but if you're so all-fired dug in on the idea I hope you'll at least let me help you get down to the livery."

Josh managed a weak smile. "I'd be much obliged."

And with that Josh and Ma exited the back of the sheriff's office. Josh towered over Ma, but with his left arm resting across her shoulders, it was just enough to help him keep his balance. They kept to the trees and brush behind the houses along the main street of Bear Creek. It was slow going but eventually they reached the livery. The smithy had Thunder saddled and ready to go.

"Thanks, Ma," said Josh as he stood next to Thunder. "I don't know if I can ever repay you for this. You saved my life."

"Ah fiddlesticks, you best get outa here."

"What about you?" asked Josh with concern in his voice. "Ain't you afraid Hollis will come after you?"

"I'm thinkin' he's gonna be more concerned with nailin' your hide to the barn door than roughin' up an old lady," replied Ma.

"I hope you're right," said Josh, and with that he bent down and gave Ma a kiss on the cheek.

Ma blushed. "You better get going."

Josh pulled himself up onto Thunder. The walk from the jail to the livery had actually seemed to help his equilibrium some, but he was by no means back to normal. Once in the saddle, he paused momentarily to assess how he felt. It wasn't good but it'd have to do. Turning his upper body slightly, he looked down at Ma standing in the shadows of the lantern light coming from the big open doors of the livery. Josh raised his right hand in a gentle wave good-bye and then set out for Lester's.

Chapter Twenty-Five

It was the beginning of the moon's phases—not much more than a sliver of light—but the night sky was cloudless and the stars which seemed to go on forever were doing their best to make up for the moon's shortcomings. Nonetheless Josh took his time, allowing Thunder to go at his own pace and hopefully avoid stepping in a badger or ground squirrel's hole as they skirted around the town in the hills surrounding it. Thunder had been Josh's horse the entire time that he'd been in the cavalry. They'd been through a lot together and the bond between them was strong. It'd been a stroke of luck that shortly before his discharge, the Army had deemed Thunder too old to be of further service and put him up for sale. Josh, of course, was at the auction and paid nearly two month's wages for him. And so it was, on this mostly dark night, Josh was looking out for the both of them.

Josh's head still ached terribly, but the wound caused by Hollis clubbing him with his pistol barrel had stopped bleeding. He supposed that he could take some comfort in this, but it was still going to be a long ride to Lester's place. Under other circumstances, it might have been almost pleasant riding at a leisurely pace with the stars overhead. For a time he fantasized about Sarah being there to share the experience with him and more, but all too soon that was ruined by the recurring pain in his head. The night wore on and the travel had become easier once he had intercepted the road going south. He had mixed feelings about the darkness. It required him to go slower, but at the same time he questioned whether he could stand the additional stabs of pain in his head that the jostling of riding at a quicker pace would cause. On the other hand, the darkness was his friend, allowing him to travel covertly.

The night had finally given way as Josh started down the ridge above Lester's cabin. There was no sun yet and the light was poor, but Josh could see an unorganized column of blue smoke gently surging from Lester's stovepipe. There would be hot coffee soon and maybe bacon and eggs. He could taste it now. It would be good to see Lester and Rufus and Sarah—especially Sarah. As odd as it may sound he liked the way she looked early in the morning in her men's pants and shirt and her hair in somewhat disarray. It gave her a look of innocence. He had missed her—more than he'd realized until just now.

The solitude of the birds singing was disrupted by Rufus barking wildly as Josh neared the cabin. Lester was the first to emerge with rifle in hand. He was followed by Sarah. And even though Josh was still about fifty yards away, the expressions of happiness and relief on Lester and Sarah's faces were gradually being replaced by concern. Josh wasn't wearing a hat as he usually did, and there was something about the way that he was sitting in his saddle that just didn't seem quite right. And then Sarah saw it: the caked blood and dirt on the side of Josh's head. Instantly, she began to run towards him. Josh reined Thunder in and dismounted as he turned to look down the road as a somewhat out-of-breath Sarah stood before him. Her eyes and her body language were desperate to touch him, to put her arms around him, but she respected the barrier that Josh had seemingly insisted upon before he had left. "Oh Josh, you're hurt bad," said Sarah in an almost sobbing voice. "What happened to you?"

"Had a run-in with the law in Bear Creek," replied Josh humbly.

"That damned Hollis did this to you?" said Sarah angrily.

Josh smiled weakly. He'd never heard Sarah swear before. "Hollis' day is coming." And then seeing Lester and Rufus come up behind Sarah, Josh said: "Morning." Reaching down he rubbed Rufus' head, who had come up alongside of him. "Hey, Rufus dog. How are you?" Josh had missed the three of them; they were like family to him.

"Boy, you look like crap but I'm guessin' you already know that," said Lester lightheartedly.

Josh managed a laugh. "Yeah, I kinda figured I wasn't lookin' my best today."

"Well come on down to the cabin," replied Lester. "We'll get ya cleaned up 'fore breakfast," he added, knowing that Sarah would be the one in charge of that.

"Much obliged," said Josh.

"It's just good to have ya back," replied Lester.

"Yeah, we missed you," added Sarah.

"Well, I'm thinkin' I can't stay long," said Josh with some hesitation in his voice.

"What?" said Sarah almost immediately. "Why not?"

Josh sighed and then he said sarcastically: "I expect as soon as Hollis and his chief deputy retrieve this gold that Hollis stole they're gonna come huntin' for me. I don't wanna bring that pack a varmints down on you guys. They're my problem."

"Boy, that knock on the head has affected your memory," said Lester in his usual gravelly voice. "You done forgot what friends are for. If that bunch a riffraff comes up here we'll all deal with'em."

"I can't ask ya'll to do that," replied Josh, "especially with Sarah here."

Sarah was quick to jump in: "Don't you worry about me. I can take care of myself."

"How 'bout we do this," said Lester calmly. "We'll clean up your wound, Josh, and have a little breakfast and you can get a little shut-eye and then we'll talk."

Josh was too overwhelmed by the pain, fatigue, and hunger that he was feeling to argue with Lester's logic, and so he said: "Alright, you win."

"Good," said Lester, "now why don't you let me tend to Thunder and Sarah can tend to you. I'll be along in a little while."

Just being back at Lester's place seemed to ease Josh's pain. It was peaceful there amongst the big ponderosa pines; there was a wholesomeness to it that Josh never felt in any town. And truth be told, there had been a restlessness within him while he had been gone; it was especially bad when he allowed his mind to dwell on Sarah for too long.

As they entered the cabin Sarah pulled a chair out from the table. "Sit yourself down and I'll see what I can do to clean up that wound."

Josh did as Sarah had asked without a word of protest or false stoicism or macho nonsense. He was anticipating her touch and the feeling that it gave him. Already, he had the beginnings of some goose bumps and his heart was beating a little faster.

There were two coffeepots on the stove; one much bigger than the other contained water for washing the breakfast dishes, and the other coffee; neither had come to a boil yet but that was okay. They were humming along in a halting staccato, endlessly trying to gain momentum. There was steam coming from their spouts—steady but not forceful. Sarah poured some of the hot water in a porcelain washbasin and immersed a rag that was normally used for washing the dishes in the water. She wrung it out and began to gently wipe away the dried blood on Josh's head. Josh grimaced and recoiled slightly as she attempted to clean the wound itself. "Sorry," said Sarah as she looked intently at the wound in the poor light of the cabin.

"It's okay," said Josh. "I appreciate your doing this."

"Well, I don't know about you, Mr. Morrow," said Sarah in a teasing tone. "This is the second time I've had to patch you up. What would you do if you didn't have me around to take care of your bullet wounds and knocks on the head?"

Josh paused before responding to Sarah's playful inquiry. He knew what he felt and what he wanted to say, but verbalizing it wasn't that easy. The chasm of silence was widening between them. It was nearing the point of social uneasiness when Josh finally said: "Hopefully, I'll never have to find out."

Sarah's immediate reaction was one of joy that Josh didn't want to be without her, but then almost as quickly she thought, maybe he's hoping that he never gets shot or hit in the head again. And so she continued to work at removing the dried blood, dirt, and horse manure from his scalp and face. However, momentarily she saw Josh's left hand slowly come up and grasp her hand with the rag in it. He lowered her hand and looked her in the eyes. "What I meant to say was, I can't imagine being without you."

Sarah's eyes began to well up with tears. She'd been hoping to hear these words or something similar for some time, but she'd pretty much given up on that ever happening because of her past. But now that she had she was uncertain as to how to respond. The stigma of having been a whore had left her doubting her self-worth not just as a person but as a lady. She felt as if everything that she said or did now was subject to being judged by others. But then it became a moot point as Josh gently sat her down on his lap and kissed her softly. And then he said: "There'll come a day, not long from now I hope, when we'll be shed of this country and all of this stuff will be just a bad dream."

Sarah wiped away some of the tears that had now run down onto her cheeks with the back of her hand. "I hope you're right, Josh. This country is just so wicked. I sometimes think we won't survive it."

Josh sighed. He often wondered the same thing but he said: "Better days is comin'. Ya'll just gotta believe in that." And then he kissed Sarah again. It felt better than he ever imagined it would, and that was good, he reckoned, as there'd be no turning back with her now—not without a lot of hurt.

After breakfast, Lester and Sarah convinced Josh to lie down on Lester's bed and get some sleep. His head still throbbed unmercifully, but maybe a little less so than before he had gotten there. Once he was lying on the bed, Josh could feel the fatigue and stress flow from his body. Sleep quickly overtook him, and it wasn't until late afternoon that he got free of its grasp. He'd slept hard. Lester and Sarah had gone on about their day, checking periodically on the slumbering Josh. They'd worked the sluice box together until about four o'clock, when Lester suggested Sarah try her luck at catching some fish for supper. There was a decent-sized beaver dam up the creek a ways that never failed to surrender a few trout, and so Sarah set out with Rufus for the pond created by the beavers. She had her willow pole, an extra hook, and a shovel for digging worms. It was a warm, sunny day and her spirits were high—not at the prospect of catching fish but rather her future with Josh. Except for the occasional raspy calls of a couple of ravens circling overhead and the high-pitched chatter of a pine squirrel in a big Douglas fir tree behind her, it was a quiet setting. And then it happened—the tranquility was broken by the loud report of a rifle. It had come from down by the cabin. Sarah pulled her line out of the water. Her heart was out of control. She'd been expecting something like this to happen but she had tried to bury it in the back of her mind, hoping that it wouldn't. She had no weapon, but nonetheless she started towards the cabin and the men who had given her respect and a new life. She'd taken only a few steps when there came another single gunshot and then in rapid succession another four or five shots. And then silence. Sarah paused to listen. She could hear shouting but she couldn't make out what was being said. And so she went on cautiously paralleling the creek in the aspen and intermittent pine trees, uncertain but fearful of what awaited her at the cabin. She was near the icehouse when she heard a voice that she thought was Hollis' shout: "Eddy's dead." And then there came another rifle shot from the cabin, which provoked a barrage of eight or nine gunshots from three different directions. The gunfire excited Rufus, who began to bark. Sarah, who was kneeling on the ground beside Rufus, put her arm around him and whispered frantically to him: "Quiet, Rufus. Be quiet." But it was too late. She'd been spotted.

It was Jake who alerted the others: "Hey, Sheriff, I spotted the whore," he shouted. "She's right above the cabin.

Why don't you and Edgar keep them boys busy while I see if I can capture her."

"Sounds good," shouted Hollis. "We'll use her for bait."

Josh knew that Jake would have the upper hand, as he only had to make it about thirty yards and then he would be out of view of the window on that side of the cabin. He'd seen Edgar pop up to take a shot earlier, so he had a good idea of where he was at and what he would probably do when laying down a covering fire. He figured that both he and Hollis would be concentrating their fire on the open windows and not the closed door. Josh carefully unlatched the door and opened it about an inch. He stood back from the door and sighted through the crack at where Edgar had been hiding. It was just enough to shoot through. Josh had no sooner lined up his sights when bullets started pinging through the window and into the dishes, boxes, and cans on the shelves. Sure enough, Edgar rose up just enough to fire at the cabin's east window, which was all that Josh needed to put a bullet in his head. Edgar crumpled immediately, but not before Jake had made his dash towards Sarah. Josh couldn't see what was going on but he could hear Sarah scream. And then Hollis, realizing what had happened to Edgar, began putting bullets through the door, one of them grazing Josh's right hip. It spun him around and onto the floor.

"You okay?" shouted Lester, who had blood trickling down his right cheek from an earlier ricochet that had nicked him.

"Yeah," hollered Josh excitedly, "but I'm not sure about Sarah."

"Ain't much we can do for her now without gettin' killed," said Lester, clutching his rifle.

And then both Lester and Josh heard Jake shout in a frantic voice: "Get off a me, you damned dog. Quit it." Suddenly, there was a gunshot and almost simultaneous to that a loud yip and then silence. Josh made eye contact with Lester. The hurt was visible on both their faces. "I'm sorry, Lester," said Josh.

Lester nodded his head. "Me too, just hope Sarah is alright."

"Yeah, I do too," said Josh.

And then from outside came Hollis' voice. "Jake, did ya get the whore?"

There was a short delay and then an angry, frustrated Jake shouted back: "No, this damned dog attacked me and while I was fightin' him off the little bitch went and locked herself in the old-timer's icehouse."

"Well, bust the door in," shouted Hollis.

"Can't," replied Jake. "The place is built like a fort."

Inside the cabin, Jake's predicament brought a chuckle from Lester. "Thata girl, Sarah. Those two dumb asses'll never get ya now."

Josh was about to ask Lester what he meant when Hollis sounded off again. "Jake, never mind the whore. We'll burn these two yahoos out and be done with 'em."

"Sounds good to me," hollered Jake. "This whore ain't goin' no wheres 'cause there's a crossbar on the outside a the door and I done put the bar across it. I guess the dumb bitch didn't figure on me lockin' her in there." Jake's laughter could be heard all the way back to the cabin.

Lester smiled and shook his head. "Well, Mr. Deputy, we'll see who gets the last laugh."

It was dark as molasses and real quiet inside the icehouse. After Jake gave up pounding on the door and making threats, there had been no sounds that Sarah could hear except her sniffles. She was sad that Rufus hadn't made it into the icehouse with her. He'd been right behind her but had turned on Jake when he was about to catch her. Rufus had saved her. And now she knew she had to do what she could to try and help Josh and Lester. All of the good things in her new life were about to be destroyed. It was fortunate for her, however, that she had a couple of stick matches in her shirt pocket from earlier that morning when she had been starting a fire in the cabin's stove. She knew that there was a candle on a stool in the corner of the room to the left of the door, but where could she strike a match? Sarah stood for a moment facing the door, trying to recall if there was anything in the room that she could use for this. The day she and Lester had come to the icehouse, he had lit a match by running it vigorously several times back and forth on the leg of his Levis and it just popped to life. She'd seen other old-timers light a match this way and she marveled at their ability, but she wasn't wearing those new kind of pants and she had only two matches. But then it came to her: the smell of venison off to her right. There were a couple of quarters of a deer hanging from iron meat hooks that were attached to the ceiling. Turning to her right, Sarah started slowly forward with her hands out in front of her. She'd taken only three steps when her left hand bumped into one of the quarters of meat, causing her to instantly stop. The meat was cold and firm and it had kind of a sweet musky smell. Keeping her hand on the meat, Sarah felt her way up the leg to where the meat hook had been inserted. She grasped the shaft of the hook where it came out of the ceiling; it was rough. Holding onto the shaft with her left hand, she fished one of the two matches that she had from her pocket with her right hand. She ran her finger along the shaft to get a sense of it, and then she carefully placed the match head against the shaft and made a striking motion. Nothing—the match had broken and the head was lost somewhere in the darkness on the floor. Sarah continued to cling to the meat hook with her left hand, the meat only inches from her face. She allowed her head to tilt forward and rest against the meat in frustration. "Dammit," she said aloud. "How could I be so stupid?" She sighed deeply and then reached into her pocket for her last match. She felt the match and positioned her fingers about midway along its length. She attempted to rest the match head on the meat hook's shaft, but her hands were trembling and she couldn't do it on her first attempt. Sarah lowered her hand with the match so as to collect herself. She knew that she had to have light; without it she'd never be able to get out, at least not through the tunnel, and going back out the front door was not an option. She felt like crying and almost did but then she caught herself. Images of Josh and Lester came into her mind. She had to do this for them, and so once again, she positioned the match on the meat hook's shaft. This time she applied less pressure and then struck the match. Nothing. Instantly, fear began to envelop her. It was like being buried alive. Sarah knew that she could remove the bar from her side of the door and in due time Jake would remove the bar from the outside and open the door, but that would be like surrendering to the devil; she'd rather be dead. And so after saying a quick prayer she applied the match one more time to the meat hook. Much to her relief, it burst into flame. Cupping her hands around the burning match, Sarah turned and moved towards the candle on the stool near the door. She moved slowly so as to not accidentally extinguish the flame. Still, the end of the natural life of the match's flame and Sarah's lighting of the candle were almost simultaneous. The candle's flame was tenuous at best and Sarah knew that she would need to work quickly, but carefully, to remove the ice blocks so that she could exit her icy tomb through the escape door. She grabbed ahold of the first ice block. The coldness stung her hands and its weight buckled her knees slightly. Moving just one block had left her slightly out of breath; nonetheless, she turned and grabbed a second and a third and so on until she had methodically revealed the escape door. Dropping to her knees, she opened the ground-level door. She was greeted by darkness as black as coal. She rose from her knees and retrieved the candle from the stool. She could see Lester's "go-to-hell" shotgun and his stash of gold. She would need to take both out through the tunnel. She had barely started when she was struck with just how small the tunnel was. To say that it was claustrophobic would be an understatement, especially if it was dark, and it was almost a given that the candle would never survive the crawl out with dirt falling from the roof of the tunnel. But what choice did she have, and so off she went, sliding the shotgun in its wrap and the bags of gold before her, being careful to always place the candle in a safe place. The tunnel was far more claustrophobic than the icehouse. It was just big enough for Sarah to move on her hands and knees. In places there were roots protruding from the walls, mostly small stringy ones that appeared to have grown after Lester had dug the tunnel; where they hung down from the ceiling they would grab hold of Sarah's hair. The first time that this happened she screamed—her scream, of course, was heard by no one. The tunnel seemed to go on forever, which only worsened her claustrophobia. Her fear of the tunnel caving in grew as she slowly moved her cumbersome procession of the shotgun, gold, and candle before her. Her heart was pounding loudly and her breathing had quickened. She began to imagine an awful scenario of where she would find the tunnel already collapsed in front of her. The tunnel was too tight to turn around in so she would have to back out, but what if the tunnel was to cave in behind her? She would be trapped, buried alive. The thought caused her to whimper and take several rapid breaths. Still on her hands and knees she froze in place, fearful that her movement might make her terrifying fantasy a reality. She began to cry. She first hung her head between her arms and then she surrendered to the paralyzing fear and lay flat on her stomach, her face cradled in the cool soil. She lay there for a moment and sobbed quietly. She could feel her tears blending with the dirt on her cheeks but she didn't care. Her mind had traveled back to better times at home in Boston. She could see the blue sky and the sun and her family. Life had been good—or at least a damned sight better than it had in Bear Creek. Sarah dug the fingers of her right hand deeply into the soil; she clenched it tightly as if to vent her frustration. "I should never have come west," she said to herself. But then, just as quickly she thought of Josh. He had been the one good thing to come from her agreeing to leave Boston. Deep down she knew that she had to compose herself soon, if she was to be of any help to Josh and Lester. And so once again Sarah got on her hands and knees, and after taking a deep breath to calm herself she started her slow crawl. She tried to concentrate on staying calm and not thinking bad things. It seemed to be working—she was making good progress. Finally, she reached a point where the tunnel started to go up. She was elated as she recalled Lester telling her this was where the tunnel was close to the exit. After steadying the candle she shoved the shotgun in its wrap ahead of her. She had almost reached the full extent of her reach when the gun barrel bumped into something. Instantly, she heard a hiss and in turn she screamed. "Oh shit," shrieked Sarah in an angry, trembling voice. Her heart was in her throat, pounding furiously. Slowly, she held the candle out in front of her so she could see better and there it was: a snake. It was good sized, maybe four feet long, but it was not making any rattling noises. Sarah knew next to nothing about snakes except that a rattlesnake was poisonous and it rattled when it was upset. This snake had hissed once but it didn't appear to be aggressive. It may have been because her fear was turning to anger and defiance that gave Sarah the courage, but she jabbed the snake hard with the barrel of the shotgun. Immediately the snake slithered away into the darkness, but in the same direction that she had to go. The snake's reaction bolstered Sarah's resolve to move forward. And so she started out again, slow and methodical, pushing the shotgun, gold, and candle in front of her. She'd gone only five or six feet when the tunnel turned fairly sharply to avoid a huge root of one of the ponderosa pines. The height of the tunnel was lower here by almost half, causing Sarah to lie flat and pull herself over the surface of the ground. She'd just cleared this low spot when she saw it, but she wasn't sure due to having looked into the candle for so long that her eyes had bright spots when she looked into the far darkness. And so she closed her eyes for a moment and then opened them. There it was: a faint shaft of natural light. The tiny opening must have been how the snake had gotten into the tunnel. Sarah's spirits were soaring. She quickly got to her hands and knees and started forward. She'd gone only a few feet when in her haste she brushed the candle's flame against a root and it went out. "Dammit," said Sarah aloud. The darkness was overpowering except for the tiny slit that she could see directly ahead. Seemingly oblivious to the snake but hopeful that it had exited the tunnel, she crawled as fast as she could into the near darkness. The tunnel was quickly getting steeper as the shaft of light grew stronger. And then finally, Sarah was at the end. She was directly beneath the rock slab. Eager to be free of this underground prison, she pushed up on the rock. Her first effort moved it six or eight inches, exposing the sky and trees above. Sarah put her face close to the opening, wanting a breath of fresh air that didn't smell of dirt; she was greeted instead by smoke. An adrenalin rush fueled by concern for Josh and Lester immediately shot through her.

At the cabin, things had taken a turn for the worse for Josh and Lester. The cabin had windows on the east, west, and north sides, with the south side being the only blind side. And so with some harassing fire from Hollis on the east side where the door was and on the north occasionally, he was able to keep Josh and Lester confined to the cabin while Jake built a large fire against the south wall of the cabin. It wasn't long after this fire was rolling up flame lengths of eight to ten feet and the logs of the cabin's back wall were clearly on fire that Jake decided to add the final touches to his pyrotechnic handiwork. He had to skirt wide of the cabin out of view in the trees to where they had tied their horses. In his saddlebag he had a long-neck whiskey bottle that contained moonshine that would burn a blue flame. It made for a powerful good drunk and he really hated to part with it, but he reckoned it was for a good cause. And so after he had maneuvered back around to the south side of the cabin, he tore a piece of his shirt off and soaked it with some of the shine. He then inserted it into the mouth of the bottle. After making eye contact with Hollis and a few hand signals, Jake then touched the wick in the bottle to the flames at the back of the cabin, and then staying as close as he could to the east wall, he ran forward while Hollis provided cover fire and hurled the flaming bottle through the window. It apparently hit the stove as breaking glass could be heard, and then frantic shouts from Josh and Lester.

"Hey Tex, can ya hear me?" shouted Hollis.

Josh and Lester were working frantically to smother the flames created by the moonshine torch. Between that morning's leftover coffee and a blanket, they were able to douse most of the flames but the larger problem, the back wall and now part of the roof, was a lost cause. Maybe it was time to bargain with Hollis. And so Josh said: "Waddaya want, Hollis?"

"Things ain't lookin' too good for ya. Thought maybe we could strike a deal."

Josh knew that Hollis was totally untrustworthy, but he had no choice but to play along. "How's that?" hollered Josh.

"Simple," shouted Hollis. "You and the old man come on out. You tell me where the gold is that you stole from Leroy and Edgar and I'll let all of ya ride outa here."

Josh knew that would never happen, but they couldn't stay in the cabin much longer. The smoke was so thick that both he and Lester had dropped to the floor to breathe the air there. It wouldn't be long until the flames would become a factor. His best bet was to try and leverage some advantage from the fact that Hollis still believed that he knew where Seth's gold was. To come out guns ablazing against two well-concealed shooters would likely get him and Lester killed. Sarah, he hoped, would be able to escape out the tunnel. Josh looked over at Lester, who lay face down on the cabin floor across the room. He had a bandana tied around his face, as did Josh, to help filter the smoke from his nose and mouth.

"Whaddaya think, Lester?" Lester's eyes were telling; as might be expected there was anger and frustration radiating from them. "I can spit farther than I'd trust either of them two vermin," he said spitefully, "but I don't see as where we got much choice. The sonsabitches pretty much got us."

"I reckon you're right," said Josh bitterly. "Ya'll ready?"

"Yeah, let's do it," replied Lester. "Least I won't die like some damned fricasseed squirrel."

Josh nodded at Lester and then he got to his knees. "Hey, Hollis," he shouted.

"Yeah."

"We're comin' out."

"Throw your guns out first and then come out with your hands up," commanded Hollis.

"That wasn't part of the deal," shouted Josh.

"It is now," interjected Jake. "We ain't stupid."

Josh had assumed that Hollis would demand that they come out unarmed, but he figured it was worth a try to keep their weapons. He knew it was pointless to argue with him, especially with time not being on his side. Josh looked over at Lester. He was getting to his feet. Josh did the same and moved to the door. "Alright, Hollis," he shouted as he opened the door about a foot. "We'll do it your way," and then Josh tossed out his rifle followed by his pistol.

Hollis and Jake watched the guns land in the dirt about twenty feet in front of the cabin. Both of them had nervous smiles on their faces but they were smug, almost joyful, in getting the upper hand on Josh and Lester. "That's good, Tex," shouted Hollis, "now come on out with your hands in the air, and no sudden moves or I'll shoot your ass deader 'n' a skunk in a trash heap."

Josh pushed the cabin door open and then slowly stepped outside. He was perfectly framed in the doorway and he half expected for them to shoot him down, but instead Hollis yelled: "Alright, step to the side and let's have the old man toss his guns out."

There was a long pause and then finally Lester's guns came tumbling through the air and landed in the pine needles and dirt beyond Josh. Hollis and Jake remained partially concealed, one behind a big rock and the other behind a tree, until Lester stepped from the cabin. Not until then did they step into plain view and begin walking towards Josh and Lester with their rifles trained upon them. Both of them wore cruel expressions.

"I don't like the looks of this," said Lester to Josh in a low voice.

"Me neither," said Josh quietly. And then he shouted at Hollis: "Remember, Hollis, a deal is a deal."

"Ya know, Tex," said Hollis, who was now within about

twenty feet of Josh and Lester. "I kinda figured on the way up here that ya was tellin' me the straight of it about Leroy and Edgar's gold. But I thought I'd set you and Edgar down together and compare stories whilst I was lookin' ya both in the face just to be sure, but you had to go and kill Edgar so that ain't an option anymore. So, to tell ya the truth I just ain't got much use for either you or the old man."

"I believe they aim to kill us," said Lester glancing over at Josh.

Hollis and Jake both laughed. "You catch on pretty fast," said Jake. "So which one of ya wants to go first?"

The roar of Lester's old twelve-gauge caught them all by surprise, but probably Jake most of all as its mass of buckshot hit him in the belly and nearly cut him in two. Peripherally, Hollis saw the smoke coming from the branches of a juniper tree about forty feet to his right. Instinctively, he turned in this direction and fired his Sharps rifle from the hip. He was in the process of levering in a second round when the shotgun roared again and he was slammed to the ground by a load of buckshot in his chest.

Josh and Lester looked at one another as if lightning had struck in their midst. Their sense of relief was nearly overwhelming, but paled in comparison to the emotions that Sarah was feeling at having just killed two men. Josh and Lester were nearly to the juniper tree when Sarah emerged from behind it. She was crying quietly but her whole body seemed to be trembling. Josh gently took the shotgun from her and handed it to Lester. Sarah collapsed against Josh's chest and Josh put his arms around her. They all stood there in silence for a moment and then Josh said: "It'll get better in time."

Sarah didn't move from Josh's embrace. "Right now I just need for you to hold me."

"I'm gonna go look for Rufus," said Lester sadly.

Josh nodded as Lester turned and slowly walked away. Sarah continued to cry quietly, her head resting against Josh's chest, not wanting to look beyond him and at the grotesqueness of the two dead men sprawled in the dirt. The image of the two men was bad enough, but knowing that she was responsible for it made it almost unbearable. She felt as if her mind was about to explode with the revulsion of it. And then, as if God knew that they'd all been put to the test that day and were in need of an emotional lift, one was provided: it was the unmistakable bark of Rufus. Sarah stepped back from Josh and turned uphill. Rufus was limping from a wound on his left front shoulder, but he was wagging his tail and making his way towards them. Instantly, Josh hollered for Lester as he and Sarah rushed towards Rufus. It was a joyful reunion with lots of licks, tail wagging, and pets. As they all sat on the ground near Rufus, they were now enveloped by the smoke from the burning cabin. It occurred to Josh that the wickedness of Bear Creek had finally come home to roost with the deaths of Hollis and his deputies. But for him the country around there would always be tainted by everything that had gone on. He'd done what he could to avenge Seth's death; it was time to move on. He had one last obligation, and that was to turn in his badge to Judge Higgins.

Chapter Twenty-Six

They were a banged-up bunch, both physically and mentally, but they had one another. And so the little caravan set out about midmorning the next day from Lester's still smoldering cabin, with Josh riding Thunder and Lester driving his team of mules pulling the freight wagon. Sarah rode her horse and Rufus lay on the wagon seat next to Lester. The preceding night had been one of mixed emotions for all of them. Josh felt responsible for everything that had happened. If it hadn't been for him, Hollis and his men would never have come to Lester's. The scene there now would be one of peace and quiet instead of the smoke that still hung in the air and the pall of death that lingered over the fresh graves. It was a place that would never be the same, not even in memory; violence and wickedness had a way of doing that—destroying good memories. It was time to move on in search of a place where good memories would last.

It was shaping up to be a hot day. For some time now they had moved along at a pace that was comfortable for the mules and pretty much in silence, each of them processing yesterday's events in their own way. Josh and Sarah were riding next to one another and within easy shouting distance of Lester and Rufus, who were directly in front of them. Josh could see the troubled look on Sarah's face. He knew what was on her mind. They'd talked well into the night before falling asleep in one another's arms. But things like this weighed heavy on a person's mind, and the only solace to be had was that over time, the load would get lighter. On the front end of this process, however, there was little comfort, and so Sarah said pretty much out of the blue: "You know, Josh, since coming to this godforsaken place I've had to sell my body just to be able to eat and have a roof over my head. And now I've had to kill two men to save the people that I care most about in this world. It doesn't seem fair."

Josh had mostly exhausted all of his "make-it-better words" last night. But in the past he had been where Sarah was at, and so at the risk of plowing the same ground, he said: "Sarah, you came to this Bear Creek country when it was just flat out a bad place to be. The both of us did. And like it or not, if you're gonna be a survivor you're gonna have to do some unpleasant things. The way I look at it, you've had more 'n' your share a muddy water comin' down the crik, but I got a feeling it's gonna clear up for ya'll." Josh paused and looking directly into her eyes, he winked at her and said: "We'll just make it happen."

Josh's words brought a slight smile to Sarah's face. "I hope you're right," she said.

"If I was a bettin' man, I'd put money on it," replied Josh. And then he extended his left hand to Sarah. She grasped it with her right, and for a moment they held hands before Josh squeezed her hand and said: "I'll be back in a minute. I need to talk to Lester." And with that Josh prodded Thunder into a trot and caught up with Lester.

"Hey, Lester, how ya farin'?" said Josh as he reined Thunder to a walk alongside the wagon.

"Well sir, I'd be doin' a mite better if the damned badgers would quit diggin' holes in the road."

Josh laughed politely and then said, "Yes sir, they appear to be workin' Sundays on that job."

Lester leaned forward and spit a stream of tobacco juice down in front of the wagon and behind the mules. Some of the juice splattered on the wagon's tongue on top of tobacco stains from past trips. Sensing that Josh wanted to talk, Lester said: "What's on your mind?"

"Well, I been thinkin' 'bout something that Ma there at the café in town told me about that Edgar fella. She said he come into the café early one morning with charcoal smudges all over and smellin' like smoke. This woulda been back about the time he lit out with the gold from Seth's claim. She never told me this until just a coupla nights past when she helped me bust outa Hollis' caboose."

"OK, so you're thinkin' he went to where there'd been a fire," interjected Lester.

"Yes sir, I am," replied Josh.

"That could be a lotta places,"

"It could," said Josh, "but I'm thinkin' I may have it narrowed down to one."

"How so?"

"Well sir, based on what Ma told me, after his run-in with me, Edgar must have hightailed it straight back to Bear Creek to get protection from Hollis. And if ya think about it, there's an old lightning strike up that little no-name draw about two miles outside of town. It kinda makes sense that Edgar could've gone up there to hide the gold on his way back to town. He then lies to Hollis about me takin' the gold so he doesn't have to split it with him. He probably figured that if he got Hollis to take care of me, that he could go back and work the claim and never have to share this little nest egg that he stashed."

Lester moved the reins of the mules to one side and spit another stream of tobacco juice. "You might be on to something," he said. "I know the burn you're talkin' 'bout. Lightning started it last summer but then a hard rain come and put it out. It ain't no bigger than your average-size garden. Ya thinkin' a pokin' around in it?"

"I reckon it couldn't hurt none," replied Josh.

"Alridey then, we'll just do that," said Lester.

It was going on five o'clock in the afternoon when they came to the no-name draw. It was only a few hundred yards off of the road. As they proceeded to the burn, Josh's confidence that this was a wise decision soared. There in the soft soil were the hoofprints of a horse that appeared to have lost a shoe, just as Edgar's had. The trio continued on, following the tracks to a burned tree where the horse had apparently been tied. From there the boot tracks in the soft ash led them to the big hollowed-out ponderosa lying on its side. Josh couldn't help but smile. Edgar had left a trail that a blind man could follow. It didn't make any sense, but then thinking back on that day when Edgar had made good his escape from Seth's claim and the amount of time that it would've taken him to get to this burn, it would've been close to dark when he got here. Couple that with the fact that Edgar had decided to double-cross Hollis and that he was probably looking over his shoulder, wondering when the deputy marshal was going to catch up, he was most likely not paying attention in the growing darkness to the obvious nature of the tracks that he was leaving. He no doubt wanted to stash the gold as quickly as possible and get into Bear Creek and the protection of Hollis. Add the darkness to Edgar's fear and it became more logical to Josh how Edgar had done such a foolish thing. And so it wasn't long after getting a fairly liberal coating of charcoal that Josh had the saddlebags with the gold in hand. As he looked down at the gold, there was no joy—if anything he felt sadness, but relief too. He could now leave this Bear Creek country knowing that he had avenged his friend's death. The gold seemed inconsequential given the fact that it had come with such a heavy price. Josh would get a check for it and send it to Seth's parents. It would in no way make up for the loss of their son. There was nothing that could do that, but they would hopefully have memories of better times and be able to take solace in those. That's generally all the living ever had. Josh's debt to Seth for having saved his life was paid in full. He could now move on to that ranch in the Salmon River country with a good woman and a new friend.

CPSIA information can be obtained at www.ICGtesting.com
Printed in the USA
LVOW08s1145220516

489437LV00001B/37/P